ST. MARTIN'S

MINOTAUR

MYSTERIES

Other titles from
St. Martin's **Minotaur** Mysteries

St. Martin's Paperbacks is also proud to present
these mystery classics by Ngaio Marsh

THE SUN WAS STARTING TO SET, TURNING ORANGE AND MASSIVE AT THE edge of the world. All my time in Orsino, and I had never once seen the sun set from the cliffs. It was dinnertime, when jesters make their living or die hungry. So many years looking at audiences through thickened lashes, hiding behind the double artifice of masks and words. Rare to have this moment of isolation, God's glory on full display, the waves crashing below and the wind whispering through the woods behind. "Fool," I thought it whispered . . .

But it wasn't the wind. A man laughed somewhere in the woods behind me . . .

There was a large boulder, about twenty feet to my left. I took a step, and something went whistling by my ear and out to sea.

"Stand still, Fool," said a voice from my past. "I want to see what Time has done to you."

The fastest I've ever seen a man reload a crossbow was to a quick count of four. I made that boulder in about three and a half, diving into a somersault and rolling behind it in a tight ball. Something clattered off it an instant later . . .

Thirteenth Night

ALAN GORDON

St. Martin's Paperbacks

THIRTEENTH NIGHT

Copyright © 1999 by Alan Gordon.
Excerpt from *Jester Leaps In* copyright © 2000 by Alan Gordon.

Library of Congress Catalog Card Number: 98-44612

ISBN: 0-312-97684-4

Printed in the United States of America

St. Martin's Press hardcover edition / February 1999
St. Martin's Paperbacks edition / November 2000

10 9 8 7 6 5 4 3 2 1

To my best friend, fellow traveler,
fellow parent, lover, wife, and in-house Muse,
Judy Downer

FOOL: And thus the whirligig of time brings in his revenges.

MALVOLIO: I'll be revenged on the whole pack of you!

Twelfth Night, V, i

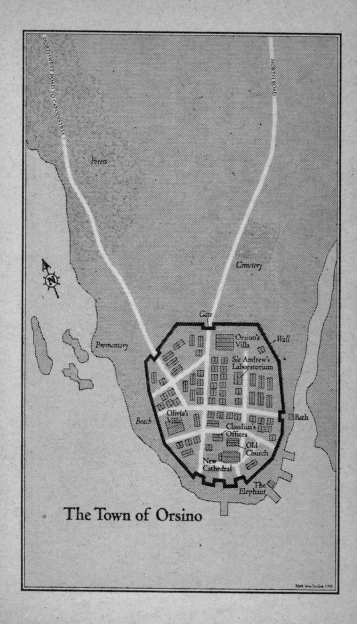

NORTHWEST ROAD TO CANOSSILIA

NORTH ROAD

Forest

Cemetery

Gate

Orsino's Villa

Wall

Promontory

Sir Andrew's Laboratorium

Beach

Olivia's Villa

Claudius's Offices

Old Church

Bath

New Cathedral

The Elephant

The Town of Orsino

Mark Stein Studios, 1998

ONE

We are fools for Christ's sake . . .
1 CORINTHIANS 4.10

We were gathered in the tavern to taste the new beer. I had just taken a deep, satisfying draught when a stranger entered and drew our attention. To say that he stood out would be strange, for he was an ordinary-looking fellow—a dull gray cloak over sweat-stained breeches and weary brown eyes over a drooping brown mustache. But an ordinary-looking man will stand out when he enters a room filled with jesters, much as a single sparrow will seem bizarre when surrounded by peacocks and popinjays. His garb bespoke trade; his bearing, a soldier, but in these perilous times it is a small step from merchant to mercenary and back again. Amidst the exchanges of song, dirty jokes, and routines new and ancient, my colleagues and I sized him up as he picked his way through to see which one of us he would bless as a target. Then he sat next to me and begged my pardon.

"Pardon?" I said. "Name the offense before I determine whether it is pardonable."

"I am looking for someone," he said. He spoke passable Tuscan but with a pronounced Slavic accent. "A fool."

"Look past the barkeep," I said. He did and saw his reflection in the glass. "You have found him."

"I seek a particular fool," he continued doggedly.

"Then you seek nothing," I said. "He cannot exist. If he be a fool, then he cannot be particular. And if he be particular, he is no fool."

"These are but feeble japes," he said. "I would expect better of one of the Fools' Guild."

"I am between engagements," I admitted. "When the time comes, I shall fetch the whetstone of my wits and hone them to rapier sharpness. But what fool do you seek? Perhaps I know him."

"He has been described to me as a whoreson mad fellow, all in motley, with a dry wit that improved upon wetting."

All laughed.

"Look about the room and you will find twenty such fellows. And fifty more passed out in the Guildhall."

My colleagues saluted him with an astonishing variety of rude noises. As I said, off duty. Saving the good material for the paying customers. The stranger smiled wanly and spoke again.

"His name is Feste."

The noises continued without interruption, nor was there any reaction to the name. Years of training to hide our emotions.

"I have heard the name," I said, "but he has not been seen here in some time. Does anyone know where he makes his living nowadays?" None did. I turned back to the stranger. "All I can say is that he passes through at irregular intervals. A message left here will reach him by and by."

The man studied me carefully. "I bring it only as a favor to a lady. I cannot tarry here, for I have business in Milan. The message is short."

"The easier to remember. Out with it."

"Orsino is dead."

No reaction, no reaction, I admonished myself. "Of natural causes?"

"No."

"How then?"

"His body was found at the base of a cliff. He had been known to wander along the edge of it, deep in thought. It is believed that he missed his footing and fell. An accident."

"And the Duchess?"

He looked at me sharply. "What do you know of the Duchess?"

"Where there's a Duke, there's usually a Duchess. How fares the lady?"

"She mourns him. For seven days she stayed by his casket, watering the flowers with her tears. Then she took to the villa and has not emerged since."

"A sad state of affairs. And the affairs of state, state how they fare?"

"When I left, they were being held in abeyance. The young Duke is but eleven years of age, and a regent has not yet been chosen."

"When did this occur?"

"He was found three weeks ago."

I sipped my beer idly as if I were memorizing the message to pass on. "Well, if that is all you have to tell me, I shall spread the word. If this Feste comes again and is sober enough to hear it, and I sober enough to tell it, then he shall hear and I shall tell. More than that, I cannot tell."

He looked at the barkeep. "Can this man be trusted?"

"I trust him in all matters, as long as he pays up front," answered the barkeep. I lifted my tankard in salute.

"And, sirrah," I added as the stranger turned to leave. He looked at me, and I waved my hand through a slovenly sign of the cross. "I pardon thee. Go and sin no more."

He looked less than satisfied but left nonetheless. The sounds of my comrades' revelry followed him out the door and continued until he was safely out of earshot.

"Niccolò!" I called, and one of the younger fools cartwheeled up to the bar. "Follow him, would you?"

He dashed off, and I placed a silver coin on the bar.

"Am I covered?" I asked.

"Until you come back," said the barkeep, placing it in my tankard and putting it on a shelf next to those of other colleagues on missions. "It will be waiting for you."

I made my farewells quickly and walked briskly towards the Guildhall, thinking. It was an unusually cold December in that first year of the Thirteenth Century. We had somehow made it through the Twelfth without the world coming to an end, much to the disappointment of those hoping for a better one. There was one overly devout sect that calculated the world would last a century for each of the Disciples. They are now recalculating. Last I heard, they had decided it would take another century for the Apostle Paul. Their membership is dwindling rapidly as no one expects to be around that long. Anyway, as I fully expect to fry when my time comes, I am just as happy to keep the present situation going. Especially when the new beer is coming in.

Nevertheless, my head cleared quickly in the chill, and I thought back fifteen years. A good man, Orsino, once he had been shown his folly. And with her . . . Enough. No time for reminiscences.

The village was not exactly off the beaten path. In fact, there was a very fine beaten path that took one southwards through the concealing forest. We were tucked into a fold at the beginning of the Dolomites, and a traveler would have to go well out of his way to find us.

The Guild had quietly bought up the area over the centuries, funded by the erratic contributions of its members and the odd bequests from some grateful benefactors. There was just enough farmland and mountain pasture to sustain us without resorting over-much to trade. The village contained a crossroads surrounded by a minimal number of shops: a wheelwright, a carpenter, an apothecary, the all-important tavern. North, the direction I was walking, led to the Guildhall itself, a large, irregular structure on the western slope of a smallish mountain. It had been built centuries ago, burned down once or twice, rebuilt several times, and added on to so that not even our historians could point to an original timber. The main hall, which towered some fifty feet high, was used for instruction and performances. Sleeping quarters were to the rear, stables to the right, although more than one of us has confused the two after a day of carousing and ended up sleeping in the stables.

Brother Timothy was conducting a juggling clinic when I entered the main hall. The young initiates sat enraptured as he flipped four clubs through increasingly intricate patterns. I thought he had not noticed me, but as I passed some twenty paces from him, a club came flying at my head as if by mistake. I caught it instinctively and tossed it back. Another came at me, then another, and before I was quite aware of it, I was in a duet.

"With two jugglers, six clubs should be the absolute minimum," said Brother Timothy as he brought two more into the pattern. "Simple, really, it just involves an outward throw instead of a vertical one, and an inward catch as well. You should practice with each hand. . . ." The thrown clubs shifted from right to left and back again, and I had to scramble to make the returns. "Now, for seven . . ."

"Wait!" I yelled, but his assistant had already tossed him another, which immediately came to my left hand in a perfect arc.

"It's all a matter of rhythm," continued Timothy calmly. "You should learn to feel a natural seven, rather than dividing it into twos and threes. It will make for a smoother transition. Don't you agree, Theophilos?"

I was starting to sweat new beer. "I've always thought of seven as eight with one missing," I panted as the pattern started to get ragged on my end.

Timothy shook his head. "You see the error of his ways. He's losing the rhythm and overcompensating to keep the clubs in the air. But since he's more comfortable with eight . . ."

"I didn't say," I started, but another club was already flying through the air. I was moving as fast as I could, but each catch was a close call. I threw them at odd angles to throw Timothy off, but he caught them adroitly and whipped them back at me even faster.

"Now, with nine," he said, slipping one foot out of its sandal and maneuvering a club onto his toes.

"I can't do nine," I implored him, but it was too late. Desperately, I tossed two high above me, hurled one back at Timothy, flipped the club in my left hand to my right, and caught another in my newly emptied left. That meant that the sixth club, which had been given an extra hard toss, caught me squarely in the chin. I stumbled backwards, and the remaining clubs rained ignominiously down on my embarrassment.

"You're right, you can't," observed Timothy as the apprentices laughed. I stood up with as much dignity as I could muster, took a step, and promptly returned to a supine position as I slipped on a club. As they laughed some more, I used my momentum to carry me through a series of backwards somersaults ending in a flip into a handstand. They applauded as they realized that the second fall was no accident.

"Theophilos will be giving a demonstration on pratfalls next week," announced Timothy as I regained my feet. "Or, for the price of a drink, anytime you like."

"Thank you, thank you all," I said grandly, waving my scarf. "And now, I leave you in the competent and roving hands of Brother Timothy."

An unimposing wooden door led me to a pantry. I lit a candle, then slid back a section of the wall and descended a stairway carved into the mountain on which the Guildhall perched. A rough tunnel snaked through the rock for perhaps five hundred feet to the monastery on the eastern slope. I passed through it, ducking occasionally, for it had been excavated by shorter men than myself. At the other end, I opened the door and walked down a hallway until I found Father Gerald's rooms and knocked quietly on the door.

"Come in," he called, and I entered to find him poring over a sheaf of yellowed papers, the red string that had bound them lying crumpled by the candle. Hundreds of others filled pigeonholes built into one wall of the tiny room, sorted by a system known only to himself. No one knew his true age, though all agreed that there could be no one older. His face at this point might have been shaped by the same ancient tunnelers whose handiwork I had just traversed.

"Theophilos, good," he said, waving me to a bench with his gnarled hand. "You've saved me the trouble of sending for you. Sit, boy, sit. You've come to tell me of the death of the Duke Orsino."

"Do you keep spies in the tavern?" I asked as I sat down.

"I do, but that's not your concern. As it happened, this messenger came to the Guildhall first with his news. Looking for Feste. Imagine that."

"Imagine that."

He looked at me sharply.

"Now, why do you suppose anyone would want you?" he asked.

"Because Orsino was murdered."

"That's not what the message said. But let's assume that it's true. You suspect this man Malvolio."

"Naturally. Who else?"

Father Gerald glared at me. "Who else? Do you think perhaps there could be another reason why anyone would kill Orsino?" He motioned me over to his desk and pulled out his map. Never a good sign when an Irish priest pulls out a map. "Orsino, Orsino," he muttered.

"The Dalmatian coast, below Zara, above Spalato," I said helpfully.

"Of course," he said, stabbing at it with his finger. "I remember being irritated that you called it Illyria in your report. Only you would use that antiquated name. No one's called it Illyria in centuries."

"I like it better," I said, shrugging.

"To start with, Orsino owed his allegiance to Hungary. But Hungary is far, and Venice is close. It's on the Adriatic, so any intrigue is likely to originate from the Doge. Or from Pisa or Genoa, if they thought Orsino was favoring Venice. Or from Rome or Hungary, if they thought he was favoring Constantinople."

"Or from the Saracens for all of the above reasons, or just to cause trouble. Or maybe the Catholics thought him a Cathar, or the Cathars too much a Catholic. Or the Guelfs thought him too Ghibelline, or the Ghibellines too Guelf." I continued in spite of his deepening glare. "Maybe a jealous husband caught him unawares. Or a jealous wife or mistress. One of his heirs with precocious ambition. Maybe he died by chance, by happenstance. Maybe he was drunk. Maybe the gods looked down and flicked him off of the cliff to amuse themselves and tantalize the rest of us. But it was none of these."

"Your reason, Fool?" snapped Father Gerald.

"Because I was sent for."

He nodded slowly. "Aye, there's that. Had there been correspondence before this?"

"I left fourteen years ago. A few letters reached the Guildhall but none in over a decade."

He leaned back and held up the sheaf of papers. "I've been reading your reports from that assignment, but I'd rather hear it from your own sweet mouth."

I took a second to collect my thoughts. "The town is by the mouth of a river. It lives off the barges coming from inland and the boats arriving at the port. Much of the commerce was controlled by two families, one headed by Orsino, the other by a young woman named Olivia. At the time the Guild assigned me there, the late Duke was obsessed with the Countess. She spurned his love, for she was in mourning for her late brother. He was so wracked with melancholy and she with grief that they completely neglected the affairs of the town. The Guild, concerned that a strategic port could become vulnerable to Saracen piracy or even invasion, sent me."

"With an eye towards encouraging the alliance of the two families," remembered Father Gerald.

"Yes, only she didn't want him, which was just as well. They would have been wrong for each other even in the best of circumstances. As it stood, they were paralyzed. She was attended by this man Malvolio, who I discovered had his own designs. At first, I thought he wanted her for her wealth, but after observing him closely I began to suspect that he may have been an agent for someone."

"Did you ever discover who?"

"No. He was very secretive. I believe that he practiced on the Countess to encourage her despair. He may even have been administering some subtle drug that sapped her will. I decided that outside intervention was needed. I learned of a suitable pair of siblings, a young man and woman of good family. Through the Guild, I arranged for them to be shipwrecked and guided towards the town by our agents, hoping that their arrival would rouse either the Duke or the Countess."

"One of your typical, harebrained schemes."

"Thank you, Father. But something odd happened. The sister, Viola, proved to be unusually resourceful. Fearing for her safety, she disguised herself as a man and found employment as Orsino's servant. He used her as an emissary to the Countess, but the Countess took one look at her, or him, and fell in love. Viola subsequently fell in love with the Duke but feared discovery. Things were getting complicated but fortunately her brother Sebastian finally came on the scene. I managed to intercept him and divert him to the Countess. She mistook him for his sister and promptly married him. Orsino, the scales fallen from his eyes, returned Viola's love. Happy ending."

"Except," prompted Father Gerald.

"Except for Malvolio. I took him out of the picture by a trick which I suggested to Sir Toby, a relative of the Countess. By various ruses, he and other members of her household convinced Malvolio that the Countess loved him and would respond to certain bizarre behaviors we invented. He fell for it and was promptly imprisoned as a madman and remained so until events had safely taken their course." I paused, hearing again Malvolio's chill curse as he stormed away, *I'll be revenged on the whole pack of you!*

"Did he know about you?"

"I don't think so. I was too lowly a creature for his concern. He suspected Viola, certainly. He discovered one of our agents, who was the captain of the vessel she arrived on, and had him locked up on some pretext. He was clever, but so full of himself that he was fairly easy to gull."

"Did you consider the threat to be serious?"

"Certainly. After what we had put him through, I thought him capable of any rash act. But he simply packed his bags and rode out of town, to the south as I recall. I would have followed, but my performance was required for the nuptial festivities, so I had our captain make certain that he left for good."

"And then?"

"Standard procedure. With Pantolino, who was traveling the troubadour route at that time, I composed a rhymed account of what happened that minimized my own part in it. And he took with him a description of Malvolio to circulate among the Guild in case he turned up anywhere. That was the last I heard of him. A year later, I left."

The old priest removed a single page and handed it to me. "This came a year after I received your report."

The letter was in Greek. It still bore the splatters of ink from someone writing in haste.

"Dear Uncle," I read. "Spotted someone who looks like this Malvolio fellow you wrote me about. I've been keeping an eye on the *Tigris*, which pulled into harbor three days ago. The ship's Genoese, but trades openly with the Ayyubids and is generally suspected to spy for Saladin. Malvolio has arranged passage to Beirut. Think I'll do the same. The crew could use a little entertainment. I'll get in touch with our man there once I arrive. Must dash, yours in Christ, Sean."

I looked up. "So he was working for Saladin."

"We received this from Damascus four months later," he said, handing me another report.

I write to tell you a curious set of circumstances, and how I responded to them. I hope I did well. They occurred rapidly, and only now do I begin to wonder at them.

You know by now of Saladin's victories at the Horns of Hattin and Jerusalem. The troops exhausted, he decided not to lay siege to Tyre and has returned to Damascus, where I had been forced to remain for the pendency of the campaign. I have again waited upon him, enlivening his days while gleaning what I can of his plans. He looks weary, and it is whispered about the town that he is not long for this world. It is unfortunate—he was provoked to this last war by wrongful actions of the so-called Christian Reginald of Karak, and many lives have been lost as a result.

On the fourteenth of March, if my calendar still be accurate after so long a time in Islamic lands, a Christian prisoner was brought before him, shackled, dressed in sailor's garb. Black-bearded and dark-visaged, he seemed almost a madman, his eyes casting about in every direction. To my surprise, Saladin began railing at him in Arabic, and the fellow replied fluently in the same tongue. He was being dressed down for failing in some mission—the details were not discussed. Mostly, he was begging the King for mercy and another chance to serve him. I was ready to dismiss him as no more than a common spy when I spotted a Guild ring among the many that bejeweled his hands. It was of iron, with a single small blue stone set in an ass's mouth. I conjectured that the fellow was one of us, and sought an opportunity to speak with him.

This was easier said than done. Saladin had him imprisoned in a dungeon in an area I am normally not privy to, but I wheedled and joked with the guard until I was able to gain access to the fellow's cell. I whispered the password, *"Stultorum numerus . . . ,"* but he failed to reply. He came to the front of the bars and stared at me for a long time. "You're a fool!" he said in astonishment. *"Stultorum numerus . . . ,"* I whispered again. *". . . infinitus est!"* he replied, and clasped my hand.

"I didn't know there were any fools here," he said. "Praised be Our Lord Jesus Christ."

"Praised be," I replied. "Few in the Guild know of my mission. Good for you that I was here, and that I spotted the Guild ring."

"The Guild, yes. Of course." He paced about the cell, running his hands though his hair. "Forgive me, I am much distracted. I did not stand up to torture as well as I had hoped."

"Poor fellow. Is there anything I can do to help?"

He seized the bars and hissed, "Can you get me out of here?"

I was somewhat taken aback. Normally, our training is to resign ourselves to whatever end Fate brings us when a mission fails. Freeing him meant jeopardizing myself and my mission. I explained this to the fellow. "After all, the Guild comes first. I am sorry."

"But don't you understand? The Guild itself is threatened."

"Explain."

He paced back and forth. "I was taken when a fellow fool, one who purported to be of the Guild, gained my trust and then betrayed me. I discovered too late that he was a Saracen spy, sent to infiltrate the Guild and learn its secrets."

"Impossible," I said. "It takes years of training to become a fool."

"He had it," insisted the prisoner. "He could sing, play instruments, rhyme *ex tempore* in several languages, juggle, tumble, dance, and recite. He took me in completely, and after I was imprisoned on the ship that took me here he came and boasted of his plan. He's an assassin, I tell you, and the whole Guild is at risk. And only I know what he looks like."

Needless to say, I was horrified by his report. I agreed to help him escape. By constant observation, I discovered which slave brought the dungeon guards their meals. I slipped a slow-acting sleep potion into their dinner, then crept down late at night and freed our comrade. I took him from the city through one of the water tunnels, and provided him with enough food for three days' journey. It was all I could do.

The uproar over his escape has died down, and fortunately

suspicion was never directed towards me. Upon reflection, I wonder at the man and his story. He did not, despite the ring and the password, strike me one of our brethren, though I well know the diversity found within our membership. Perhaps his ordeal as a captive soured his personality.

I send this warning to you in the event that he fails to return to the Guildhall. There is a traitor amongst you, Father. Take heed. Al-Mutabbi.

I handed the report back to the old priest, who was gazing sadly at the fireplace. "Sean was never heard from again," he said softly. "Al-Mutabbi was denounced as a spy by an anonymous letter to Saladin and beheaded. They say he was laughing when the axe came down."

"Sean was your nephew? I never knew that."

"I put that ring on his finger myself when we initiated him into the Guild. A boisterous, impetuous boy. He looked like my brother at that age." He sat in silence as the flames flared suddenly. "We'll send someone to Orsino," he said finally.

"We'll send me," I said.

He shook his head. "He'll be expecting you. It's too dangerous."

"It will be dangerous for any fool who goes rushing in. At least I know the territory and the players."

"Knew them, Theophilos. That was fifteen years ago. Everyone's gotten older, including you."

I didn't like it. "You don't trust me."

He wouldn't look at me. "As you said, I have spies in the tavern. And they report to me that you have been doing prodigious feats of imbibing, such as would dwarf the legends of Heracles."

"That's here. That's between assignments. I have too much time on my hands. Why haven't you sent me out?"

"They also say that when you aren't drinking, you're brooding, which then leads you straightaway to drinking again. I conclude from all of this that you haven't recovered from your last mission."

"My failure, you mean."

He shook his head. "Theo, my lad, you have to accept the fact that our role will always be one of subtle influence, and when the target is an old man who had the misfortune to turn dotard before giving away his power, then it's not your fault that it turned out badly."

"I should have stayed."

"It would have made no difference. And until you realize that and regain some semblance of your old self, I'm going to keep you here. You are still one of my best men, which is precisely why I am not sending you into a new situation while you're mooning over the last one. I'm sending someone else."

I stood up. "In that case, Father, I regret to say that I am resigning from the Guild."

He looked up at me in surprise. "I won't permit that."

"It doesn't matter. If you won't send me on behalf of the Guild, I'll go on my own. These are people that I care about, and if it is Malvolio, then I am responsible for what is happening to them. I'm going."

He turned back to the fireplace and thought. I didn't interrupt him. "Did any of them ever see you without your makeup?" he asked abruptly.

"No, Father. I was scrupulous about that."

"Then I propose the following. You go, but not as Feste. Not even as a fool."

"But . . ."

"Don't interrupt, lad. I'm trying to save your life. You go as a merchant. Invent some plausible story that will take you there and keep you for a while. I'll have someone else arrive a few days later as a fool. That way, we'll have two men on the scene, and Malvolio will concentrate his efforts on him."

It was a good plan, though it irked me that I would be working outside of my profession, as a common spy rather than a fool. I could have just as well become an actor if that was all I amounted to. "Whom will you send?"

"I'm not sure, yet. I'm expecting someone in from Toledo who might be good for the job. You don't know him. Whoever it is, he will be wearing this ring." He held up an intricate silver filigree shaped in the head of an ass. "When you see him, use the password."

"Fine. Um, if I'm to play the merchant, I'll need money. More than usual."

He reached into his desk and pulled out a small purse. "This will get you as far as Venice. Brother Timothy will give you a letter of credit on our account there."

"I'm going to Venice? That's a little out of the way."

"Not necessarily. Even this late in the year you can probably find a boat to take you across. It's safer than by land. Word has reached us that the Serbs and the Croats are at it again."

"What's the Guild position on them?"

"Ah, I wish one of them would do the other in so we could stop worrying about it," he grumbled. "No, I never said that. The Guild takes no position. We're trying to get them to come to terms. In the meantime, that road is risky, so go to Venice. Check in with Domino while you're there. He'll have the gossip on Orsino if there is any."

"All right, Father." I turned to leave, then turned back somewhat guiltily. "I'm afraid I'll have to miss the Feast."

He nodded sadly. "I heard you were going to portray me," he said. "I was looking forward to that. But there may be nothing to miss."

That was disturbing. "What do you mean?" I asked.

He stared at the fire again, absentmindedly massaging his brows. "Nominally, Rome thinks that it controls the Guild, and we prefer to let it think so. But there's been an unusual amount of backlash against the Feast, more than just that idiot bishop in Paris. Our Pope Innocent is turning out to be anything but. The Church is under attack because people are finally wondering why they have so little while the wardens of Christ have so much, and His Holiness is becoming very sensitive about ridicule. And that includes the Feast of Fools."

"But that's ludicrous. It's a harmless ritual."

"Not a bit of it, Theo. It's subversive. It undermines the foundations of the edifice even while they pile more gold leaf on the dome. Which is precisely why the Guild developed the Feast. Rome doesn't know that, but it knows it doesn't like it. We're using what influence we can to keep it from issuing an absolute ban. If it merely expresses disapproval, we'll be all right, but it could get very dicey for us. That's another reason I wanted to keep you around here. However, I think I can spare you for a little while. When you see Domino, fill him in so he can use his influence in Venice on our behalf."

"Yes, Father." I turned to go.

"Theo. There is one more thing."

I turned back again. He came around the desk to take my hand between his.

"I would like you to come to confession before you go," he said.

My heart sank. "I can't, Father. I have yet to absolve myself. How can I go to you?"

"It's not just your life that I worry about, my boy. I have to worry about your immortal soul. And I do care about what happens to you."

"I'm not ready yet, Father. Maybe when I return."

He patted my hand and released it. "Then make sure you do return, Theo."

"And you make sure you're still alive when I get back."

He laughed for the first time. "Go on, lad. It's a pact." I turned once more. "Theo," he called as I left the room. .

"Yes, Father?" I replied, leaning into the doorway.

"Find Malvolio. Find out what he knows of the Guild, and who he's working for. Then give him a good Christian burial."

"Yes, Father." I walked down the hall.

"Theo!" he called.

"Yes, Father?"

"It doesn't particularly matter to me whether he's alive or dead when you bury him."

"Yes, Father." And I walked towards the tunnel as his door slammed shut behind me.

Two

Behold, I send you out as sheep in the midst of wolves;
so be wise as serpents and innocent as doves.

MATTHEW 10.16

When I returned to the Guildhall I found Brother Timothy by himself juggling six clubs while the novitiates were off to their evening meal. He varied the pattern with every cycle, the clubs following routes that seemed chaotic but were mathematically precise. He nodded at me as I approached, and three of the clubs detached themselves from his ambit and hurtled in my direction. I was ready for him this time, and sober as well, so I caught them easily and set them aloft again over my head.

"I'll go easy on you," promised Timothy. "Now, breathe. And . . ." We threw from our right hands and circled an imaginary point between us as the clubs passed one another over it.

"Time was when you could keep eight in the air by yourself," commented Timothy.

"Time was," I agreed. "Time was when I could run for leagues without stopping. Time was when I could drink any man under the table. Not anymore."

"Then you shouldn't be going out," he said bluntly. I didn't ask him how he knew. He had a knack for knowing things before they came about.

"How bad is he?" I asked, indicating the passageway to Father Gerald's cell.

"I don't know what you're talking about," he muttered, altering the pattern to distract me.

"His eyes," I said. "When did they start to go?"

"What makes you think that?"

"Can't find Orsino on the map. Wants me to rehash my report verbally when he has it right in front of him. Delegates the drafting of the letter of credit to you. He never used to do any of this. He's going blind, isn't he?"

"Blind or not, he's as sharp as ever. If you're so concerned, stay here and help me watch over him."

"Can't do that. I'm off to Orsino."

"Leaving the Guild for a personal matter in a time of crisis. You're acting like a schoolboy, Theo, when we could really use you here right now. We may have to relocate on short notice."

"As bad as all that?"

"Rome being Rome, yes. As bad as all that."

I was stunned. I had no idea things had gotten to that point. "You'd think they'd know better. Makes you want to leave the Church and join the Waldenses."

"Ah, the Waldenses," mused Timothy fondly. "Lovely little group. Rome could learn much from them if it were willing. Makes me proud when I think how we caused all that."

"We did? I never knew that."

"It's a pretty story. Peter Waldes heard a troubadour singing the 'Lay of Saint Alexis' one day in Lyons, and before you know it he's sold his goods and preaching poverty. The troubadour was one of ours, of course."

I laughed. "You mean we're taking credit for a coincidence?"

"It's hard to tell the rocky ground from the good soil nowadays," he replied solemnly. "So we sow our seed everywhere and hope for the best. I tell you what, if you run away to the Waldenses,

I might go with you. Only if Rome is worried about us, God knows what they'll do to a competing sect, especially one that preaches ecclesiastical poverty. Speaking of which, I suppose you'll be needing money for this adventure of yours."

"Yes. And a horse."

"An ass is good enough for a fool, fool."

"But I am going as a merchant. A horse, decent clothing, and enough money to travel in style. So decrees the good father."

He scowled. He kept an iron grip on the Guild's purse strings, and this was clearly an extravagance. But I was still feeling insulted by being forced to abandon my motley for the journey, so I would be damned if I wasn't going to make them pay for that.

"All right, Theo," he conceded. "Are you going through Venice?" I nodded. "Come with me and I'll give a letter of credit. Are you sure you can handle this job?"

His eyes widened as my dagger split the air a hand's breadth from his ear and embedded itself in a post behind him. The clubs maintained their pattern on both ends.

"I haven't completely lost my skills," I drawled, and then I dropped my hands, stepped back, and let the clubs clatter to the floor around me. He slammed down his remaining club, pulled the dagger out, and whipped it back. It passed by my ear by a finger's width. I bowed to the master and retrieved it from the opposite wall.

Niccolò intercepted me as I walked to the stables, my newly filled purse jingling happily at my waist.

"Your mysterious messenger has a very good horse," he reported. "Much better than any of ours. He went in the direction he said he would at an unreasonably fast pace. I could track him, if you like, but I doubt that I could catch him with any of the swaybacked nags we have here."

"Thank you, but no. He doesn't matter. The man I want will be waiting for me at my journey's end." He held out his hand, and I took it. "You'll have to take over Father Gerald's part in the Feast."

"I don't imitate him as well as you."

"You'll be fine. Try stumbling and bumping into things. If he asks you why, tell him I suggested it. He'll understand."

Brother Dennis was shoeing a bay mare when I came in, a leathern apron over his cassock, the nails tucked in the corner of his mouth. "Be with you in a minute," he muttered. The mare was struggling, but he had her leg immobilized in one immense arm. He drove the nails home with one blow each, then released the mare and slapped her affectionately on the rump. She snorted and trotted away. "What can I do for you, Theo? I have the donkey trained for the Feast."

"Thank you, but unfortunately I won't be here. I'm off on the morrow, and shall require one of your finest Arabians."

He snorted much as the bay had. "What's the setup? Too good for an ass?"

"I go in the guise of a merchant. I also need some speed."

He motioned me inside. "Mostly packs and drays right now, but I've got one that might do the trick. Cantankerous bastard, I'll be glad to get rid of him for a while."

This didn't exactly inspire me with confidence. The beast itself turned out to be a large, shaggy gray that cast a malevolent glance in my direction.

"How do you like him?" asked Dennis.

I reached my hand out to touch him and pulled it back in time to keep my fingers. "I'm supposed to ride this thing?"

"Ah, don't bother yourself. You said you wanted a riding horse with some speed to him. Old Zeus here will give it to you, once you get the hang of him."

"And if I don't?"

"He'll still run fast. It's just a question of which direction is all. I'll have him saddled and ready for you tomorrow."

I thanked him and backed carefully away from the stall. I then climbed a nearby ladder to the large storeroom over the stables, where Sister Agatha could usually be found plying her needle. She was sitting at her worktable by a large window, taking advantage of the last rays of the sun to complete some immense white structure. She had been recruited to the Guild twenty years before as a fool, but her prowess as costumer soon proved to be more valuable. The passing decades had left her hands quick yet scarred with a thousand pinpricks, but the round, red-cheeked face that peeked out from under her coverchief was as merry as when she first arrived.

"Agatha, sweet virgin, abandon your vows and romp with me in Cupid's fields or I shall die of heartbreak."

She dimpled as she always did when I flirted with her and looked twenty years younger for a moment. "Go on with you," she chuckled. "As if an old man like you could do anything for me." She held up her handiwork to the light, and I realized it was a giant miter, grossly distorted. "For the Bishop of Fools," she said. "Watch." She pulled a string at the base of it and a panel sprang open revealing a small compartment. "The doves will be in here. When they get their cue, they'll fly out and perch on the rafters. I don't plan to be sitting under there, by the way, and I recommend you don't either."

"It's brilliant. Unfortunately, I won't be sitting there or anywhere else in the neighborhood. I'm off in the morning."

Her face fell. "And you'll be missing the Feast! Now, that's a shame, Master Theo. We were all looking forward to your joining us after such a long time away. It's been ages since we've seen you do Father Gerald."

"Then let the memory of me suffice, dear heart. Rejoice that I am still worthy of a mission at such an advanced age. And I need your needle to prick me on."

She sighed wearily. "All these costumes to make, and you can't even mend your own motley. Really, Theo."

"Motley? Not me. I go in the guise of a merchant this time, and require the appropriate wardrobe."

She shot me a sharp glance. "They're not sending you as a jester?"

"No. Bright colors make a better target. So sayeth the good Father."

She shook her head and stood up. "It's shameful how they treat you. You're one of the best."

"Nostalgia, my dear. It takes more makeup than it once did to smooth my flawed visage for public consumption. The cracks, crannies, and crevices run deep."

"You're talking nonsense," she scolded as she vanished into her racks of costumes. "But then, that's your job," she added as she emerged with an armful of dull brown garments. "Stand still." She held up a pair of breeches and eyed me critically. "I'll have to let these out a bit. There's two pair, one for travel, one for proper. The tunics are cut from German fustian. Could you be a German merchant?"

"As good a choice as any."

"Good. Here's a new cloak. The lining's sheepskin and the trimming's fox. I've put in a few secret pockets. Do you need a money belt?"

"I have one."

"How are your boots?"

"In decent enough shape."

"Then that should hold you. Try the cloak."

It was black with a large hood. I draped it across my shoulders and took a few steps.

"Not like a soldier," she said. "Merchants always look tired. They huddle inside themselves and check their purses too many times because that's what they live for."

I hunched slightly and retreated into the cloak like a tortoise into its shell. She reached around and pulled the hood up, then stepped back and appraised me.

"How long will you be traveling?" she asked.

"Maybe ten days."

"Stop shaving," she advised. "You'll have a good enough beard by the time you get there. Looks like it will come in gray."

"Looks like my life is coming in gray. Promise you'll wait for me, sweet Agatha."

"I promised myself to another long ago, Theo. But you'll always be second in my heart."

"Knowing the competition, high praise. Good night, Sister."

I climbed back down and went to the kitchen to scrounge some late dinner. Word had gotten around, of course, and a few of the older fellows came to wish me luck. Most of them were retired from the game and were now passing their skills on to the new generation. I couldn't tell if they envied me for going out again or thought I was mad.

By the light of a single taper in my cell, I packed two large saddlebags. Optimistically I included my motley and jester's gear; who knows where I would be going after this venture? I reached under my pallet and removed my scabbard and sword. I pulled the weapon out and examined it closely, then swung it experimentally about the room a few times. It felt heavier than I remembered, and long-unused muscles in my arm and shoulder complained about the un-usual strain. I was an adequate swordsman at best, but my best was a long time ago. I hoped I wouldn't need to use it.

I closed the bags, pulled them onto the floor, and fell onto the pallet. I turned onto my side and gazed out the window. The moon was out, about three-quarters full, and the sky was filled with stars. I hoped that the weather would stay clear at least until I reached the other side of the Adriatic. Winter crossings were bad enough when the weather was good. I thought briefly about praying, but didn't. I expected that my prayers would be given the consideration that they deserved, and that every day that I lived was just another brief postponement of the fire and brimstone that awaited me. Then I thought of the dead Duke, and of the living Duchess, and of the fat drunk and the skinny scarecrow and the passionate Countess and the lucky twin and the black-bearded, black-hearted steward of their destinies. And of mine, if I wasn't careful. Shivering, I fell asleep.

The cock crew immediately after, or so it seemed to me. My entire body resisted as I dragged myself onto the cold flagstones. My bags awaited me, the sword resting on top. I strapped it on and became a gentleman.

I lugged the bags down to the stable, where Brother Dennis was already up and about, stoking the fire of his smithy. He lifted the bags like they were feathers and threw them across Zeus's rump, startling the sleeping horse into a fury of stamping and neighing. Dennis winked at me, which did nothing to help my confidence.

I climbed the ladder to where Sister Agatha waited in the chill air, basking in the first rays of the sun. She tossed me my traveling clothes. "Go try them on," she ordered. I went obediently behind the screen and changed. I added the sword and cloak, slipped my dagger into my sleeve and a larger knife into my boot, then became hunched and tired, which took no effort at all.

"Blessings upon this weary traveler," I intoned, using a German accent.

"God speed you on your journey," she returned gravely and to my surprise embraced me, then patted me on the cheek. "Come back and tempt me some more, you old scoundrel." Then she turned quickly so that I wouldn't see the tears.

Timothy looked at me critically when I came out in my new guise. "You look ordinary," he said. "Not like yourself at all."

"That's the idea," I replied. He gave me a leg up, then leapt to seize the reins as Zeus tried to throw me off.

"Don't you just love them when they have this much energy?" he gasped as the horse struggled in his grasp. "He's champing at the bit already."

"I'm the one he wants champed and bitten," I yelled, but I managed to get a grip on the reins and yanked them sharply. The horse backed up into the stable door and almost shivered it but finally realized that I had him on short rein and that he had better do what I wanted. "This ride is going to be fun," I predicted gloomily.

"That's the spirit," said Timothy. "I'd shake hands, but you'd better keep them both where they are for a while. Good luck, Theo."

I took the horse at a brisk trot out of the stable yard into the courtyard of the Guildhall. Niccolò was out, leading a group of initiates through early-morning tumbling exercises. He waved to me, then quickly mimed a doddering old man and stumbled over a bucket. I nodded approval and left. I cast a longing glance at the tavern as I passed by, but it was still closed.

Just before I reached the edge of town, I had a curious encounter. I was hailed by a rider headed in the opposite direction.

"Ho, Sir Balaam!" he called, and I looked up to see a young man dressed as a troubadour riding a beautiful chestnut stallion. I say dressed as a troubadour, but his garment was richly colored and would have been half a year's wages for most of our lot. "But you should be riding an ass, not a horse," he continued, drawing closer.

It was the greeting that led me to him. I had used the name Balaam once, while passing through Umbria. I recognized him at last. Young de Bernadone, son of a well-to-do merchant from that area. I had met him a few years before and encountered him once or twice since.

"Well met, Monsieur Francesco," I greeted him cordially. "Have you come to join the Guild at last?"

"Alas, no," he said. "Father won't permit it. But he did let me come to see the Feast of Fools done by the masters. My last indulgence of youthful folly, he said. Tell me you aren't leaving."

"Unfortunately, I am," I replied. "A new post. A jester cannot choose his employment and must go when called. But you should find more than adequate entertainment without me."

He looked sad for a moment, then dismounted and came up to my horse. "But where did this magnificent creature come from? I'm used to seeing you on foot."

"A gracious gift from a wealthy patron. He's called Zeus, for his lightning speed and capricious temperament. I have yet to see his prowess with the mares."

Francesco took the horse's head between his hands and examined him critically. The beast submitted to it, to my surprise. The youth looked him directly in the eyes.

"Bear him well," he instructed him. "He has walked farther in his life than you have and deserves a comfortable journey. Treat him gently, for he is a friend of mine. God grant you both safe passage." The benediction completed, he reached up and clasped my hand. "Godspeed, good Balaam. Come back to Assisi someday and we will have our conversation."

He mounted his horse and continued on.

I stopped by the guardhouse at the gate and tapped on the door. The guard peered out sleepily, "You're up early, Theo," he observed.

"The youthful troubadour who passed a few minutes ago is not one of us," I told him urgently. "Get word to the Guild. He is probably harmless but should be watched nonetheless."

"All right, Theo. I'll tell them."

I thanked him and left. Oddly enough, Zeus had calmed down and was carrying me quite nicely. Maybe it was Francesco's doing, maybe not. All I can say is some people have a way with animals.

Ͼhree

Foolery, sir, does walk about the orb
like the sun; it shines everywhere.

TWELFTH NIGHT, III, i

A day's brisk travel brought me to Verona, where I was able to find a small convoy of three barges taking a load of larch and pine down the Adige to Venice. They were glad to have me as I represented both a paying fare and an extra sword. Although piracy on the rivers was less frequent now than of old, a harsh winter always brought the wolves down from the mountain, and many of them walked on two legs.

Zeus, to my secret satisfaction, was most unhappy to be traveling by water. He whinnied and shifted nervously as the barge rocked back and forth. I scavenged an old blanket and threw it over him to protect him from the winds whipping across the deck. "Don't worry, old Greek," I whispered to him. "We'll be going on a real boat next." This didn't seem to comfort him. I strapped his feed bag on and walked to the bow.

We were going deceptively fast. There must have been a brief thaw, because the river was high and huge chunks of ice swept by us. The bargemen kept a steady pace. I let them. I have a healthy respect for the musculature of others, and these sturdy Lombards looked as if they could have used the logs they were transporting for barge poles.

We tied up at night and made camp on shore. We didn't lack for firewood, of course, having taken a healthy supply of that as well. I took my turn on watch with the others, chatting quietly and occasionally tossing another log on the fire. The smell of burning pine on a clear winter night is wonderfully restorative, and despite the hard ground, I felt more and more limber with each passing night. Perhaps just being on the journey was all that I needed.

By the third day, my beard was starting to thicken into something passable. Protective cover for the winter, as if I were some kind of weasel. We were starting to come into the coast. The river widened, and we began spotting boats and docks more frequently. As we rounded one curve, I heard from a distance a huge gabbling, as if a learned convocation of geese had forsaken their southward migration and had decided to discuss Plato instead.

As we drew closer, I realized that the sound came from a veritable army of washerwomen, squatting by the river and chatting away, oblivious to the combined chills of water and wind. In the distance, I saw a small encampment. I recognized the colors of Flanders, Champagne, Montferrat, and a few others. A handful of men were up, desultorily exercising their horses or practicing their swordplay while their pages huddled by the cooking fires.

"Look there," said the chief boatman, pointing at another camp situated nearby. I followed his direction and saw another group of women, younger and prettier than the ones beating blankets in front of us.

"The next Holy Crusade?" I asked.

"And their holy whores right behind," he said. "If you give yourself to Christ, they'll give themselves to you. Well, not give, exactly."

"And they invade the Holy Land in the spring?"

He laughed. "We'll see. When the Pope pays as well as the infidels, I'm sure we'll all be better Christians." He spoke no further on the subject.

We made Chioggia by noon and anchored close to shore. A customs official came out to inspect the spike that marked the load line and verify that it was above water. The chief boatman unloaded a small boat and rowed off to find the Master of the Lombards while I bade my companions farewell and led Zeus back to land. I found a stable to take him while I was in the city proper and then traveled by *traghetto* to Venice.

There are many who love Venice, who find the whole idea of the city built on a collection of misshapen mudflats romantic. I hated it. It was dirty, and it stank with the inhuman fumes from boiling pitch, glass furnaces, soap makers, and metal refineries. I had performed in a minor parish there once, and it was all I could do to keep my whiteface white. I was glad for once that it was winter, so that I could at least avoid the miasma of the marshes.

I made straight for the Bacino San Marco, where I discovered that the *Ursula*, a roundship of some one hundred and twenty tons, had been laid up for repairs and would be leaving in the afternoon of the following day, hoping to take advantage of the clear weather to make its way down the Adriatic to winter in Cyprus. I found it aswarm with caulkers, carpenters, and sailors scurrying through last-minute preparations, tying down barrels, lowering cargo into the hold, testing the rigging. I arranged my passage with the ship's scribe, who was, like the bargemen, more than happy to take on a paying passenger during such an unprofitable time of the year. I gave my destination as Zara and paid one of the sailors to transport Zeus on board, a task I was happy to delegate.

As I passed by other shipyards along the Grand Canal, I saw boat after boat being constructed at a frenzied pace, many with broad bows that could handle the easy loading of horses. All connected with the encampment I had seen earlier, I surmised. I passed by a series of wooden footbridges to the Castello at the eastern end of the city, where I took a room for the night at an unprepossessing sailors' hostel. Once inside, I wrote a brief note to Domino and gave it to a boy with instructions to find the fool at the Ducal Palace along with a small penny for his pains, then journeyed to the Rialto.

Under the portico of a church near one end of the drawbridge several tables stood in a row. Behind each table a fat man sat, glumly surveying the passing traffic. Behind each fat man stood a small, thin man holding a ledger and a large, armed man holding an iron chest. The fat men were the most important people in Venice. They were its bankers and controlled the loans to the government, the letter of credit, occasionally even actual money. I presented my letter of credit to the keeper of the Guild's account. He read it impassively, then motioned to his assistants, who placed the strongbox and the ledger onto the table.

"How do you want it?" he asked.

"What do you recommend?"

"That depends on where you're going."

"Zara, perhaps Spalato."

He nodded and began placing a small pile of silver in front of me, carefully noting the amount in his ledger. "Some Venetian coin, some Genoan, a few Pisan. Silver's pretty much silver the world over. Do you want to weigh it?"

"I wouldn't dream of insulting you. Should I take some gold?"

He shook his head. "Too unsteady right now. No one's chancing it. Stick with silver, it won't fail you."

I thanked him and walked back to my room.

As I lay down to catch a nap, I heard someone tapping lightly on the door. I drew my knife, stepped to one side of the doorway, and asked, "Who is it?"

"*Stultorum numerus . . . ,*" came a whisper from the hall.

" . . . *infinitus est,*" I responded, and pulled open the door.

Domino stared at me for a moment, then squealed, "It *is* you!" and leapt into my arms. He hugged me tightly, then drew back and looked at me critically. "Well, you haven't aged much."

"Neither have you," I replied tactfully. He looked hearty for all of his sixty-odd years and was magnificently attired in his customary black-and-white motley, with an ermine cape that he swirled imperiously about him as he entered the room. I've often wondered if I could live the life of a big-city fool, mostly when I was sitting in some tree hollow with the wind and the rain beating down, sewing yet another scrounged bit of fabric onto my own threadbare costume. I figured it had to be decades since Domino last picked up needle and thread himself.

"What liars we both are, Theo," he said as I closed the door. "I'm practically in the grave and I look it. Thank God I'm in a profession where I can wear makeup. I'd hate to have my natural face afflicting the world. By the First Fool, Our Savior, it's good to see you again. It's been years. How long will you be in Venice?"

"Just until tomorrow. I sail on the *Ursula.*"

"Sail? At this time of year? What can you be thinking about? And what is that hideous growth doing on that divine face of yours?"

"I'm traveling incognito. And I must say you certainly have a fine way of arriving at a clandestine meeting."

"Oh, don't be ridiculous," he huffed. "I am Venice. I come and go as I please. If I'm seen wandering into a hostel in the Castello, they'll merely say, 'There goes Domino off to another assignation with a sailor.' But if I took off my makeup and motley, the news would be in the Doge's ear within minutes."

"My apologies."

"Accepted. Now, why are you sneaking around here?"

"What have you heard about the death of the Duke Orsino?"

He sat down and stroked his chin, thinking. "Interesting that you bring that up. We've heard about it, of course. Perhaps two weeks ago. No one wept at his loss, I can tell you that, but it did seem to take people by surprise, which leads me to believe that it didn't originate from around here."

"Why would Venice want to see him dead?"

"He was considered a strong and capable man. Venice doesn't like strong and capable men when they rule across the Adriatic. They have this nasty tendency to be independent. Orsino would have opposed our upcoming adventure quite fiercely."

"Which adventure?"

"You mean you haven't heard?" he said in astonishment. "What have you been doing at the Guildhall, stuffing your ears with wax? I've been sending reports almost weekly."

I mumbled something about living in the tavern, and he glared indignantly.

"A fine thing, loafing about in a stupor while the world is about to undergo a genuine sea change. Sea change, yes, that's exactly the word."

"You mean the Crusade that's being launched."

"Pfaff!" he said, or something to that effect. "My dear, you have no idea about the marvelous scam that's being perpetrated here. A swindle of historic proportions. The Count of Champagne and Geoffrey de Villehardouin decide in the best French tradition to retake the Holy Land, either directly or by way of Egypt. Everyone thinks it's wonderful. The Pope gives his blessing, which is exactly what you would expect of a pope. They gallop off to Venice and say can you take us to Beyond-the-Sea? When? says us. How's next spring? says them. Fine, says us, and how many will be going? They puff out their chests and say thirty-three thousand valiant sons of France and their beloved steeds. And the Doge, who benefits from being blind, never blinks and with a straight face says, 'Very good.

That will be eighty-five thousand marks in silver, payable prior to departure.' And to our astonishment, they agreed straight away!" He chuckled. "Oh, Theo, how we all laughed when they left. There's not eighty-five thousand marks in silver in Europe. And now, they can't even raise the men. So as a result of all of this, the Doge has an army of frustrated Frenchmen camped by the lagoons, and they all owe him money."

He shuddered suddenly. "It's horrible, Theo. Christian soldiers tricked into mercenaries. Enrico Dandolo turned out to be more than anyone expected when they elected him Doge. They thought, 'He's over ninety and blind, he won't last long,' and now he's on the verge of taking over the world."

"What do you mean? They're not invading Palestine?"

"Of course not, you idiot. Venice has been trading quite nicely with the Muslims, thank you very much. No, they have much bigger ideas."

"I see. They want control over the whole Adriatic. Zara, Spalato, Durazzo, Orsino, the lot."

"Oh, but you're not thinking grandly enough, Theo. Forget your background, be greedy."

I shook my head. "Tell me."

He leaned forward and whispered, "Constantinople."

"What?"

"Yes, Venice is so in love with its Byzantine past that it seeks to recapture it. Think of it, Theo. For the very first time, a Crusade against Christians. Our French patsies pay off their debt with the plunder, Venice rules the seas, maybe the Church is reunited under Rome." His face fell and for the first time he looked his age. "I'm doing everything I can to stop it, but this is too big for the Guild to fight. Greed and zealotry are powerful enough forces by themselves but when combined . . . There's an army ready to wage battle and a debt to be paid and they have the momentum now."

He sighed. "Well, enough about my little problems. I've been very depressed lately. Probably the time of year. Nothing's more useless than a jester during Advent. I can't wait for Christmas. I'm preparing the festivities, of course. We don't do a full Feast of Fools here, but we do a nice little Festival of the Ass, and I'll have my usual responsibilities for the New Year. So, you're off to investigate the death of Orsino. I remember, you were involved in that part of the world once. Charming story, I still sing it every now and then. Was the verse yours as well?"

"Yes, mostly."

"I thought as much. It has your style. Do you at least have time for a dinner's worth of gossip? There's a nice little inn just across the bridge."

I agreed, and we ambled arm in arm to a house near the Arsenal that had several steaming kettles suspended over a fireplace that filled an entire side of the room. Over a pitcher of wine and a hearty fish soup we dished the dirt. When I brought up the threat from Rome, he pounded his fist on the table and shouted, "Never!" The room fell silent as they realized who was there, and he did a quick, imperious bow with such intricate flailings of his arms that he immediately became tangled in his cloak. His efforts to extricate himself set the room to paroxysms of laughter, which peaked as he finally collapsed to the ground. It was a signature move of his, and I applauded along with the rest of the diners when he finished.

"Should be enough of a distraction," he muttered as he sat down again. "Dear boy, you've upset me with your news. By all that is laughable, I shall fight for the Guild here, you can count on it. I'm owed a few favors, and I know a few secrets. I might as well cash them in now. I'm too old to use them for anything else. I'll start with the wives, that's always the best way. My reputation in this city is so debauched that the men trust me absolutely to pay court to their ladies. If I get them on our side, the men will surely follow."

He fell silent, a bit morose. "I'm so tired, Theo," he said quietly. "I've been training my replacement, and there's just so much to learn. This could be such a remarkable city, the closest thing to an Athenian democracy since, well, Athens, but this latest leap into folly . . ." He trailed off.

"Your replacement? Nonsense, you have years left."

"No, I haven't. Father Gerald, bless his calculating mind, sent me an assistant. Everyone here thinks he's my little rearboy, which should help him down the road. I'm teaching him how to gossip with the ladies. He's a talented lad, but there are so many nuances and shifting alliances. It's positively Byzantine, which isn't surprising. You have to know how to tell the Dandolos from the Tiepolos from the Zianos and a hundred other families besides. I'll hold on until I can get them to support the Guild, but then it's off to the farm with Domino."

"You've earned a peaceful retirement."

"Have I?" he mused. "There's so much to do, it seems impertinent to just quit in the middle. But that's life, a never-ending middle. It's only stories that have endings."

"Sometimes not even them."

"No, I suppose not. Well, young Theo, help this old fool to his feet. I've drunk rather too much from the twin cups of nostalgia and introspection, and I want to embrace you one last time."

I pulled him out of there and we walked for a while until we came to the bridge that led out of the Castello. We stood for a while, watching the shimmering light play along the gleaming marble.

"There's no witty way to bid farewell to true friends, Theo," he said. "One night is not enough, but that's how it goes. Wander back this way, and comfort me with your success. There are songs I've never taught you, bits of business and cunning effects that maybe you can pass on to the young fools so that I may live on in them."

"You live on, Modesty," I reassured him. "Your legend is secure."

"But you should have seen me in my prime, Theophilos."

"You mean there was a time when you were even more brilliant?"

He smiled and embraced me, then crossed the footbridge. I watched him until he disappeared. He was a legend, I thought as I made my way back to the hostel. His work behind the scenes brought the great reconciliation of Pope Alexander and the Emperor Frederick Barbarossa. Whoever was the Doge at the time got the credit, but that's how we work. A legend within a secret society. Would that guarantee his immortality? Did it matter? I wondered if I would be remembered as well in Guildlore.

In the morning I gathered my bags and walked to where the *Ursula* was docked. The Master Caulker emerged as I arrived, having inspected the work of his guild and finding it satisfactory. The sailing master paid him and he left. A sleepy priest staggered up and perfunctorily blessed the ship and crew. The sailing master paid him and he left. A representative of the Doge then strode up to inspect the crew and their armor. The *Ursula* carried about thirty men. I lined up with them and presented my sword when the official came to me. He sniffed disdainfully.

"Don't travel much by sea, do you?" he commented. I confessed that I did not. He pointed at my weapon. "By the time you get a chance to use that, it will be too late. The idea is to stop them before they board. Do you have a bow?"

"No, but I can use one well enough."

"You'd better get one. I'll let you off because you're only a passenger, but I'll remember you."

He walked off, and we boarded. I went into the hold to visit Zeus. He was tethered inside a makeshift stall filled with straw, and it was clear that whatever goodwill had been imparted to him by de

Bernadone had long gone. I went aft on the lower deck and stowed my gear, then up top to see our departure.

A longboat with twenty-eight men pulled us from the wharf into the harbor. The side-rudders were carefully lowered and a large, triangular cotton sail was raised on the forward mast. It bulged slowly outwards, and we began to move eastwards.

The pilot, a Venetian who knew the harbor inside and out, maneuvered us slowly through the channel until we passed the bar at San Nicolò. The cotton sail was lowered, and several small canvas sails were hoisted up. Our speed picked up, and we were in the Adriatic.

We made Capodistria in a day and a half and anchored there for the night. In the morning, a boat came out to pick up the pilot, and we were off. The sailing master kept us within sight of the coast, directing the crew to raise and lower sails as the winds shifted. We were fortunate to have a calm passage. As night fell, I was surprised to see the ship continue on even though the stars were concealed by the clouds. I wandered towards the forecastle and found the sailing master and his assistant huddled by torchlight over a small box lined up with the keel. The sailing master nodded at me and beckoned me forward. I looked inside the box and saw a small metal needle mounted on some kind of pivot. It moved slightly every now and then, and the sailing master would issue commands to his assistant, who went running down to the steerage gallery to alter the course appropriately.

"An Arab invention," said the sailing master. "I don't know how it works, but the needle points north. If you're brave enough to trust it and smart enough to know which direction you want to go, then you don't even need the stars."

I expressed my amazement.

"We should reach Zara in another day," he continued.

"I wanted to talk to you about that," I said. "I'd actually like to go a little further than Zara."

"Oh? Where?"

"Orsino."

He thought for a minute. "That suits me. I hadn't intended to stay in Zara, and it's a difficult entry. Orsino's easier. I'd just as lief take you in by small boat, if you don't mind."

"I don't mind, but someone will have to break the news to my horse."

He chuckled quietly. "I suppose your reasons for this are private."

"Private but obvious. I have certain competitors who I'd rather be kept in the dark as to my whereabouts. Markets are so volatile nowadays."

"Of course. You'll find that when you pay your fare, you also buy our discretion. Frankly, we don't care all that much what you do. All right, we should make Orsino by evening if the wind stays as it is."

I looked across the bow into the darkness. Suddenly, a light flared up on the coast to the east, then another and another. A string of bonfires had sprung into existence.

"What is it?" I asked him. "Some kind of signal?"

He looked at me strangely. "Aye, it is. Have you so lost track of time that you don't know what it is?"

"I suppose I have."

"There'll be bonfires all over Europe tonight. It's Christmas Eve."

The next day, as the coastal islands slipped by us, the crew wished one another a joyous Christmas. The cook prepared a particularly sumptuous late-afternoon meal, with a bean soup filled with chunks of salt pork providing the main course. I followed the crew's example and picked through my biscuits for vermin before eating them.

One of the sailors pointed to me and laughed. "He's an experienced traveler, this German."

"Friend, I've been on voyages where the vermin were the best part of the meal," I responded.

"Aye, we must have been on the same ship," agreed the sailor.

Just then, the sailing master's assistant came down to advise me that we would be arriving at my destination soon. I hurried to collect my gear, then went amidships, where Zeus was being led onto the deck. The sails were lowered and several anchors dropped, and the *Ursula* was at rest. A small boat was winched over the side. I tied a scarf over Zeus's head so he wouldn't see his next mode of transport and maneuvered him into it. No small task, I can assure you, but somehow we got it done. I clambered in and was joined by three of the crew. I waved to the rest, thanked them, and the windlass was slowly turned.

We hit the water and released the ropes, then two of the men took up oars while the third manned a small tiller. We crested over the surf for perhaps a mile and came up on shore on the west side of the town. I removed the scarf from Zeus, who took one look at the solid ground and leapt from the boat with a neigh of relief. I distributed some extra silver to my most recent transport, hauled my bags out of the boat, and threw them across Zeus's rump. The boat pulled away, and that was the last I saw of the *Ursula* and its crew.

Zeus condescended to let me mount, and we trotted through the southwest gate into the town proper. The sun was beginning to set across the water. As we entered the square, I saw a large flag on a pole depicting a giant bear, fierce of expression, cradling the town protectively in its arms and staring out to the world as if daring it to attack. Little did it know that someone already had.

I was back in Orsino.

ƒOUR

The toil of a fool wearies him,
so that he does not know the way to the city.

ECCLESIASTES 10.15

The square was quiet as I trotted across. The market, normally bustling, was abandoned, its stalls shuttered, its banners furled. The true test of a religion is its effect on commerce.

It was much as I had remembered, with one notable exception. Next to the church was a massive portico, surrounded with scaffolding, with marble columns and an impressive flight of steps that upon closer inspection led nowhere. Behind this imposing facade was a huge pit, lined with stone and dotted with ladders and ramps.

So they got the bishopric at last. It had been the subject of much debate and outright envy when I last lived here. The local merchants, as they grew ever more prosperous, sought validation for their good fortune from Rome. Apparently, the Pope's blessing had been obtained, although I shuddered to guess at what cost. The cathedral in progress looked decades away from completion.

As Zeus carried me past the old church, which despite its Byzantine dome looked cramped and squat next to its grandiose shell of a neighbor, I saw the Bishop himself emerge and squint into the west, surveying the square for lost sheep. He frowned when he saw me, and I hastened to salute him.

"Greetings, holy Father, on this holiest of days," I said, dismounting. "Blessings upon a weary traveler."

"Blessings upon you, my son," he replied. "You're a stranger here, I believe."

"Indeed I am," I agreed. "May I humbly present myself. I am Octavius, a merchant of Augsburg."

"Ah, I thought from your speech that you hailed from that part of the Empire." Score one for the accent, I thought. "What brings you so far?"

"Business," I replied with a vague wave. "But I won't bore you with details. I seek lodging for a short period. Does your worship know of an inn where an honest Christian soul may find safe haven?"

"If you were a pilgrim, I would direct you to the monastery. If you were a student, there is a hostel maintained by the town. But if you are like every other honest Christian merchant I have met, I would put such holy endorsements aside and recommend the Elephant. They set a good table and could accommodate both you and this fine steed of yours. You should bring him by the church tomorrow, by the way. It's Saint Stephen's Day, and we will be blessing the animals."

"I would be delighted," I responded sincerely. "He could use a good blessing." I patted Zeus on the muzzle, and he nearly took my hand off.

"Indeed," said the Bishop, moving a safe distance away. "And if that doesn't work, I also perform exorcisms."

I got a better grip on Zeus's reins and pulled his head down. "Thank you," I gasped. "I regret missing services this morning. May I make a small donation in honor of my safe arrival?"

"Of course," he replied, and the transaction was completed. He gave me directions to the Elephant, and I led Zeus toward the southeast gate.

As I approached it, I heard hoofbeats behind me. I turned to see a soldier of some kind, modestly armored but with a gaudy red plume decorating his helmet. "Hail, stranger," he said quietly, his right hand resting near his sword.

"Hail, good soldier," I replied.

"That would be Captain to you."

I espied the insignia. "My apologies, Captain. I am unfamiliar with the symbol of your rank in this town. No offense was intended."

He studied me closely. He seemed to be about forty, and boasted a magnificent mustache that curled up at each end. His bearing was somehow both erect and relaxed, as if it took only a small amount of his strength to maintain that posture even under the weight of his armor.

"Your garments are German," he commented. "Your speech as well."

"Correct on both counts, good Captain. I am from Augsburg. My name is Octavius. I am a merchant."

He continued to stare at me. "You're a bit late for the fair," he said. "It was in July. But as you have no goods to sell, perhaps you are here to buy."

"Perhaps," I replied, and then decided to match his silence.

"You come by way of Zara, I assume?" he said finally.

"No. I came by sea."

"I saw no ship in our harbor."

"I was brought in by small boat. The ship's destination was farther south. I was let off on the shore west of the town."

"And where did you board this accommodating vessel?"

"In Venice, some days ago."

This elicited an arching of the eyebrows but no further comment. This time, I broke the silence.

"I will be staying at the Elephant, Captain. My whereabouts will be evident at all times, and I expect to leave once my business here is concluded."

"And that business is?"

"That business is business. And as you are no doubt a busy man as well, I will take my leave of you."

I led Zeus away and felt the Captain's eyes marking a target on my back the whole way to the gate.

The town was situated on the north bank of a river that widened as it entered the Adriatic from the northeast. An old Roman wall encircled it, rebuilt many times since the first pensioned soldiers settled here, broken by three gates to the harbor, one to the riverside, and two more for the main roads leading to Zara and the interior. The Elephant was outside the southeast gate, situated equally close to the barge landings that accommodated the river traffic and the wharves for the oceangoing trade.

The old sign still hung from the second story of the inn, badly needing paint. On it was an enormous elephant, purportedly one of Hannibal's, crossing the Alps while dark-skinned men dotted its back like ants. I remembered, as a boy, reading an illustrated account of the Punic Wars that included a similar drawing, with the men dangling from the side of the beast and a small town perched on its back. The creature haunted my imagination for years. When I was in my early twenties, on a mission in Alexandria, a traveling circus came to town, and their criers proclaimed an actual elephant in captivity. I immediately threw all my responsibilities to the wind and hurried to the outskirts of the city to buy my admission. Upon entering the ratty tent, I saw, rather than the monster of my nightmares, a large but pathetic creature, flies buzzing around the scabrous sores caused by the iron shackles imprisoning it on the platform, its tusks sawed off, its skin hanging in folds. It cast a bleary, yellowed eye in my direction, then managed a feeble bellow after being prodded by a small boy with a stick who then held his hand out to me, expecting to be paid again for the favor. I hurried out of there. That memory replaced the fierce, heroic one in my dreams, and I've never been able to recapture the original.

The inn was a two-story log structure, tavern below and a few rooms above. It was hung with laurel wreaths on the outside in honor of the season, and a fire beckoned from within. I tied Zeus to the rail, removed my bags, and entered. A Christmas cake with a cross carved on top was placed on a small table by the door. Three long tables filled the front half of the room, while the rear was taken up by a stove and several casks mounted in a frame against the wall.

I didn't recognize the tapster, and fortunately he didn't recognize me. He was a stout man of florid complexion and wore an ancient apron of uncertain fabric and color. He was certainly surprised to have a stranger come in at that time of day. Or year, for that matter.

"Any room at the inn?" I asked.

"Come in, good sir," he said, recovering quickly. "Welcome to the Elephant. And a joyous Christmas to you. Is it dinner or lodging you want?"

"Both," I replied. "And stabling for my horse."

"Newt!" he bellowed suddenly behind him. I looked past him to the curtain separating the tavern from the family's living quarters, and a small boy of about ten years dashed in, wiping his mouth on his sleeve. "Take this gentleman's horse and put it in the second stall." The boy looked around the room uncertainly, and the tapster cuffed him gently. "Outside, Newt, outside." The boy brightened and dashed past me. I heard a yelp of fear, but somehow he got Zeus under control.

"Well, sir," said the tapster, turning his attention back to me. "My name is Alexander. Let me show you to your room, and then you can come back down for dinner. It's a long ride from Zara, and I'm sure you must be exhausted."

"I didn't . . ." I began, but he had already seized my bags and was tromping up the stairs, humming to himself. I followed him into a short, dark hallway.

"As you can see, sir, we do have room," he said with an exaggerated sweep of his arm. "No need to send you to the stables. You'll sleep in better accommodations than Our Lord on His first Christmas Day. It's lucky you arrived at such a slow time of year. You can have your choice of rooms. A view of the harbor or a view of the town?"

"Harbor, please, as long as the shutters keep out the wind."

"Oh, they do, sir. And a good thing, too. There's snow coming tonight. You can see it on the horizon. Fresh from the Marches, and who knows where before that. You may have to stay with us more than the one night."

"I was planning on it."

That brought a pleased grunt. He opened a door to the right, revealing a space with a bed and enough room to pace beside it. "Here's your pot," he said, gesturing under the bed. "And I'll send up my daughter Agatha with a washbasin. We have a nice stew cooking if you're hungry. And there's wine, ale, cider, perry, and some mead brewed special for the holiday. How about I heat up the cider? That's best for a winter traveler."

I agreed to the last, both to stop the torrent of words and because it sounded delicious, and he left me to my unpacking. I immediately cast about for a decent hiding place for my jester's gear. I didn't know who might decide to poke through my belongings, but the Captain looked like a thorough man, and who knew what spies Malvolio had? Rejecting the floorboards as obvious, I stood on the bed and pulled myself up onto the rafters. Where they met the roof beams, I wedged the bag in. I dropped back onto the floor and was satisfied that it was not immediately visible.

A girl of twelve knocked on the doorway and carried in a basin of water and a cloth. She had long brown hair plaited untidily behind her and was wearing a brown gown that had been tied in haste. "Father wants to know if you'll do with just the heel of the bread," she said nervously. "If not, he'll send me to the baker, but I don't know that there's any left."

"Tell him that would be fine," I reassured her. "I had an ample lunch and just want enough warm food to take the chill away. You must be Agatha."

"Yes, sir," she said, and curtsied prettily. "We saved you some of the good parts in the stew. It's heated up now."

I followed her down and sat at a table near the fire. There were squid and mussels and bits of fish mixed together in the bowl, and the cider was flavored with lemon and spices. Apart from my host and his daughter, I was alone in the room.

I was puzzling over in what manner I would approach my former patrons, direct or indirect, when the door swung open and the decision was made for me.

"Barkeep!" bellowed Sir Toby as he lurched in, angling his great bulk in order to get it through the doorway. "It's Christmas, Alexander, and it would be a sin to pay for a drink on this day. But just in case you have no charity in you, we brought old Isaac along to foot the bill." He dragged in a Jew, a long-bearded fellow about my age, who forced a smile. Then a gust of wind blew Sir Andrew stumbling in behind them.

They were fat and thin when I knew them, and they were fatter and thinner now. Sir Toby had spent so much of his time drinking the health of others, and eating to keep pace, that he now looked as if he could feed the town for a month, were it permissible to cook and divide him. Sir Andrew, on the other hand, was barely a mouthful now, not even enough meat on him to make a passable soup. Aguecheek, people used to call him, and he had become so gaunt of frame that a medical school could have used him for a lesson on the skeleton, so sharply defined was every bone. A pronounced tremor possessed his body so that it was surprising that he didn't make a constant rattling noise. The stringy yellow mop of hair was now streaked with gray. Time's palette had found less inspiration in Sir Toby's thatch, on the other hand, and had contented itself with lopping it off. The man was stone bald, and the light from the fire reflected merrily off of his pate to cast a second glow in the room.

"Good evening, Sir Toby, Sir Andrew, Master Isaac," said Alexander, placing three tankards on the table nearest the stove. Agatha came in with a pitcher and filled it from one of the casks.

"Let's see them, my pretty one," cried Sir Toby, pulling her onto his lap and pawing at her blouse. She turned beet red but submitted to his inspection. "Not ripe enough for marriage yet," he pronounced. "But we'll start looking for a husband for you. You don't do your sainted namesake justice, dear Agatha. Her breasts were huge and holy, if the legend is correct."

"Were they?" asked Sir Andrew. "I thought she was the one who gave the apples to the lawyer."

"No, that was someone else. Saint Clare or somebody."

I cleared my throat. It seemed as good an opportunity as any. "Excuse me for interrupting your pious and learned conversation, but the saint you refer to is Saint Dorothy. She promised a lawyer who was a disbeliever that she would send him apples from Paradise upon her arrival. The apples appeared by his bedside at her death, and he converted and became a martyr himself."

"A holy lawyer!" exclaimed Sir Toby, clapping Isaac on the back. "Then there's even hope for you, Isaac. Be a saint, man, and repay your debt to Our Savior by buying a drink for this gentleman."

"I owe your savior no debt," said Isaac. "I owe you none as well. In fact, you owe me. But I will welcome the gentleman as I would any traveler. Sir, my name is Isaac. I am the assistant to the Duke's steward. Please join us if you would."

"Your servant," I said, bowing. I picked up my cup and moved to their table. "I am Octavius of Augsburg."

Sir Andrew greeted me haltingly in German, and I replied fluently in the same tongue. He looked at me uncomprehendingly and blushed.

"Marvelous, isn't he?" commented Sir Toby. "Speaks a dozen languages with as much wit, and can still turn a lady's head after all these years. Isn't that right, Agatha? I have it, we'll marry you off to him. What do you say, dearest?"

Agatha looked as if Sir Andrew turned her stomach rather than her head. "Oh, he is much above me and deserves better," she said gratefully. She pulled herself up from Sir Toby's lap to fill my cup with wine.

"I don't know what I deserve anymore," mused Sir Andrew. "I didn't think I deserved bachelorhood for so long, yet here I am."

"Perhaps if you didn't waste so much time on your damn fool experiments," scolded Sir Toby. "Puttering around your cellar making those foul stinks. Meandering through the woods picking up pieces of bark and stones." He leaned towards me to roar confidentially, "Man thinks he's a sorcerer."

"I'm an alchemist," retorted Sir Andrew. "I'm searching for the eternal verities of the world. What higher calling could there be?"

"Aye, you're an alchemist now. And before that it was lapidaries, and before that hydromancy, pyromancy, necromancy . . ."

"Don't forget the haruspicy," added Isaac.

"Ugh, I wish I could. All those entrails you made us look at. I tell you, friend Octavius, this slender fellow will follow any mancy that takes his fancy."

"But alchemy is no fancy," I protested. "It is a true science."

"Exactly!" shouted Sir Andrew. "Well spoken, stranger."

"Well, enough of this," rumbled Sir Toby. "Brother Octavius, as a visitor and guest, I leave the next toast to you."

"You are most kind," I said, lifting my cup and considering. "To our new friendship, to your generous welcome, to the spirit of the season, and finally, to the memory of your late Duke."

They stared at me as I drained my cup. Sir Andrew's jaw hung open, completing the fishlike appearance begun by his pale skin. Isaac leaned back on his stool and lifted his cup to his lips while observing me thoughtfully through half-closed eyes. Sir Toby cast his eyes downwards.

"Well, sir," he said, subdued for the first time since he came in. "Those were kind words. He was a friend of mine and kin by marriage. We drank together, we traveled, we fought side by side in the Holy Land against the armies of Saladin. I drink to his memory." And he drained his cup in one prodigious quaff.

"Did you know the late Duke?" inquired Isaac.

"I cannot say that I knew him," I replied. "But I met him once years ago. I was passing through the area, and he was kind enough to invite me to sup with him. He asked me about myself, which is the mark of a gracious host. I found him to be a knowledgeable and generous man on short acquaintance."

"And the Duchess?"

"There was no duchess that I recall, although there was some talk about a countess who lived in the town. Did they marry finally?"

"You mean you don't know the tale?" exclaimed Sir Toby. "Well, I'll tell it to you. I was intimately involved." And he regaled me with a version of the events that did violence to my memory of the role he played.

"Remarkable," I said when he finished. "The whole town must owe you a debt of happiness, Sir Toby." Isaac and Sir Andrew rolled their eyes. "But is there an heir?"

"There is," replied Isaac. "The young Duke Mark inherited his father's title and lands. A fine boy. He'll be a fine leader someday."

"How old is he?"

"Eleven."

"And is there a regent?"

"Not yet," said Sir Toby curtly. I guessed that he had volunteered unsuccessfully for the position.

"Unfortunately, the death left a great void in the town," explained Isaac. "Normally, the Duchess would be considered, but she is foreign-born and not trusted by the wealthier families of the town, the Countess Olivia excepted. Likewise, the Duke's steward, Claudius, is a newcomer."

"He is someone I may wish to meet," I said. "Will he be joining you tonight?"

"Ha!" snorted Sir Toby. "The man is inhuman. I've never seen him eat or drink anything. He disappears into that office and emerges the following morning. If he didn't have such an aptitude for business, you'd think he was a damn anchorite."

"You're not far off the mark, Sir Toby," said Isaac. "He is a deeply religious man and spends much of his time in solitude and prayer. Although it is not my faith, I respect him as a learned and holy man. If you wish, I will try and arrange an appointment for you. Not today, of course. He will be at prayer at some chapel right now."

"Perhaps tomorrow. Shall I come by your office?"

"Please do. I am at the north end of the market. If Claudius is not there, we shall discuss your business until he arrives. After your services, I should think. Around noon? Good, it is agreed. My turn to toast, gentlemen." He lifted his cup. "To peace and to prosperity, for one cannot exist without the other. To long lives and noble deaths. To the Duke who is past and the Duke who is present. May he reign as well as his father did."

We drank again, and Sir Toby refilled our cups, slopping some wine on the table, which he mopped up ineffectually with his sleeve. "My turn," he said, and he raised his cup high. "To women!" he shouted. "To Agatha's future husband, whoever he is, and to the marvelous wench who still shares my bed for reasons she alone knows. To Maria!"

"To Maria," echoed Sir Andrew. "And now it's my turn." He lifted his glass, then looked puzzled. "Dear me, you've done all the good ones. To the Church, the Pope, and whatever's left to toast."

We finished the pitcher, and the three got up to leave. As the Jew settled with Alexander, I tapped Sir Andrew on the shoulder. He glanced at me quizzically.

"I would like to visit your laboratorium," I whispered. "I, too, am a student of the Four and the Three and the Two."

"Wonderful!" he said fervently. "It's been so long since I've had an intelligent conversation about it. Later in the week, if you plan to be here that long."

"I do."

"Then come by in the afternoon. In the mornings, I search for the Stone."

I promised that I would, then the three left. Alexander emerged from the doorway and began cleaning the table while I finished the last of the wine.

"How did the late Duke die?" I asked casually.

He shook his head sadly. "Fell from the cliffs overlooking the town. You can see them from the beach if you go seaside."

"Accident or suicide?"

He drew in his breath sharply. "That's a sinful thing to say, sir, and I suggest you not repeat it in town. No, there was no question it was an accident. There was a man who saw it."

"Really? Astonishing. Who was it?"

"Old Hector. He lives in a shack at the end of the beach. Pans salt, collects driftwood, spreads his nets in the tidal pools. Drops off a bucket of crabs here once a week, so I usually send Agatha out there with a bottle of something to keep off the chill. Anyhow, he saw the Duke fall, so it was an accident."

"Why was the Duke up there at all?"

"Oh, he always goes there towards sunset. Looks across the sea for ships or looks across the town. Master of all he can see. And where did it get him? Dead on a slab like everyone else. But a good man while he was alive."

"Did he always go alone?"

"Usually either the Duchess or that steward fellow would walk with him. Kind of a daily ritual. But that day he was alone, as it happened. Why are you so curious about it, if you don't mind my asking?"

I shrugged. "It's the news of the town. I just wanted to hear the latest gossip, and that's as good a story as any. It also helps a man of my profession to know who's in charge here. Is Claudius the man to see?"

"If it involves business, I'd say so. And there's Fabian. He manages the Countess's estates, and she's next to the Duke as far as being rich and all."

"Good to know. Now, may I rely on your discretion as to a particular matter?"

He sat down across from me and leaned forward. "Depends what you're asking for. I don't keep a bawdy house here."

"Content yourself, good barkeep. I shall not scandalize you. I only wish your aid in finding a particular person, should he arrive here. My brother, in fact. We had arranged to meet in Orsino come the New Year, but my affairs were settled early enough for me to get a head start. He's about my height, a year younger, and when I last saw him sported black hair and a beard. However, that was three years ago and he may be gray, bald, clean-shaven, or one-legged by now, for all I know. He may be traveling under an assumed name, as well. His given name is Heinrich."

Alexander shook his head. "Doesn't ring a bell. Why so secret?"

"Because of our competition. A certain Venetian *colleganza* would be most unhappy if we succeeded, and the stakes are high enough that they may try to interfere. I sense that you are a man of honor, and I am counting on you."

He stood up beaming. "Well, there's counting, and there's accounting, if you take my meaning. I'll keep my ears peeled in the meanwhile."

I thanked him, then decided to stretch my legs before curfew was called.

I passed through the gate and found the north road. Without thinking, I wandered up the hill and found myself in sight of the Duke's villa. It was perched on the highest point in the town, giving view to the harbor and the outlying estates. It was a grand, sprawling, stone structure, with three levels to the main house and lengthy wings on either side. The east wing had been started when I was last here and still seemed incomplete at the far end. The front gates were open, and servants were distributing food and coins to the poor. I watched as the haughtiest of the servants shooed away an excessively thankful woman. He appeared to be the chief almoner. I approached him.

"Here you are, Merry Christmas," he muttered, thrusting a roast joint into my hands. I handed it back.

"Save it for someone who needs it," I replied. "Is the Duchess at home?"

He looked at me for the first time, sized up my merchant's costume, and sneered. "The Duchess is not receiving visitors. She is in mourning, as you have no doubt heard."

"I have, and I wished to pay my respects. I knew the late Duke many years ago."

He looked at me again. "I don't know you," he said.

"Nor I you. The Duke's man was named Valentine, as I recall. His steward was Curio, and I don't recall the chief servant, but he was an older man and I suspect has either died or been pensioned since then."

"Dead, five years ago. His name was Malachi, as is mine. I am his son."

"My belated condolences on the loss of your father. I hope you are up to his standards of service."

"Frankly, sir, I have surpassed them. The Duchess is not receiving anyone. Good evening."

He closed the gates, and I heard the bars fall into place behind them.

"And a Merry Christmas to you," I murmured. There being nothing else I could accomplish, I returned to the Elephant and collapsed into a profound sleep.

ƒIVE

The life of the world is only play,
and idle talk, and pageantry.

KORAN, LVII, 20

The snow came during the night, a heavy one, covering the streets to about mid-shin. Force of habit woke me at dawn. Force of habit left me singularly unrested. Alexander kindly let me borrow some blankets from the unoccupied rooms, and within them I had made myself a burrow with just the slightest crack to let the air in. My jaw, unaccustomed to being bearded, itched. Perhaps some quilt-dwelling mite had made its way into my whiskers. I resolved to wash it if I could find some hot water on this cold day.

There was a soft but heavy thudding going on outside. I dressed and opened the shutters to behold a strange sight. On the other side of the wall, the market was bustling, but with animals outnumbering the people. Cattle, horses, goats, and sheep flooded the square, with dogs nipping at their hooves and children dancing fearlessly among them. I blinked with astonishment, then remembered what day it was and hustled downstairs to fetch Zeus over to the church.

Outside of the Feast of Fools, the blessing of the animals on Saint Stephen's Day is my favorite ceremony. It is the acknowledgment, the recognition of those simple creatures who give us their lives. I was especially glad to see the goats getting their fair due. The Gospel of Matthew to the contrary, there was many a time when I was poor and hungry and found hospitality in a goat shed. Nothing like cuddling up to some warm goats on a cold night. And if you're lucky, you can sneak off with a cupful of milk before the farmer discovers you. On the other hand, sheep have never done me a bit of good. I shall rewrite the parables someday, get them to make more sense.

I worked my way through the milling herds to a cluster of horsemen. I nodded cheerfully to the Captain, who scowled back. A beautiful little girl of perhaps eight years trotted up on a white mare. The horse was grandly festooned with ribbons and dried flowers. The girl was dressed simply but elegantly in a white cloak trimmed with ermine. She was hatless and wore a wide-eyed expression of the utmost solemnity. She took her place at the head of the riders and waited with the rest of us.

The doors of the old church were flung open, and the Bishop himself came out to beckon us in. "Horses first!" he shouted. The girl rode carefully up the steps. We followed at a respectful distance.

"Who is she?" I asked a farmer riding next to me.

"Celia, the daughter of the Duke," he answered, then caught himself. "No, I mean the sister of the Duke. I keep forgetting the old man's dead." The old man was younger than me, but I decided not to mention that fact.

The Bishop bowed to the girl. She nodded and to the crowd's delight had her mare bend a foreleg to him. The crowd cheered. The Bishop took her reins and led her to the altar. There before the plain wooden cross he sprinkled holy water over a barrel, blessed it, thrust his hand in, and scooped out some oats. He held them up to the mare, who lapped them greedily, then threw another handful over both horse and rider. She guided her mount off to one side, and one by one we approached to have the ceremony repeated.

I looked to the front pews and recognized two of my dinner companions seated with a heavily rouged woman that, with a start, I recognized as Olivia. Nature no longer did all. Seated next to her then was Sebastian, looking stout and unhappy, and the crowd of children fidgeting on his right were theirs.

I looked across the aisle to the Duke's pew to see a woman in black, veiled to the point of opacity, watching the girl rider. Viola, still trim, still with the bearing of a youth. Next to her was a severe-looking man, with long flowing brown hair streaked with gray and a beard as grizzled as mine. He beamed as he watched Viola's daughter, then settled back into a frown when he saw me looking in his direction. Claudius, I guessed. I did not see the young Duke. I turned my attention back to the Bishop.

He smiled when he saw me. "Good morning, traveler. Did the inn meet with your approval?"

"Yes, indeed, your Holiness. We both thank you for your recommendation." He turned his attention to Zeus, who looked at him balefully.

"In the name of the ass, and of the ass and the colt, and of the white horse that is to come, I bless thee in the name of Our Savior and Saint Stephen," he intoned. He held out his hand fearlessly. Zeus sniffed it suspiciously, then gobbled up the oats. We were dusted with a few more, then followed the other riders back outside.

"Now, good souls!" shouted the Captain. "Three times around the church."

We took off at a reasonable gallop, skidding and colliding as we turned the corners. I remembered that local custom had turned the traditional three circuits into a friendly race. I was interested to see what Zeus could do when challenged. The first two laps we ran together, with the weaker or more cautious horses drifting to the rear of the pack. Some couldn't handle the corners and slid into the adjoining buildings or lurched into the crowd. Miraculously, there were no fatalities, although one soldier pitched over the side of an unfinished wall of the nascent cathedral. From his laughter, I gathered he landed uninjured or was too drunk to care.

As the third lap began, the Captain was a length ahead of the rest of us as some fierce wagering went on in the market. I gave Zeus his head just to see what would happen. He shook it happily and shot past the pack until just the Captain was ahead of us. He glanced back, saw us gaining, and spurred his mount onward.

"Go, you wretched beast!" I yelled. "I give you a bushel of apples if you win!"

The crowd roared as we rounded the last corner neck and neck. The Captain spurred his stallion so hard that blood ran down its flanks. He thrashed it with the reins, cursed it and its lineage. I took the opposite tack and let go of the reins. The crowd scattered as we hurtled into it, and Zeus was first by a head.

It took us to the other side of the square to rein in our steeds. I was breathing harder than Zeus was. The Captain looked at him appraisingly.

"Faster than he looks," he said. I nodded, still out of breath. "And you weren't wearing armor. That gave you an advantage." I nodded again. "But not for this." His sword flashed under my chin before I could even blink. "You've cost me a small fortune today, merchant."

"Good Captain," I gasped. "This was merely sport. This is a holy day, a festive day. I intended no disrespect. I just wanted to see what the animal could do."

Slowly, too slowly for my taste, he returned his sword to its scabbard. "It would be a sin to challenge you on a feast day. And there are several more to follow. So, my sportive merchant, you are safe for now. I suggest that you complete your business here by Twelfth Night. Otherwise, you will take up my gage and meet me in combat." If a man on a horse could be said to storm away, the Captain did so.

I was angry at myself for drawing this unnecessary attention. Until I knew who all the players were, it was foolish to make enemies. Then again, he was a man who didn't need much of an excuse.

Some happy winners offered to buy me a meal and drink in honor of my triumph. I decided to let them. We trudged back to the Elephant. I sent Newt out to purchase some dried apples for Zeus, then sat down to lunch and conversation. I quickly gathered that the Captain was not much beloved in the town, which was hardly surprising.

"At least when the old Duke was alive, he held him in check," said a farmer. "He's getting out of control, now."

"Hush, you don't know who's listening," advised a dockhand.

"Am I in any real danger?" I asked.

They shrugged. "He had wagered pretty heavily on winning today," said the farmer. "But that's hardly a matter of honor. Just stupidity. It wouldn't benefit him to challenge someone over money."

"Doesn't he still owe fealty to the young Duke?"

"Of course," said a blacksmith. "But the Duke's a child, and he's been sick. Captain won't accept orders from Claudius or the Duchess, and they haven't made anyone regent yet."

"The boy's ill? I hadn't heard."

"Nothing to hear. He's always been sickly, and the cold took him badly this year. And the shock of losing his father, they say."

"No, he was taken ill even before that," said the dockhand. "I heard that from one of the cooks when she was down buying fish."

"Dear me, this is frustrating," I said. "My business requires someone in authority. I hope any arrangements I make will be valid after the regent's appointed."

"It depends on the regent," said the farmer.

"Well, I'm going to stretch my legs," I said. "Thank you again for your generosity."

"Thanks for beating the Captain," said the dockhand, grinning. "Even if I hadn't bet against him, I would have enjoyed seeing him taken down a peg or two. Watch your back, friend. And I'll keep an eye on it as well."

I shook everybody's hand and left.

Zeus had gorged himself on dried apples and looked sleepy and almost pleased to see me. I patted him on the neck.

"You are the unluckiest horse I've ever known," I told him. "Even when you win, you bring me misfortune. Let's walk off our meals." I saddled him and rode along the docks until I reached the beach where I first landed.

The winds had pushed the snow towards the town wall, leaving the beach relatively clear. As we left the town behind, the cliffs rose to our right, climbing to well over a hundred feet.

I didn't remember any "old Hector" from my stay in Orsino, but he may not have been so old then. I gathered he was one of those beached mariners who couldn't tear himself away from the sea and eked out whatever living he could from its edges. It couldn't have been much, I realized, as I came upon a shack that was not much bigger than a coffin, hammered together from odd bits of driftwood. Some ratty nets were piled on one side, and some large pans lay nearby. A small boat was perched upon some ill-made trestles. The boat itself was such a misshapen vessel that I would have been afraid to sit in it on land, much less take to the crashing waves.

I saw a wisp of smoke rising past the shack and followed it down to a small fire. A wisp of a man squatted by it, covered with blankets that were in such a shredded state that he might as well have been wearing the nets for all the good they were doing. He had a small fish spitted over the flames and was eyeing it with more resignation than appetite.

"Greetings, Tatterdemalion," I said, alighting from Zeus. "I seek a sage named Hector."

"You found him," he said. "What's that word you called me?"

"A term of respect, given to the elders in my part of the world."

"Ah. Thought it might be something insulting. Have you brought something to drink, pilgrim?"

I reached into Zeus's saddlebag and pulled out a jar of wine and half a loaf of bread. He opened the jar, inhaled deeply, and nodded.

"From the Elephant," he said. It was a statement, not a question. "You've got time to waste and thought you'd amuse yourself by bothering me for some stories."

"Am I bothering you?"

"Not in the winter. Talk's my stock-in-trade this time of year. Too cold for crabs and mussels, too cold for panning salt, and the ships have gone south with the birds so there's no salvaging. So the folks with time on their hands come to visit old crazy Hector to listen to him babble on."

"No one called you crazy."

"But they called me old," he said sharply. I shrugged. "Well, I am old. Too old, and my legs hurt when the cold comes in. But my eyes are good as ever. You and that nag of yours came in by boat yesterday from a merchantman."

"Correct."

"So you have money."

"More expectations than silver."

"I have none of either. Shall I talk about my life? The forgotten beginnings, the fascinating middle, or the dull end?"

"Not so dull recently, from what I heard. You saw the Duke die, they tell me."

He decided to inspect his cooking, holding the fish up to his face and sniffing it from every angle while he peered at me suspiciously.

"I saw it," he said curtly. "And I'd rather not think about it. It was horrible. Why do you want to know about it?"

"You are a teller of tales. I am a collector of tales. I promise not to intrude upon your territory, but I would like to report back to my employer."

"Why?"

"He loves the local gossip." I held up a coin. "Do I need a better reason?"

He eyed it greedily. "Well, now that you mention it, it was quite a sordid experience." He sat back and looked at the sky, pretending to summon up the memory. "He always used to walk along the cliff path, looking out to sea. Sometimes the Duchess would be with him, sometimes his son, sometimes that steward fellow. He'd walk up to that spot there." He indicated a point where the cliff jutted out over the sea and then continued on to the northwest. "I'd usually be around here that time of day. He'd wave to me, he would, say, 'Good evening, Old Hector,' and I'd say, 'Good evening, Your Grace,' and he'd say, 'How are you today, Hector?' and I'd say, 'Very well, Your Grace, and I thank you for asking,' although sometimes I wouldn't be feeling so good, but there'd be no point in bothering him about it as I'm sure he was asking just to be polite. Still, it was nice for the likes of him to take an interest in the likes of me, all things considered. Then he'd say, 'Anything unusual today?' and I'd tell him if I saw any strange ships and whatnot, odd things washed up, portents in the weather. He was a good one, was the old Duke, and sent me the odd gift of food and drink. Many is the time that . . ."

"This is fascinating, but I'm interested in the last time, not the many."

He glared at me. "A good story's in the telling, and if you ever get to my age, you'll appreciate that. And when you get to my age, you don't like to be interrupted. And when you get to my age . . ."

I was beginning to think I would get to his age by the time he finished, but rather than risk interrupting him again, I waited until the harangue had finished.

"Now, where was I?" he said.

"The night the Duke died," I prompted him.

"Yes. I was mending my nets. He waved to me, and I waved back. He shouted, 'Good evening, Old Hector,' and I shouted, 'Good evening, Your Grace.' "

I gritted my teeth and kept listening. He stood.

"Then he suddenly yelled, 'O Hector, I am undone!' and he fell forward like this." He leaned forward with his arms out to either side. "Like a fallen angel, he was, still trying to fly. 'I am doomed, Hector!' I heard him cry in a tone that froze my blood. And as he fell to the earth, his last words were, 'Tell the Duchess I love her.' And then he struck, and his voice was stilled. I ran, oh, how I ran, as fast as I could on these gouty legs, but it was no use. He was dead. His face was frozen in a look of horror, such as I have seen on men who have glimpsed the infinite ahead of them and didn't like what they saw. I covered his face and ran to the town and that was the end of it. Give me that coin."

He snatched at my hand. I closed it around the coin and pulled it away.

"What cheat is this?" he howled.

"When I said I wanted the story, I meant I wanted the true story," I said. "That little oration of yours may be good enough to cadge a drink out of a simpleton, but it won't do me any good at all. I want what you saw and heard, unembellished. No false heroics, no invented dialogue. Then, and only then, you shall be paid."

He was still staring at the coin. I indulged in a bit of tregetry, rolling it from knuckle to knuckle, making it vanish and reappear in my other hand. His eyes followed it involuntarily. I repeated the process with the other hand, palmed it, passed it back to the first, and suddenly snapped my fingers. He started at the sound, then ogled the coin, which was now betwixt my thumb and forefinger.

"One more snap, and it disappears forever," I said.

"What are you?" he asked hoarsely.

"A professional gossip who can entertain with words and cheap legerdemain. Watch the coin closely as it vanishes before your very eyes." I started to pass my left hand over my right.

"No!" he shouted. I stopped and waited. He hesitated and I began to move again.

"No," he said in a whisper. "All right. I did see him every day, but we never spoke. There's no way he could hear me from up there, with the waves crashing and all. But I'd give him a wave, and he'd wave back, and that's the truth of it."

"The day he died," I prompted him.

"The day he died, he was by himself. I wasn't mending my nets, I was drinking to keep away the cold. It was a cold day, first freeze and my fingers were too stiff to do anything other than hold a cup of wine. I saw him up there. He looked at me and waved. I waved back. Then his knees bent and he fell. Didn't make a sound until he hit those rocks. I thought I was dreaming it. I ran to where he struck the rocks, but there was nothing I could do. His face was caved in, and so was his chest. I pulled him off the rocks and dragged him to higher ground, then ran to town. They came and took him away. That captain fellow thought I had killed him at first, but the Duke still had his purse and jewelry. Captain looked around my shack for some kind of weapon, but there weren't none. He finally decided I was telling the truth, which I was, and I am, so give me the damn coin."

He held out his hand defiantly.

"Not just yet," I said. "Show me where he landed."

He took me a short distance to an outcrop of rocks at the base of the cliff, worn smooth by the sea but still hard enough to smash a fallen Duke. "Show me how he lay when you found him." He stretched himself out carefully, face on a rock about the size of his head, chest on a larger one, arms and legs sprawled in different directions. "Show me how he fell," I commanded, and he stood on the shore, looking out to sea, and slowly toppled forward, his arms out. "Did he fall like that or tumble end over end?"

"Straight out," he said. "And he fell. He didn't jump, or dive, or leap, or anything like that. I don't know why he fell, but he fell and landed on his face, and that was the end of him. Enough. I'll do no more."

"For your pains," I said, and I plucked the coin out of his ear and put it in his outstretched hand.

"I would check my pockets after meeting the likes of you," he said, showing the gaps in his teeth as he bit the coin. "But I have no pockets and nothing to steal. Get out of here, and bother me no more. And thanks for the wine."

I glanced behind me as I rode back, but he had his face in the jar and looked to stay that way. "What did you think of his story, my lord?" I asked Zeus. He snorted. "Perhaps, perhaps not. He lacks sufficient imagination to be a good liar. Unlike myself. Well, my lord, I am abusing your goodwill on the one day of the year in your honor. Allow me to conduct you to your lodgings, where you may find shelter. The wind blows where it wills, as the good book says, but you can still put a door between it and your rump."

I left him in the stables and wandered into the square, searching for Isaac's office. I found it on the north side, a modest, two-story, wooden building with the Duke's insignia carved over the door. I kicked the snow off of my boots and went in.

Isaac was at a large oaken desk in the front of the room, surrounded by ledgers bound in leather. He was reading from a sheaf of papers and making entries on both sides of the page. He waved me to a seat without looking up.

"I'm almost done," he said. "A minuscule error made in April has through my faulty oversight grown into a discrepancy of cataclysmic proportions. I am restoring balance to this precarious world." A few more strokes, then he underlined something, blotted it, and laid his quill to rest.

"Now, my foreign brother, what brings you from Zara in this time of the year?"

"Zara?"

He smiled. "I make it my business to know what's going on. Your innkeeper mentioned it. Wonderful place. Going to be quite the crossroads if they succeed in unyoking themselves from Hungary. How were events shaping up when you left?"

"Good sir, I fear you have been misinformed. I arrived from Venice, not Zara."

His eyes gleamed for a moment, and he leaned forward. "Venice, in truth. Well, that does put a different complexion on things. What news on the Rialto? Is the next holy war prepared? Are the Christians ready to fight the Muslims for the Jewish city? And when?"

"I'm afraid I did not tarry long enough for the Doge to share that information with me."

He nodded, amused. "I am in correspondence with cousins in Venice. We try to keep each other posted on the progress of the Crusades."

"That's good business, certainly."

"No," he said. "That's survival. My people have an unfortunate habit of being in the way of these fanatics. If they can't find any Muslims to kill, they turn their attention to us. And they've been known to burn down the occasional synagogue on their way, just for practice. So, we keep each other warned."

"Interesting. How far does this network of informants extend?"

"As far as my great-grandfather was able to distribute his seed. He was married four times and had a legion of descendants. It would take the very best Arab mathematician to plot our family tree.

But here I am talking about my poor self when I have a guest, one with a business proposition, yes?"

"Indeed. But I was hoping to speak with the Duke's steward as well."

"And so you shall," came a voice from above. I looked up the stairs to see Claudius descending, the scowl from his first view of me in the church still in place. He favored black, bringing up unfortunate memories of another steward I once knew in this town. But any thoughts I had that he might be Malvolio were quickly dispelled when he reached the bottom step. He was too short by a head, looking me firmly in the neck as I stood to greet him. He glided silently by me, smelling faintly of pine, and settled behind another desk at the rear of the room, placed on a low platform so that he could command a view both of the room and of the square beyond the windows. He greeted me in German so superior to Sir Andrew's that I worried for a moment that he would realize it was not my first tongue.

"Your proposition, if you please," he said in a voice that was unpleasantly oily.

"You may find it a bit speculative," I began hesitantly.

"Come, sir, that is no way to begin," Claudius interrupted sharply. "Men of business are men of action. Life itself is a bit speculative. Let us be the judge of whether you are worth a small investment."

"It would require no investment on your part," I said. "Merely an accommodation. A permission, as it were."

"To do what?" asked Claudius.

"To have one, perhaps two boats harbor here on an irregular basis, to unload their cargo onto a waiting wagonry, and to guarantee safe passage to the end of your domain."

"A simple enough favor, so simple that I wonder if the cargo be disproportionately complex. What is it that you are smuggling?"

"Smuggling?" I said aghast. "Sir, you do me much wrong. I merely wish to bypass the Venetian tariffs."

An unspoken communication seemed to go on between them. Claudius nodded finally. "Pray continue," he said.

"The cargo is spice," I said.

"Nothing unusual about spice."

"The spice isn't unusual, the route is," I said. "Rather than pick it up directly from Egyptian ports, my brother has ventured into Arabia itself and established contact with certain merchants in Siddiq."

"Ah," breathed Isaac. "That saves twenty percent of the cost right there if he's successful."

"But we hope to save still more. In the past, spice has come, as all our imports do, through Venice, then through the Brenner Pass to Augsburg. Venice exacts an exorbitant tariff for the accident of its geography."

"You propose to unload here and do what?" asked Claudius. "Go by wagon through dangerous country until you reach the Danube? That will take you months out of your way. You've saved your twenty percent, go through Venice and pay the price."

"Only as far as the Drava," I replied. "The main point is to avoid Venice. Even with the time lost, we save another fifteen percent. You don't know how much spices sell for in Augsburg. In Munich, even, we could make our fortune with one ship's worth. And of the cost saved, we would pay you a fee of five percent, as an accommodation."

"For which princely reward, we receive the undying enmity of Venice," commented Isaac.

"A valid point," said Claudius. "Our percentage on two shiploads of spice may be amply outweighed by making ourselves a larger plum for the plucking. We've maintained a delicate balance between independence and servitude."

"Surely Orsino is known for its autonomy. Why do you fear Venice? You didn't under the late Duke."

"But we are no longer under the late Duke," replied Claudius. "And events across the sea dictate the choice for the regency."

"Would either of you gentlemen be a candidate?"

The two began to laugh, not a reaction I was expecting. "Isaac will not be selected because the wealth of the town will not tolerate a Jew in that position. It's one thing to have one work here, as we trade with Christian, Jew, and Muslim alike. But as regent, never."

"And yourself?"

"I am not a candidate because I do not wish to be. I have my reasons. They do not concern you."

"Then there's little point in talking to you until that is resolved. You won't be able to make a decision until a regent is chosen to approve it."

"Correct. But that doesn't concern me. I wouldn't make it until your brother showed up with something in hand, anyway."

"Stalemate."

He chuckled softly, his eyes fixed on mine. "Stalemate? My dear fellow, we don't even have enough pieces to begin the game. Until then, I wish you the joy of the season, and I will devote a portion of my prayers to your brother's safe arrival. Good day, Signor Octavius."

I bowed and left.

Traversing the muddied square, I sorted through the muddle of my thoughts. Neither Isaac nor Claudius seemed likely to be the Duke's murderer, since their livelihoods depended on his existence. Unless he had decided to change them for some new managers, in which case they may very well have wanted to be rid of him. A theory worth investigating, especially since I had yet to find any hard evidence to support my suspicions, although my chat with Hector convinced me that the fall was neither accident nor suicide. I suddenly was very curious about the minuscule error Isaac was correcting. Perhaps a surreptitious visit to his ledgers after hours could be arranged.

One more thing. Although Claudius lacked sufficient height to be Malvolio, the Jew did not.

Ⓢıx

Let Paradise be set up in a somewhat lofty place.
STAGE DIRECTION FROM *JEU D' ADAM,*
A TWELFTH-CENTURY PLAY

The next morning, I presented myself humbly at the gates of the Duke's villa. After too long a time, Malachi came from upon high to speak with me, taking particular satisfaction in telling me that a humble merchant such as myself could not possibly have anything of interest to the grandness within, and would I be so kind as to not try his patience anymore.

Kind or no, my nose was once again in intimate contact with a closed gate. Apart from the retreating rear of Malachi, I could espy no activity within the house. Well, where one door closes, another may open. I skulked to the back of the premises and waited patiently. Sure enough, a woman emerged from the servant's gate, carrying a large basket. A cook, I guessed, on her way to the market. No better source of gossip in my experience than a cook in a great house unless it's a nun in a large abbey. I trailed her from a distance as she made her way first to the square.

The market was in full bustle. The stalls were filled with handicrafts, made by farmers at a time when it was too cold to farm. Vendors hawked roasted nuts, wheels of cheese, ingenious wooden toys, family heirlooms, and Turkish rugs. I saw the woman pick carefully through tables of nuts and dried fruit, then followed her through the southeastern gate to the docks.

A fishing boat had come in, and its crew was rolling barrels of salted fish onto the docks. She singled out the sailing master, who pulled at his cap respectfully when he saw her. He signaled to one of the crew, who staggered out with an armful of sturgeon. She sniffed at it approvingly, and it was added to her basket.

She was heavily laden now, and I saw my opportunity. I fell into step alongside of her.

"Madam, I find myself with some time on my hands," I said. "And I could think of no better use to put time or hands than to offer them to your service."

She dimpled. "That would be a kindness, sir. It's cold enough for these fish to keep until I come home, but there's still the weight and the hill and the wind and the ice and all."

I shouldered the basket and we began to walk.

"Truly a feast you are preparing. How big is your family?"

She laughed. "Oh, this is too fine a meal for my children. They'll have to content themselves with some scraps of salt herring later. I am a cook in the Duke's house, and there'll be eighteen to dinner tonight."

"Ah, I had the pleasure of dining there many years ago. It was a fine table. The cook's name escapes me, but the dessert lingers in my memory, an orange custard, delicately spiced, that tantalized the eye, seduced the nose, and enslaved the mouth. I've never had its equal. Say you're the warden of the recipe, and I'll marry you on the spot. Look, here's the church now, Mistress Cook."

She laughed merrily. "And what should I tell my husband and children then? Nay, the sorceress of the hearth then was a woman named Katrina, and that recipe was passed to her daughter, who is the inheritor of her position as well. The recipe is kept within her bosom to be handed on to her own daughter someday."

"Then I shall wait for her daughter to come of age. How fares the young Duke? Will he partake of your basket tonight?"

"Alas, the poor boy still ails. He's on the mend, I'm happy to say, but he can only keep down broth and a bit of gruel."

"What afflicts the lad?"

"The doctors don't know. Something in his gut, and it's a wonder we didn't all get it, for that's usually the case. And his father dying, well, that was a blow to all of us, but especially to him. To fall so ill and lose him practically at the same moment, well, it's no wonder that he nearly followed him to the grave."

"Were the two events so close? I hadn't heard that."

"Certainly, it was the same night. We had a large group of people for the dinner, the main families of the town, and all of a sudden Mark gives a scream and falls, clutching his stomach. It was right after the third toast, a merry one by Sir Toby, and some thought maybe it was just too much wine for a boy his age, and he had been gorging himself on nuts and sweetmeats before. He always liked to come down to the kitchen when we were preparing large dinners, to watch how we did things and to snatch whatever his nimble fingers could. Yet there he was at the table, moaning and heaving like a drunk man until he collapsed on poor Sir Andrew. Mercy, I thought the knight would make a second when the boy did that, he turned so pale. They took the boy to his room, and the Duchess and his nurse were up all night with him."

"And then they heard about the Duke. The shock must have been considerable."

"Oh, the boy worshiped his father, as boys do at that age. And there was the grieving, and now all the fuss over who's to be the regent. Why they just don't make it his mother is beyond me. She has a better head then all of them, foreigner or no. Everyone's coming to visit him, which is nice, but some of them are trying to insinuate themselves into his good graces, if you take my meaning. Using a sick child like that just to be regent for a few years."

"But he's improving."

"Yes, by Our Savior, he is. With luck, he'll be well enough for the play, though Count Sebastian is standing in for him now."

"Ah, a Christmas play. What are they doing?"

"It's *The Harrowing of Hell* this year, and he was to be the Savior. He was so excited, it was the first year his father was to let him play the part. And now neither old Duke nor new may be there. Such a pity." She chattered on, telling me of Silvio's gout, Anna's latest pregnancy, and such other servants' matters until I could have probably walked in and identified the entire staff. Finally, we reached the villa.

She wiped her nose on her sleeve. "Well, sir. Here we are, and the walk was a quick one, thanks to you. Nothing like the conversation of a gentleman to pass the time. Blessings upon you, sir."

"And you," I replied. "And on your house and your feast."

She dimpled again and went in.

The Harrowing of Hell. An odd choice. The town was not large enough to do a full cycle during the season, so they always put together one for the last day. I wondered which version they'd be using. Not much of a play, more like a quick debate between Jesus and the Devil, which He wins, naturally, then the righteous Jews parade about and thank Him for saving them.

I came back down the road into the square to find a number of laborers erecting some small platforms on and about the steps of the new cathedral. The market stalls were being pushed back to the western side of the square to make room for the upcoming festivities, though the vending continued uninterrupted. As I drew closer, I recognized some of the scenery in progress. The Cross and the Sepulcher were easy enough to figure out. Two poles with a rope dangling loosely between them were at the highest step. I assumed that would eventually be Paradise. The most elaborate setting was for the gates of Hell, a crude head of Satan with his jaws open wide enough for a man to walk through without stooping. Red damask curtains concealed the interior. To the right of that were a pair of thrones, one painted white, the other a deep red.

A man was turning a windlass that lifted a small, frightened boy into the air. He kept flipping over, which did nothing to assuage his fear.

"No, no, no," scolded an imperious man who seemed to be in charge. "That won't do. The Angel of the Lord must be upright when flying. What can we do?"

"How about we weight his feet?" suggested the man at the windlass.

"Excellent," cried the man directing, and a pair of large stones were lashed to the unfortunate child's shoes. He turned upright, the rope now digging painfully into his armpits. He looked unhappily at the man in charge and took a deep breath.

"All harken to me now," he whined, barely audible.

"No, no, no," shouted the man. "You are supposed to be an Angel of the Lord, coming from up high to deliver a message of hope. Don't whimper, proclaim it, boy."

"But it hurts," whined the boy.

"You'll stay up there until I decide to let you down, and that will be when you give the speech to my satisfaction."

I recognized him now. His name was Fabian, and he had been one of the Countess Olivia's men when I was last in Orsino. He had played a small part in the events leading to Malvolio's disgrace. I hoped it was small enough to escape notice. He was an impudent rascal when I first knew him, and now the rascal had metamorphosed into a tyrant.

The boy struggled through his speech, scrunching up his face as if he thought it might be written on the insides of his eyelids. He did it a few more times in the same faint monotone, but the last rendition either satisfied Fabian or forced him to concede defeat, for he turned to a young deacon who was standing nearby.

"The cue is, 'As I shall now tell to thee,'" he instructed him. The deacon nodded at a shivering group of onlookers who proved to be the choir, for they launched immediately into a shaky rendition of *"Advenisti desirabilis."* Fabian immediately cut them off. "Not that one, that's for later. That 'welcome to hell' one, that's the one I mean. Good, that's it. Jesus, that's your cue to enter. Jesus?"

"Here, damn you," muttered Sebastian, huddled inside his cloak. He walked to his position in a most ungodly fashion. "Christ, why did they have to put Christmas in the winter?"

"Now, now, Count. That's hardly the spirit we want. Your first speech, if you please."

"Hard ways have I gone," began Sebastian, scarcely more audible than the angel who preceded him. There were a number of spectators openly smirking at his appearance.

"And how do you like our little production so far, pilgrim?" came a voice at my elbow. I turned and marked the Bishop, his miter replaced by a simple cap, his eminence swathed in an elaborately trimmed fur coat.

"I find it somewhat appalling," I replied. "Surely the Church does not endorse these sorry proceedings. How can you let these holy days be profaned by theatricals?"

"Nonsense. Just what we need. It brings them in, and if a little moral instruction slips in amidst the entertainment, so much the better. It's not as if they were doing *The Interlude of the Shepherdess.*"

"It smacks of bread and circuses."

"Of wafers and masses, more likely. Look you, see the high and the low mingle in common purpose. Think how grateful the lowly peasants are to be freezing their balls off in the same cold wind as a count or a duke, and to realize how little they suffer in comparison with the agonies of Our Savior on the Cross, which they see reenacted right in front of them. And then to assemble afterwards in a nice warm cathedral and give thanks that their lives are only slightly miserable and that Heaven awaits them."

"Where's Adam and Eve?" yelled Fabian. "We need to measure Paradise."

A young couple, giggling, ascended the steps and stood between the two poles. Fabian fussed with the rope until it was level with their chests. "This is the height," he said to a man who marked it with chalk on each of the poles. "Remember, Paradise must reach the ground so only their heads are visible once they enter. Demons! Mouth of hell, if you please."

"I know there are those in Rome and elsewhere who disapprove," said the Bishop a little more quietly. "But there's no reason why we shouldn't usurp spectacle to our purposes. Why should the Devil have all the good tunes?"

"Because, unlike your choir, he can sing."

He laughed. "Charity and patience, my cynical merchant. And you shouldn't be one to criticize. I've heard German music—those elevated drinking songs—and it is unfit to sing the praises of Our Lord. And you condemn actors. Remember Genesius and Pelagia were actors once, and now they're saints. Well, good pilgrim, although I'm forbidden to put my own genitals to use, that doesn't mean I want them to freeze off. I will see you later at the Elephant. I am giving the traditional blessing of the wine in there."

"If there's wine to be blessed, I will honor the sacrament," I promised, and he strolled away. An earthy fellow for a Bishop, I thought. Unusual, but I liked him the more for it.

Fabian was walking the demons through some clumsy pratfalls. "Now, remember, this is the holiest personage you have ever encountered, and it should send you into a complete panic. Astarot and Anaball on the right, Berith and Belyall on the left. Use your pitchforks, trip over them, try poking each other." Belyall slipped for real on a patch of ice and nearly impaled Astarot. The onlookers roared. "That's good," applauded Fabian. "Keep that in." Belyall looked dubious as to whether he could repeat the move. Astarot looked dubious as to whether he wanted him to. Berith belched abruptly, some more spontaneous comedy. It was all very crude and pedestrian.

"Come, demons, you can do better than that," scolded Fabian. "By heaven, if only that drunken oaf Feste were here to see this. He could teach you a thing or two about falling down."

I had decidedly mixed feelings about being invoked in that manner.

The demons finally trooped through the mouth of Hell. Jesus made another bland and pretty speech and followed them.

"Sir Andrew? Where's Sir Andrew?" shouted Fabian.

"Here I am!" shouted the spindle-shanked knight, galloping into the square precariously perched on an equally emaciated pony. The beast stopped abruptly, pitching its rider headlong into the choir. Fortunately they seemed to be expecting something of that kind, for several, in the spirit of the season, cleared a space for him to fall.

He stood up, reassembled his wardrobe, and limped over to an impatient Fabian.

"My apologies," said Sir Andrew. "You were going to tell me my cue."

"Your cue was to be here an hour ago," snapped Fabian. "Everyone else, in town and out, managed to be here, but not Sir Andrew. Oh, he was a-traipsing through the woods looking for his little stone so he could live his little life past his days. Demons!" he shouted suddenly, and Sir Andrew jumped, looking frantically about for them while the choir roared with laughter. The demons emerged. "Now, Sir Andrew, when they enter the mouth, I want some kind of smoke and flame."

"Certainly," said Sir Andrew. "I can give you red smoke, black, or a nice yellow I've been working on. The flame, unfortunately, will not lend itself to being anything other than flame-colored."

"Red would be fine. And then the second time will be when the Count enters. Count Sebastian?"

"Morning, Andrew," waved Sebastian from the mouth of the devil. "Coming for the mince pie tonight?"

"Yes, thank you," replied the knight. "I'm trying to do all twelve nights this year. Maybe my luck will change."

"Good. Come with me to the Elephant after this. I need something to take the chill off." He turned and went back into Hell.

I noticed Isaac watching from in front of his office. He caught my eye and beckoned to me. I walked over to join him, and we watched the rehearsal from the entry to his offices.

"It's not much shelter, but the wind is blowing from the north," he commented. "A sorry spectacle, don't you think?"

"Oh, I expect they'll be up to speed by Twelfth Day. And audiences tend to be very forgiving about this kind of thing. How do you like it? I supposed it has little meaning for one of your faith."

He examined me as he had that first night in the Elephant. "How am I supposed to answer that? As one of my faith, I would never criticize any aspect of your faith."

"I speak only out of curiosity. As a Jew, you must find it insulting. All of your prophets and patriarchs condemned to Hell, only to be redeemed centuries later by someone you do not believe in."

He laughed. "As a Jew, one comes to tolerate such insults. One must, if one wishes to continue to live in a Christian world. There are worse insults than this. At least this play considers us worth redeeming. Look, that must be Moses."

I turned and watched a man dressed much as Isaac was, with a false beard and a pair of stone tablets under his arm. "Lord, Thou knowest all with skill," he shouted. "The law of Sinai upon the hill! I am Moses . . ."

"He declaims well," I commented.

"Note the horns," Isaac pointed out. I squinted, and was just able to make them out buried in the curly wig.

Isaac glanced at me sideways, gauging my reaction. "Another tradition?" I asked.

He shrugged. "A trick of the light."

The Angel was raised again to deliver the Epilogue. As he completed it with, "And to Heaven wend," the choir launched into something I didn't recognize.

"What is that?" I wondered aloud.

"The Twenty Fourth Psalm," answered Isaac. "In Latin."

"You understand Latin?" I asked, slightly surprised.

"Of course," he answered. "I travel to many Christian lands. I do not speak ever native tongue. But all the educated gentry speak Latin. An agreement made in Latin in Constantinople will be honored in Latin in Bruges, and anywhere in between. A most useful language for commerce."

"You must speak all the languages of commerce."

He laughed. "Latin, Hebrew, Arabic, and double entry. I know them all. Are you sure you had no word for me from Venice?"

"None."

He sighed. "The wind seems to be blowing from that direction. Around here they say surely no Christian will attack another Christian. Not being a Christian, I lack their faith."

"Does your own faith sustain you?"

"Of course. And the faith of the Muslims sustains them. And what is remarkable is that when we all profit from successful trading, we all seem to be able to live together just fine. Perhaps that's the answer."

"Yet Our Savior drove the money changers from the Temple."

"They seem to have resettled in the Church. And they seek to reclaim Jerusalem. Why? For its holy sites or its strategic location? For whichever reason, too many people have died for it, and too many more will follow. But such is the way of the world."

"A cynical view."

"Is it? My late master sallied off to the last Crusade and was away from his wife and family for two years. Many of our best men went with him, and many did not return. He came back and dedicated part of his plunder to that pile of marble over there, displacing several dozen families in the process. Why did he do it? To buy his place in Heaven after earning one in Hell?"

"I am shocked that you could be so critical. The man employed you despite your faith. How many other princes of the realm would deign to do so?"

"Should I praise him for being neutral instead of hateful? Or because his greed outweighed his Christian scruples? I am grateful to find steady employment. I would be more grateful if I were permitted to own property and my own business. But such is the way of the world."

The rehearsal came to a close. The participants began to scatter while Fabian yelled suggestions and criticisms that were largely ignored. A substantial number moved in the direction of the southeast gate. I thought of the Bishop's invitation and found I had a powerful desire to join them at this particular occasion.

"I'm going to the Elephant for the blessing of the wine," I said. "Will you join me?"

"Respectfully, I must decline. We bless the wine on a different day. I will offer a prayer for your brother's safe return when I do."

I bowed, which pleasantly surprised him, and to the Elephant did wend. It may not have been Heaven, but with both wine and a bishop, it was the closest thing in town.

I entered as the Bishop was completing the blessing over a large cask, surrounded by Sir Toby, Count Sebastian, and Alexander. The cask was tapped and cups were passed around to the assembled worshipers.

Milling around, I found myself near the Count. I quickly introduced myself as Octavius before he could have a chance to remember me as anyone else. Fortunately, he had a head start on the blessings due to some earlier imbibing and was plunging headlong into the morose.

"Merchant, eh?" he said. "Traveler, I suppose."

"Quite a bit."

"Lucky. Get to see the world. Thought I was going to see the world once. Got as far as here."

"This seems to be a pleasant enough spot."

He laughed, a short, bitter barking noise. "Oh, it's lovely. Stay for the summer when it's at its peak. Glorious. Every summer, exactly the same. The town, that is. The people?" He quaffed his cup and filled it from a pitcher. "They keep getting older." He downed about half of the next one. "Never marry young," he said suddenly.

"I am not the right man to take that advice."

"Why? Not married?"

"Not young."

He squinted at me, and I tilted my head back and drank to conceal my face with the cup. It was good wine.

"Were you on the last Crusade?" he asked.

"No," I replied.

"Neither was I. Wanted to go. I was young and full of righteous vigor. 'You stay,' says his own puissant self, the Duke. 'Someone must stay and see to the ladies. Look after your sister for me.' And off he gallivants, and all the best folk with him, while I'm stuck with the women and children. Doing my little administrative tasks, and not many of those. His steward took care of most of them."

"Claudius?"

"No, he came later. Another fellow, old geezer. And then he

dropped dead, and my sister without so much as a by-your-leave takes over. Did a good job. I'm not criticizing, but now, not only am I left behind with the women, but a woman's running everything. Then the men come back, and they're all heroes. 'Oh, fine job watching the town, Sebastian. And I hear your sister helped. Well done, lad.'"

He finished the cup, filled it again. I decided not to keep pace.

"I'm a Count, you know."

I nodded.

"By marriage."

I nodded again.

"It was all very well at the time. Swept me off my feet. Didn't even realize what was happening, then it turned out she wanted my sister all the time. Not after, of course, but she thought Viola was me, or I was her, or something. It all happened so quickly. I married a woman who thought I was someone else. Married after only one day's courtship. I was seventeen. And I've been here ever since. With my older wife. And her money and her title. Don't marry young. I know, I know, you're old, but you can tell others about me. Make me into a cautionary fable for adventurous youths. Tell 'em to go ahead and have the goddamn adventure, even if it kills them. I have to take a piss." He rose abruptly and staggered out.

Another cask was tapped, and another after that. There was a toast from Alexander, and a toast from Sir Toby, and then from several other distinguished citizens. We continued toasting one another into the night. At some point we stopped, but for the life of me I can't remember when.

ꙅEVEN

Those women who paint their cheeks with rouge and
their eyes with belladonna, whose faces are
covered with powder . . . whom no number of years
can convince that they are old.

SAINT JEROME, *LETTERS*

I staggered downstairs mid-morning. It took me several long mo-
ments when I awoke to remember where I was, why I was there,
and who I was supposed to be. Alexander grunted pleasantly at me,
and Newt hustled in with a bowl of porridge. Then I remembered
what day it was.

"Come here, lad," I said as he turned to leave. He looked at me,
comprehension and dismay spreading slowly across his face. I
grabbed him briskly by the shoulder, spun him around, and gave
him a good hard swat on the behind. He yelped.

"Long life and joy to you, Newt," I said. Alexander applauded.

"Well done, sir," he said. "I did not say anything because I did
not know if they had that custom where you're from."

"They do," I said. "And I suppose Agatha's too old for it."

"Around here, she is."

It was the Feast of the Holy Innocents, when the children are
spanked for luck. I decided to limit my practice to the one house for
practical reasons and reminded myself to pick up some small gifts
for Agatha and Newt.

"I seem to have overslept," I said to Alexander.

"You and the rest of the town," he answered. "I think we
crammed them all in last night."

"You seem none the worse for wear."

"It's the one night of the year I won't touch a drop. It gets too crazed. I must say the choir sounded in fine form."

"Yes. Maybe you should send them a barrel before they do the play. It will improve the performance."

"You should join them, sir. Your voice was as good as any."

"Really?" I said, covering my chagrin. "I don't even remember singing."

"Oh, yes. After you had a few, of course. You seemed to know all the songs, and a few others, besides."

"I've spent far too much of my life in taverns. What language did I sing in?"

"German, I suppose that was. Sounded like it, anyway."

Well, thank Christ for that. Bad enough I reveal my foolish side by singing, but at least I kept the accent intact. I made my usual post-hangover resolution to stop drinking so much, though I expected that I would have my usual success achieving it.

I had no fixed plan for the day, which fit in nicely with my lack of a fixed plan for the entire journey. Another tilt at the Duchess's gate seemed pointless. Perhaps I should pay my respects to Sebastian and Olivia. And it was about time I started doing a little night work.

There was a flock of children running wild through the square, playing tag and gleefully spanking one another as hard as they could. Several were sliding along an icy patch near the wall, the object being to stay on one's feet as long as possible before crashing into a large pile of snow at the end. A large group of them crowded against another part of the wall, screaming with laughter. I had a sudden instinct as to the cause and sauntered over to the edge of the crowd.

He was completely bald, and his whiteface covered his scalp. There were red and green triangular markings around his eyes that echoed the pattern of his motley. In his right ear was an enameled earring depicting a death's-head. On the fourth finger of his right hand was the ring I last saw in Father Gerald's study. His eyelids were painted a deep crimson, very much in evidence as both eyes were closed. What made this significant is that, closed or not, he was having no difficulty keeping four clubs hurtling through the air.

"Do you know why I have my eyes closed, children?" he hollered.

"Why?" they responded.

"Because I'm afraid to look," he said, and they shrieked as he opened one, gasped with fright and shut it tight again. The clubs continued their gyrations uninterrupted.

A sleepy and altogether uninterested ass was tied nearby. On its head was a crushed dark green felt hat. The fool began inching towards the beast, the clubs following him at will. He opened his eyes and without breaking the pattern reached down, seized the hat, and placed it on his own head. The crowd, myself included, applauded. He shrugged nonchalantly and transferred the hat back to the ass's head, then back to his, faster and faster until his hands were a veritable blur. I tried very hard not to hate him on the spot. Of course, when I was younger I could do the same trick. Not as well, or as fast, but I could do it.

"You, Signore, come and help me," he commanded a lad of ten. The boy inched forward nervously until he was standing next to the fool. The hat appeared on his head, then red and yellow hats on the fool and the ass. The clubs continued high into the air, and the hats moved from head to head in a strange sequence. Finally, all three ended up stacked on the fool's noggin and the clubs settled gently into his hands, the fourth in a last-second catch just over the boy's head. The fool took the boy's hand, and they bowed together, the boy laughing hysterically. He ran back to his friends as a small shower of copper rained on the fool.

"Greetings, Orsino!" he shouted. "My name is Bobo, and this is my beloved Fez." The ass continued to ignore him. "We have come from Toledo for the express purpose of entertaining you. My friend Fez, he is a little ass. And I . . ."

". . . am a big one!" shouted the children gleefully as he looked shocked and offended.

"In Toledo this time of year, it is warm and sunny, and the women smell of musk and spices. Naturally, I could not stand that, so I came here for the climate. Why? Because I am a fool. Let me show you what it is like in Toledo." He reached into his bag and pulled out an assortment of scarves and wigs. He then put on a quick dumb show, mimicking the walks of the fine ladies and the serving girls, the soldiers and the priests, the Moors and the Jews, switching identities with the flick of a scarf and a marvelously changeable face. I watched him closely, observing what I could steal, guessing who he stole from. A rare opportunity, seeing a colleague in a street performance.

He went on for perhaps an hour, a most profitable one from all appearances, then bowed and collected his gear. He chatted good-naturedly with the townspeople while letting the children pet Fez, then started to load his bags back on the beast. I approached him casually.

"Good Fool, tell me the news of the world," I began.

"The world, sir? I'm afraid that is out of my sphere."

"An interesting point. Do you hold with the theory that the world is round or that it is flat?"

"Well, sir," he said. "I believe that it is both round and flat."

"Your reason, Fool?"

"It is a pretty one, sir, but requires a demonstration. Oh, that I had something round and flat to demonstrate it with!"

I held out a penny, and he inspected it closely.

"The very thing, sir." He began walking, and I fell into step beside him. "From all I have observed, men rule the world but money rules them. As the greater must encompass the lesser, so must money encompass the world. And since coin is both round and flat, so then must the world be."

"But men are not."

"True, sir. Men with coin tend to be round, while men without end up flat. It is not an argument that Aristotle would put forth, but it works well enough for the real world."

"Truly, you speak as a fool. But, as they say, *stultorum numerus . . .*"

"*. . . infinitus est.* Indeed, sir." He shot a glance at me, smiling as we turned down a side street. "So you are the great Feste," he said.

"Never call me that!" I snapped.

"Forgive me," he said immediately, crestfallen. "It's just that when I heard who I was going to be working with, well, you can only imagine how excited I was. It more than made up for missing the Feast. What name are you using?"

"I am Octavius, a merchant of Augsburg. I stay at the Elephant, an inn by the wharves. I am the only occupant of the second floor, so you can sneak up the back stairs if you need to find me or leave a message. I notice you have Father Gerald's ring."

"Yes," he said, glancing at it. "Unusually cautious for him. The password isn't enough anymore?"

"Possibly not. For a secret society, we have become notoriously penetrable. How much did Father Gerald tell you?"

"Some. I knew the basic story, of course. I've sung it enough times. How long have you been here?"

"Since Christmas Day."

"You made good time. I left the evening of the same day you did, but I had Señor Slowpoke here. I probably would have made better time without him, but I hate to break up the act."

"Really? All he does is stand there."

"Yes, but you have no idea how long it took to train him to do that."

"I liked the gag with the hats."

"Thank you. Normally, I work in a fifth club, but it's so damned cold."

"You're done. Put on a cloak."

He smote his forehead and rummaged through a pack on the donkey until he produced a cloak and scarf, which he wrapped around him. A warmer hat replaced the felt one. He almost looked like a normal human being, except for the ghostly skin color.

"What do you use for whiteface?" I asked.

"White lead."

"Really? That's unusual. Most of us think it's poison in the long run."

"It may be. But I don't expect to live that long, so I might as well look my best."

"Why the pessimism?"

"I had my fortune told by an expert, and she said I would not see my fortieth year. I am thirty-eight now. She was known for the accuracy of her predictions. She even foretold her own death to the day."

"Remarkable."

"Not really. She hung herself when it came up. Kind of a cheat, but then, maybe not. One should at least respect her professional integrity. So, I plan to be a dead fool with great makeup rather than an old fool without. But to the present matter. What have you learned?"

I sketched in my discoveries and speculations. It took all of a minute. By the end, he was shaking his head.

"You can't even prove he was murdered," he pointed out.

"Not yet."

"And you have no idea if this Malvolio is even here."

"Oh, he's here. I can't prove it, but deep in my bones, I know it."

"Deep in my bones there's marrow, and it's freezing. Where should I stay?"

"Somewhere I'm not. The hostel's your best bet."

"And what do you want me to do?"

"Find out what you can. Take a crack at getting inside the villa. I couldn't convince them to let me in."

"They have children?"

"Two, a boy and a girl. The boy is ill. I suspect they may need some entertainment."

"I'll go straight away."

"It might be worthwhile sounding out the Duchess. If the Duke was in some way lured to his death, perhaps he mentioned something to her first."

"Worth a try. Can you describe this Malvolio to me?"

"About my height, a little younger. If he's here, he's here as someone else. He's probably been here for a while, getting himself established. I'm guessing he's somewhere central where he has access to the great houses and the information he needs."

"Any candidates?"

"There's a Jew named Isaac who assists the Duke's steward. There's a captain of the guards who is itching to take my head off."

"That was quick. Most people have to get to know us first. Let me offer a suggestion, based on what you told me."

"Yes?"

"What about the Bishop?"

I thought about it. "I would think he wouldn't have enough time to establish himself in the Church that well."

"Who needs time? They appoint the Bishop, he leaves Rome, and Malvolio arrives. No one here knows the Bishop. He can pass through all doors unchallenged. It's perfect."

"All right, why not? Anyway, there may be other possibilities, and we may not have much time."

"How so? Orsino died over a month ago, and nothing's happened since."

"He was waiting."

"Waiting for what?"

"For a fool to appear."

We walked on up the hill. "Feste doesn't arrive but Bobo does," he said, thinking out loud. "Malvolio will think the Guild sent me instead of you, for whatever reason. I stay visible, draw his fire. Hopefully, he misses, and we catch him."

"Hopefully."

"And then turn him in."

"No. He disappears."

He looked away. "I see," he said quietly. "One of those assignments."

"Is that a problem?"

He grimaced. "I've killed before. So have you, I'm sure. But it always seems counter to what we stand for."

"He's responsible for the deaths of two of us."

"Maybe. Possibly. Probably. But vengeance should be the Lord's, not the fool's."

"He's a threat to the Guild—think of it as self-defense. If you don't have the stomach for it, at least help me catch him, and I'll take care of the rest."

"All right. I'll go straight to the Duchess. I'll meet you at the Elephant at sundown. Laugh like I've said something funny."

I chuckled merrily as a guard rode past, staring at us.

"You could have laughed louder," complained Bobo.

"It wasn't that funny," I said. "Until sundown. Be careful."

We parted ways, he to the hostel, I to the northwest.

Olivia's house overlooked the northern wall, halfway between the inland gates. I presented myself to a maidservant who vanished inside the house, then reappeared and bade me enter. The speed of my admission was so much more than I had been accustomed to in this town that I barely had time to prepare my story.

The Countess was in. The Count was in but out, sleeping off the previous evening's festivities in an upper room. A swarm of children passed through the rooms and hallways, in such a constant whirl that I could not possibly begin to count them.

She was seated on a pile of cushions near the fireplace, placidly working on some needlepoint. Many-hued silks were draped on the walls and on the Countess. Her unveiled face was coated with enough rouge and kohl to challenge Bobo for decoration. She indicated a large pillow decorated in some Arab fashion. I bowed and sat down.

"You're the singing German everyone has been talking about," she said, observing me closely.

"I'm afraid that I overindulged," I replied apologetically.

"The rumors have been flying about you," she remarked. "Only natural, since you're the newest stranger in town."

"The second newest," I said. "But please tell me, what are these rumors?"

"Oh, you're a smuggler, a fabulously wealthy merchant come to invest in our little town, a fortune-hunter pursuing the Duchess, the new steward for the Duke, and my favorite, a Venetian spy."

I laughed. I couldn't help it. She continued to observe me, basking in her opulence, never missing a stitch.

"The last is more than a rumor. It was propounded by Captain Perun, who happens to be an admirer of mine."

"As any man in his right mind would be, Milady."

This drew a slight smile. "A most excellent piece of flattery, Signor Octavius. You may do very well here."

"Are we speaking of commercial prospects now?"

"Perhaps. If you like. But let's speak of other things as well. You have been to Venice recently? I'm dying to hear the latest."

I had armed myself in my conversation with Domino and shot off a few choice tidbits that lasted the better part of an hour. She asked a few questions that appeared idle on the surface but in fact probed deeply into Venetian politics. Finally she nodded, satisfied.

"I'd say you have earned a reward. Ho, Julia! Something to eat and drink." A tray of dates and figs and a pitcher of wine appeared, and she dug in with a will. "Gossip is hard work," she said, one cheek bulging. "One has to mine deep to find the truth in it. Now, to your business. A new route for spice, is it?"

"You are remarkably well informed."

"I have to be. It takes a healthy estate to keep this house going. And it has to get healthier to take care of the brats."

"Are you saying that you manage it yourself?"

"Of course."

"I was given to understand that your husband did."

"Probably by my husband. When he's sober, he does. But that's less and less nowadays."

"A pity that he cannot devote more attention to you."

A turbulence of children surged through the room, screaming, hitting and biting.

"Oh, I think he's paid me enough attention," she said dryly, as several of the smaller ones tumbled over one another, hollering at the tops of their lungs. A tired group of nurses chased after them, herding them into another room. "He wants to get away from all of this. I may let him. The next Crusade if he desires. A bit less whining around the house may do us all some good. Now, spice, is it?"

"Yes, but I'm told I must await the appointment of the regent."

"Then you might as well talk to me." She started to rethread her needle, tranquilly meeting my gaze, sitting on her little island.

Well, well, I thought. Another contender, and a strong one at that.

"Will they let a woman become regent?" I wondered aloud.

"Why not?" she asked. "There's historical precedent. Irene, Theodora."

"They were Greeks. They have strange customs."

"Really, why should the raising of a boy Duke be so difficult? I'm looking after so many already."

There was a crash and a scream in the distance.

"And a fine job you're doing," I said. "Well, I have nothing to do with it. If you are going to become regent, I will happily negotiate with you. But why you and not the Duchess?"

She leaned forwards conspiratorially. "She's a foreigner, for one thing, and for another, she's a little odd. Do you know the story of how she became Duchess?"

"Yes," I said quickly in an attempt to forestall yet another retelling. She pouted prettily but moved on.

"In any case, the Five Families will want to give the responsibility to a native-born Orsinian. And I happen to be the wealthiest member of the Five Families. Need I say more?"

"I understand completely. And how would Your Grace feel about two shiploads of spice coming ashore here to evade the Venetian tariffs?"

"Would cinnamon be included?"

"I expect that it would."

"Then with a reasonable fee to the Duke and the town, all I would require is an annual chest of cinnamon. I simply adore it."

"Done, Milady. And perhaps some exotic scent on the next trip to add to your already intoxicating allure."

"My dear German, you astound me. I think I shall send my husband to Jerusalem and keep you here."

"We each have our Holy Lands to conquer, Milady."

A hoarse bellow from above echoed through the house, stifling the raucous cries of the children. Olivia barely glanced up.

"Sebastian's up," she said curtly. "Perhaps you had better leave."

"But he and I met last night," I protested.

"I promise you that he will have no memory of it. I'll have my steward show you out. You may wish to discuss the details of your proposition with him. The proposition about the spice, I mean. Ho, Fabian!" He appeared so quickly that I knew that he had heard every word. And she knew it as well and didn't care. "Treat this stranger well, Fabian. We may have much to profit by his desires."

"Of course, Countess," he said, making an impressively deep bow.

"Signor Octavius, you mentioned the arrival of another stranger. Pray, share that last bit of gossip if you would."

"Certainly, Madam," I said, rising and bowing in turn. "A jester from Toledo appeared in the square. Marvelously witty and a skillful juggler. Perhaps he could entertain your children."

"Perhaps," she said, frowning. "It's an odd omen."

"How so, Milady?"

"In my life, jesters have appeared when there's been a death. Have you ever noticed that, Fabian?"

"Certainly Your Ladyship speaks truly," he replied in his most obsequious fashion. "That drunk Feste after the death of your brother, and now this fellow after the death of the Duke."

"Two jesters only, and you see a pattern?" I said laughingly. "I need much more proof before I accept this as an omen."

"Still, the timing is odd," she insisted. "Seek out this fellow, Fabian, and find out his purpose." He bowed, then escorted me out.

As we reached the gate, I asked him, "Is she always so superstitious?"

"Don't underestimate her," he warned. "She has the best mind in town, excepting possibly the Duchess."

"Really?"

"Yes. And in the calculation of power, she surpasses her. Do you know where this fool resides?"

"I believe he said he would try the hostel. Perhaps you could find him better accommodations. The acquisition of a fool can be useful, in my experience."

"The acquisition of any man can be useful," he replied expectantly. I flipped him a coin, and he bowed at an angle calculated to reflect precisely the size of the bribe. "I am happy to make your acquaintance, Signore. Two ships, I believe. Of what tonnage?"

We walked to the square as I spun a web of mercantile lies. He had an office near that of Claudius and Isaac, furnished much more elaborately. The steward's tastes were expensive, I noticed, but he knew his business. I wondered if he would replace the Duke's steward if the Countess became regent.

I returned to the Elephant and had a light supper by myself in a corner of the room. I then went upstairs to find Bobo dozing contentedly on my bed. I kicked him gently, and he sprang lightly to the floor, dagger in hand.

"You'll have to do better than that, my lad," I chided him. "A proper assassin would have had you filleted, breaded, and in a pan by now."

"That is not how one cooks a fool," he protested. "We're supposed to be marinated. In any case, no one saw me come in, and since no one knows you're a fool, I assumed this room would be safe enough for a nap. How was the Countess?"

I told him of my encounter.

"Could anyone there be Malvolio?"

"I did not see the rest of the household," I confessed. "But on further entry I may discover more. Any luck with the Duchess?"

"Yes and no. I performed before the children of the house, including the young Duke, I'm happy to say. He seems to be on the mend. His nurse thanked me profusely afterwards, said it was the first time she had seen the boy smile since his father died."

"I'm glad to hear it. Did you speak to the Duchess?"

"I paid my respects. She was heavily veiled and remained aloof. She did not speak but handed me a silver coin at the end and had them feed me in the kitchen. Quite the elegant lady. I didn't learn much in the kitchen. The doctor had been in to see the boy, but he's there every day. The servants don't think much of him. One said the night Orsino died and Mark took ill, it took the Duchess over an hour to find the doctor. She tracked him down to the bed of some stable wench who could give him many a disease to practice upon. They have been plying the lad with broths, which has probably done him more good than anything."

"I wish we could approach her," I said. "I think she needs to be warned."

"Difficult," replied my colleague. "She is well shielded, by position, by walls, by gates, and by veils. How shall we broach her?"

"In the open," I said.

"But she's never without an escort."

"I have a hunch," I said. "Care to join me?"

He glanced out the window. The sun was below the horizon, still shooting its rays into the distant clouds. "It's cold, it's dark, and it's going to snow again. I suppose that means we're going outside."

"Yes."

"Because we're fools."

"Exactly."

Shortly thereafter, we were perched on a rooftop overlooking the villa from the north. Lights within were doused and shutters closed. Soon the dull glow of the fireplaces provided the only signs of life within.

Bobo shivered inside his cloak. "Has there ever been a winter this cold?" he muttered. "Explain why we are here before I set myself on fire."

"The Viola I knew was a woman of immense passion," I said. "She gave herself over to Orsino wholly, without hesitation. I was told that since his death she has gone every day to his grave, yet I haven't seen her do so. I expect she visits nightly, now, and in secret. We watch for her, and accost her."

"And her bodyguard cuts us in half," said Bobo. "Why can't we just drop her a note?"

"A note may be seen by other eyes."

"And a midnight assignation heard by other ears. Will you reveal yourself as Feste?"

"That wouldn't be revealing myself. Just someone I was for a while."

"And now he's gone. Will he return?"

"He's been summoned. Called forth by a malevolent spirit."

He shivered again. "We should have brought a bottle of wine to stave off the chill," he said.

"We did," I replied, producing one from under my cloak. We passed it back and forth, savoring it, making it last.

"Where did you live when you were Feste?"

"Over there, by the old church."

He looked at the unfinished cathedral, the skeletal scaffolding visible behind the completed façade. "Looks grand but a bit drafty," he commented.

Midnight came, but Viola did not.

"Home," I said finally, and we climbed down as quietly as we could.

"Anything left in there?" he asked suddenly.

"Yes," I said glancing at it.

"Then drink it and sing," he commanded, and he launched into a bawdy tune.

I joined in, slurring my words and staggering as we came upon Perun on his not fast enough steed.

"Ish the Captain," I cried, and bowed low, falling into the snow as I did.

"Good evening, Your Excellency," said Bobo. "He's had a bit too much. I was just bringing him to his lodgings, but he can't remember where they are."

I regained my feet, spitting snow and weaving slightly.

"He's at the Elephant," said Perun. "And you're at the hostel. If I find either of you out on my next circuit, I'll clap you in irons." We both bowed and carried on.

"We'll have to team up when this is over," whispered Bobo. "I'll take you back to Toledo with me. One plays the sot, one plays the fool."

"Who's playing?"

EIGHT

*Ascend with the greatest sagacity from the earth to heaven,
and then again, descend to the earth, and unite together the powers of
things superior and things inferior. Thus you will obtain the glory of
the whole world, and obscurity will fly far away from you.*

FROM THE PRECEPTS OF HERMES TRISMEGISTUS

"Here, let me help," I said.

Sir Andrew was splayed upon a patch of ice, an armful of firewood scattered about him. I started picking it up as he rubbed his nose.

"Not broken this time," he pronounced cheerfully. "There's a bit of luck. Thank you. My man is running some errands for me this morning, and I had to pick up the firewood myself. And now I have to pick it up again."

I had already done most of it. He graciously snatched the last piece from the ground and beckoned me on, making no effort to take back the rest of the load. "You wished to see my laboratorium, I believe. Come by now, and then we can have a bit of lunch afterwards."

I nodded, feigning enthusiasm. He led me to a small house near the northern gate, then around it to a poorly constructed outbuilding that was emitting a dark, noisome smoke.

"Coming along nicely," he said, sniffing it appreciatively. He pointed to the top of the door, and I saw a crude iron cross nailed to it. "Keeps out the demons," he said. "Works beautifully. We haven't had one since I put it up."

"Had you been having much trouble with them before then?" I inquired.

"No," he admitted, "but you can't be too careful. We are dealing with dark and dangerous forces here, just the sort of thing they like. No point in tempting fate." He kicked the door open and ducked inside.

Jesus, Master of Fire, I thought as I looked around. There were many fires in that stifling shack, fires that heated small furnaces, a kerotakis made of bronze with a small bronze pelican on the rim from whose beak a chunk of iron was suspended in some noxious spew or other; fires under alembics, fires under flasks both open and sealed, filled with liquids that bubbled, hissed, and spat. Smoke, fumes, and vapors of varied hues mingled in the air, causing my eyes to water and my very skin to burn, though no fire reached it. Fires tended by several small boys who glanced up fearfully as we entered, having leapt back to work seconds before our arrival. They were all covered with soot and so enshrouded by the smoke that I wouldn't have been surprised if they had been cured like hams. One had a sneezing fit that went on throughout our visit and threatened to continue to eternity. The entire room was an assault on all of the senses, individually and collectively. Its master beamed about, his pale visage mirroring the skull that grinned back from atop a pedestal at the other end.

"A little more wood on that fire, Lucius," he commanded. "No, dip it in the bucket first. That needs to be a slow heat. Philip, I pay you to pump that bellows, not to watch it. Thank you. Here, I brought you this." He tossed his single piece of wood at the boy, who caught it adroitly and stacked it on a pile next to his station. I dumped the rest of it on top.

"The level of heat is always a difficulty," he informed me. "The Principles laid down by the divine Hermes Trismegistus can be frightfully obscure, especially when there's no real way of measuring how hot things are, short of sticking one's hand into the flames themselves, which is certainly something I don't plan on doing again." He was rubbing his left hand absentmindedly as he said this, and I could see where an old burn scar crawled under the sleeve.

"Yet he had to make it obscure," I replied. "If not, anyone could rediscover his findings instead of just the chosen few. It would debase the very quest to make it obvious."

"Of course, of course," he said. "Well, friend Octavius, how do you like it? All the latest equipment, and a full range of substances to assay. I have spent many years and a small fortune to reach this point. But soon I hope to have my reward."

"Already? Then you think you have found the Stone?"

He waved at a portion of the table that was heaped with stones of all shapes, sizes, and colors. "Perhaps it lies there even now. Perhaps it is nestled safely under the new snow until spring comes. The point is, I am ready for it to be found."

"I see. Then you would have no interest in examining this?" I said, removing an ordinary-looking rock from my pouch.

He snatched it eagerly from my hand, holding it up to a lantern suspended from the ceiling that futilely attempted to shine through the smoke. "Where did you get this?" he asked, turning it round and round.

"In Cairwan, in the Dominion of the Almohads," I replied.

"It's traveled all the way from there?" he gasped in amazement.

"Even farther. It was brought by caravan from deep within Africa, where it had been buried with holy ceremony by a magician of great power and watered with the blood of sacrificial victims and aborted embryos. Or so said the man who sold it to me." I have often found that you can attribute the most outlandish stories to the African interior and you will be readily believed by Europeans.

"But haven't you tested it?"

"Alas, no, Sir Andrew. My travels have brought me far from my own equipment, and I have not found anyone with the necessary facilities. You could well imagine my delight when I met you."

He flushed with the praise, the first color I had seen to pass his cheeks since I had arrived.

"May I?" he said shyly, and I nodded. He rushed to a table, sweeping an experiment in progress to the floor in his haste. Flames shot up briefly, and Lucius staggered back in terror as his breeches started to smolder. The other boys moved quickly to quench both the fire and Lucius, then went calmly back to work as if this sort of thing happened all the time.

Sir Andrew placed the stone carefully on a ceramic dish, then removed a clay flask and poured a few drops of a clear liquid on it. Nothing happened. "So far, so good," he muttered. "That was the aqua fortis, and it withstood that. Now . . ." He took a flask filled with quicksilver, carefully removed the stopper, and dropped the stone in. Nothing happened. He swirled it around experimentally. Still no reaction. He sighed and removed it with a pair of small tongs.

"I am afraid that you were sadly deceived, Brother Octavius," he informed me. "It cannot be dissolved in the mercury, and without dissolution, there cannot be any sublimation, and without sublimation, any separation, any ceration, any fermentation, and so forth. I hope that you did not pay much for this."

"More than its true worth, I can see that now. But still worth the attempt. Much can be learned even from failure."

"If that were true, then I'd be one of the most knowledgeable men in Christendom," he said with a good-natured laugh. "Unfortunately, many would practice upon our gullibility, knowing that our haste for perfection often leads us into error."

"True," I replied. "I have seen many a clever ruse. The crucible with the false bottom, the hollow stone filled with gold, the alloy where the silver is dissolved in aqua fortis to leave only the gold . . ."

"So that's how . . ." he said with chagrin, then got up abruptly, snatched a flask from over a flame, and hurled it through a window. "I must thank you again. You have just saved me a few weeks of futile effort. If only you had come a few days earlier, I might have saved some money as well." He took a cup from the end table and faced his minions, who cringed. "Whose turn is it?" he asked. Several pointed to Lucius, who looked on the verge of tears.

"Please, Sir Andrew, I only just went," he whined.

"Nonsense," replied the skinny knight. "Drink some water, and fill it up, boy." The miserable lad took the cup and went outside while the other boys suppressed snickers. "Had I thought about it more, I would have realized that this stone could not have been the Stone," he continued. "For is it not written that the Stone cannot be found by looking but is everywhere around us? That ye shall not find it by direction but may stumble over it on the roadside?"

If that was the case, then the stone I had brought was an excellent candidate.

"That's one of the reasons I became interested in alchemy," he continued. "I'm so very good at stumbling. It's one of my strengths. And I'm always being told that I cannot see what's obvious to all. But that must mean that what is obscure to others must be obvious to me!" He beamed in triumphant conclusion.

"I certainly can't argue with that," I said honestly.

Just then, Lucius returned with a full cup and presented it to Sir Andrew, who promptly gulped it down. He made a face. "What have you been drinking?" he asked the boy. "Haven't you been taking the melted snow I've been giving you?"

"Er, yes, Sir Andrew," said the boy.

"Hmph," said the knight dubiously. "It's very important that you keep as pure as possible, lad. Otherwise, the impurities will find their way in here. Oh, forgive me, I'm being a terrible host. Would you like some?"

"Not today, thank you."

"It has medicinal qualities, you know. Who knows what kind of shape I'd be in without it? Now, lads, let's see how our red smoke is coming along."

This pronouncement met with the first signs of glee I had seen among the boys. Each gathered a small bit of powder from in front of him and hurried outside. Sir Andrew took a taper, lit it from one of the furnaces, and followed them out. The boys were lined up, each holding a plate of powder in front of him as an offering. Sir Andrew went to each in turn and ignited the powders. Flame and smoke shot up from each plate, prompting hoots of laughter from the delighted children. The plate held by Lucius produced a particularly voluminous cloud of red smoke, and he was acclaimed the winner by all.

"Well done, lads," cried Sir Andrew. "We will use the formula that made Lucius's powder. I want all of you to make a cupful by New Year's Day, and we will collect them all together. We'll make a Hellfire to astonish the Devil himself."

The boys actually cheered this little speech, and dashed back inside. But as we walked back to the house, I noticed that the sounds of activity dwindled to a halt.

"I was surprised to see you in town so early," I said as we entered the house, a dismal, ramshackle place that had not seen a housekeeper in some time. The room and everything in it smelled of must and decay. Clothes, bottles, scrolls, dishes, all were heaped in profusion on every available surface. A gray cat skulked about, as scrawny as its master, its fur coming off in patches. "I thought you devoted each morning to your searches."

"Not when the snow comes," he said, beating a cushion into submission and placing it on a chair for me. "There's not much point in it. I'll wait for the spring and devote myself to my experiments and my fasting."

"Fasting?"

"Yes. To become worthy of immortality, one must purify one-self. In addition to my experiments, which shall last me until then, I shall be meditating and praying, as well as studying the great treatises. Have you seen the new translation of Morienus?"

"No, but I have read an original copy of the *Liber Platonis Quartorum*."

"Really? You read Arabic? That is lucky. I've just purchased a translation of Geber, but I wanted to compare one passage to the original. Would you mind?"

He pulled out a chest and opened it, sending a cloud of dust into the air.

The knight found the pages that he wanted and showed them to me. They were each from the *Book of Balances*, one in Arabic, one in Latin, and the paper gave off an oily smell. I glanced over them briefly. "The Latin is accurate, I would say. Only he's made a mistake switching to the Roman numbers from the Arabic. Do you see that?"

"Yes, yes. I thought those proportions made no sense."

They still didn't, but I wasn't about to tell him that. He began rummaging around a cupboard, finally producing some very old-looking cheese. "I am afraid my hospitality is sadly lacking," he said. "Bread and cheese?" I declined graciously. "And how are you getting on with your business?" he asked.

"It's difficult with the old Duke being dead and all," I replied. "When do you think they'll appoint the regent?"

He shrugged. "I really don't pay much attention to it. I suppose it will be Olivia, but some are holding out for Viola, foreigner or no."

"Who do you think would be better?"

"Me?" He seemed astonished and flattered that anyone would even want his opinion on anything. "I think they should let the

Duke rule without interference. Mark is capable far beyond his years, and if he needed advice, he could always get it from his mother or his aunt."

"Or from his steward," I suggested.

Sir Andrew looked puzzled for a moment, then brightened. "Yes, of course. I keep forgetting about him. I don't bother about stewards. They're just servants, after all. They puff themselves up until they think they're as good as us nobility, but they're still just servants."

"I was under the opinion that the Duke's steward leads the most exemplary life, devoting his days to his service and his nights to prayer."

He looked at me oddly. "That is what they say, isn't it? Well, let him to his prayers and me to mine. But I would serve the boy with a will, if they would let him rule." He paced the room, stepping over the things scattered about the floor without even glancing down. "They all think I'm doing this for the gold," he said suddenly. "That's what people think the Philosopher's Stone is for. The transmutation of cheap ore into untold wealth. That's why no one who wishes to be rich will ever find it. It will remain as out of reach as the water does to Sisyphus."

"Tantalus," I corrected him. "Sisyphus was the one who has to push the boulder up the hill. But the metaphor is apt, nevertheless."

"Tantalus, of course. In any event, it's not for the gold, it's for the purity, the immortality, the perfection. Gold is just a base earthly symbol—once we can create gold from dross, then we can do the same to ourselves. And God knows that if ever there was a piece of human dross, I am it."

"Good Sir Andrew . . ." I admonished him.

"No, no. I am painfully aware of my shortcomings. I've lived with them long enough. My ears stick out, which means I can hear what people say about me, and they are quite right. So my life's journey has been a search for perfection. I sought it through learning, and I sought it through prowess on the field of battle. I failed miserably at the latter. Orsino himself had to rescue me from the most abject captivity." He stared out the window towards the eastern ridge and shivered. "I owed him my life," he said quietly. "And I cannot repay that debt now that he's gone. But I can repay his son, and I will. Well, I must return to my quest. Any good gossip from town before I go?"

"You've heard about the new jester?"

He sighed. "Dear me, that's unfortunate. Sometimes I feel that my life's only purpose is to provide fodder for fools. I wonder how long it will take before he latches on to me."

I felt vaguely guilty, remembering how Feste waxed satirical at the expense of the skinny knight. I clapped him on the shoulder, staggering him, and bade him farewell.

I returned to the Elephant in a quest for anything that would blot out the acrid taste in my mouth. Some ale did the trick nicely, and I repaired to my quarters to ponder a bit. The blade at my throat when I entered convinced me to postpone that plan for a moment.

"Now who's being careless?" Bobo chuckled as he slid his dagger back up his sleeve.

"I'm not the target," I protested feebly as my heart danced in my chest.

"Funny you should mention that," he said, suddenly somber. "Today I had the distinct impression that someone was following me."

"Did you see him?"

"Not quite. Just a glimpse of a head ducking around a corner. Hooded. When I looked down the street, he had vanished, but I measured from the ground to where I saw the head, and it was a tall man." He grinned. "It could be anyone, you know. Perun could have been checking me out, or one of his men. Or it could be nothing at all."

"Were you followed here?"

"No, I am certain of that. But Father Gerald's plan may be having some effect. And there's something else. I have been nosing about the docks, chatting up the locals, and there was a stranger who came to town in October and took a room in a bawdy house. He kept to himself, but they say he was a tall man with a beard, black but going gray."

"In a bawdy house?"

"Yes, and the most suspicious thing about him is that he showed no interest in the available revels. He left in mid-November."

"Which coincides with Orsino's death."

"Precisely."

"We may have flushed our quarry. I should start trailing you. Maybe I could spot him."

He shook his head vehemently. "Our main advantage is that he doesn't know about you," he argued. "If he sees you following me, he'll suspect something. I can take care of myself. I'll do better uncovering him without you cluttering the scene."

"Now, really," I protested, but he held up his hand.

"Father Gerald chose me for this mission because I'm good," he said. "You have to start relying on me if we're going to work together. I know what you've accomplished in the past, and I respect it, but you must let me do my job in my own fashion."

I was furious, partly at the lack of trust Father Gerald had in me to send such an upstart, but mostly, because he was right.

"Very well," I said, forcing myself to be calm. "Let me at least do you the favor of allowing you to nap here while I guard the door. Even you younger folk need to sleep once in a while."

He acquiesced. "There's more news," he said. "This Fabian fellow has recruited me to entertain at the house of Olivia. He also wants some help staging the play and the other festivities."

"He certainly could use some. I saw the rehearsal. Good. You seem to be having better luck getting inside than I have. Find out what you can. Now, I have a suggestion for tonight. I want to take a look around the office of the Duke's steward. I want you to check the place out, see when everyone leaves, and if there's a back way in."

"Done. Do we break in immediately?"

"No, let's do it tomorrow. I want to take another stab at intercepting Viola."

"You do that. And when I have retired from my command performance before the Countess's brats to her warm comfortable kitchen, perhaps even the company of a warm comfortable kitchen wench, I'll think of you perched on those cold slates, shivering in the frigid north wind. And I'll shed a tear, perhaps two."

"All I'm worth," I agreed. "Take your nap, fool, before I change my mind and let Malvolio find you."

He stretched out on my bed and was out in a moment. More Guild training. We work odd hours and learn to grab our sleep when we can. In repose, his perpetual smile disappeared as his mouth relaxed. The white lead smoothed out his face brilliantly. I admired the effect while wondering at the fatalism that lay behind its use. A slow, white demise, with the death mask already in place. Still, it beat my floured pan for sheer expressiveness.

He awoke refreshed and prepared to leave for his afternoon performance.

"I've worked up a routine about this Aguecheek fellow," he informed me. "Any ideas for it now that you've seen his little workshop?"

"Let him be," I urged him.

"Excuse me?" he said in shock.

"Leave him alone. He complained about being the lifetime butt of our profession. Why not give him a break?"

"Let me get this straight," said Bobo slowly. "Yesterday, you took me to task because I hesitated to commit a cold-blooded murder. Now, you scruple at mocking that vainglorious popinjay? You actually have some vague sense of compassion towards a worthless parasite who's done nothing to merit his position in life and wastes his inheritance on black magic? My brother fool, my comrade in motley, my colleague and esteemed elder, if I leave off tormenting such an obvious target, I will bring suspicion on myself and shame to our profession. Even he would expect nothing less."

"I withdraw the suggestion," I said. "It was a momentary spasm. It won't happen again. And call me your elder again and I'll knock you through that window."

He grinned. "That's better. Any more suggestions?"

"Oh, I think I'll refrain from advising you for now."

He gave what I deduced was a traditional Toledan gesture with universal meaning and left.

It was the coldest night yet, and I was out in it, sitting at my observation post without even the company of another fool to distract me. I left the bottle at the inn. I was worried that I might overdo it and end up a frozen, broken corpse in a gutter somewhere. It was an image of myself that popped unbidden into my mind more and more often. I wondered if anyone would bury me, if there would be a marker on my grave. I wondered what name would be on it. My only comfort is that there were people who would pray for me, if they lived to hear about it.

I tried to banish these morose thoughts. I heard laughter blossom forth in the distance, then a shutter closed and it was cut off. I shifted my legs, which were getting numb, and stared at the Duke's villa. I still couldn't see inside, just the flickering light through the shutters. I tried to guess where Viola's rooms would be, which gate she would use to slip out to weep by his sarcophagus, how I could approach her, what I could possibly say. Whether she would listen, or care. Whether I still mattered to her, or any of them.

It was that laughter, and its absence, that depressed me. Here I was, a jester by training and inclination, wasting away on a rooftop instead of putting my skills to their proper use in this most joyous of times. I couldn't remember a Christmas season when I wasn't wringing hysterics from families noble and common, with sophisticated wit, many-tongued puns, improvised pageantry, or the silliest of pratfalls. Spending long Teutonic nights regaling long Teutonic knights with shaggy-dog stories of ten thousand lines. Teaching children of Provence the different styles of tumbling, learning new ones from them. Leading the Feast of Fools.

Maybe Father Gerald concocted this plan to bring me back. Withdraw that best part of my existence to remind me it was there. I had been living at the bottom of a cask for too long, and from the cask to the casket is a very short step.

I made my resolution for the New Year, that I would stop pitying myself. Of course, that meant that nobody would, but that was all right. In the meantime, I had a task ahead of me, a very simple one.

I had to stop Death.

NINE

God hath chosen the foolish things of the world to confound the wise.

1 CORINTHIANS 1.27 (KING JAMES VERSION)

"What a magnificent fire they keep in that kitchen of theirs," chirped Bobo with an evil glint in his eye. "They keep it going all night, just so it will be ready to bake the family bread in the morning. Entire forests must have been denuded over the years to keep the Countess and her household toasty."

"Glad you had a good time," I muttered, suppressing a yawn. It was early afternoon, and I had just gotten up. Alexander had thoughtfully left a jug of wine by my bed last night to help me vanquish the chill of my evening adventure, and I had thoughtfully finished it, my New Year's resolution notwithstanding. Hell, the New Year hadn't started yet, I could do what I damn well pleased. Well, maybe not. The headache I had meant business.

"Did you find out anything?" I asked.

"Not much. None of the household fits Malvolio's description. None of them is tall enough. That Sebastian's a surly little fellow. Didn't crack a smile once during my whole performance, and I assure you he was the only one. The rest were rolling on the floor."

"Was he drinking?"

"Yes, heavily. Not at all a happy man, and his wife doesn't seem to care much. She spent more time ogling her oldest son's friends than she did watching the performance. I guess she still likes younger men. I wonder if it's only her eye that roves."

"Think it ever landed on the Duke?"

That caught him up short. He was perched on the end of my bed, chewing on a piece of dried meat, thinking. "I would doubt it," he said. "She made a few rather unseemly remarks about His Lateness. I flattered her in my performance, dropped some references to the regency which she liked very much. She said she'd manage things a whole lot better than he ever did. I thought that was a little inappropriate given how recently he died."

"Was murdered," I corrected him, and he glared at me.

"I haven't forgotten," he said. "I just haven't seen any proof of that yet. In any case, my performance went so well that Fabian offered me a position there, complete with lodging. I have accepted. It's a safer place to sleep than that hostel, under the circumstances."

"Sounds reasonable. By the way, I must say I am impressed with your command of the language," I commented.

"Oh, didn't you know? I was born in Spalato. I speak it fluently, I'm just using the accent for the character, just like you are. You are, aren't you? That's one of the reasons Father Gerald picked me for this assignment. That, plus my extreme talent."

"Did your extreme talent encompass surveying Claudius's offices?"

"Of course. There is an alleyway and a back entrance that should suit our purposes nicely. The Jew left at sundown. I saw an old woman servant leave shortly after that, and then the offices were empty."

"Empty? What about Claudius?"

"He must have left before that or used the back entrance. I couldn't see both at once. But he was gone, I'd swear to it. There was no fire, no candles, and when I went in back, I peeked through the shutters on both floors. No one stays there."

"That was a bit risky, don't you think?"

He waved his hand dismissively. "I was up and down in seconds. If anyone saw me, I would have been taking a quick leak in the alley."

"All right. No more conspicuous than the two of us breaking in tonight. I'll meet you in the alleyway an hour after sundown. I'll bring a lantern."

"Good. What are we looking for, exactly?"

"I haven't a clue. I'll see you then."

I emerged downstairs to some derisive applause for my late appearance. Claudius was supping at a table and motioned for me to join him. Odd experience. I've never eaten with a man I was about to burglarize.

"Any news regarding your brother?" he asked with a concern that I suspected was feigned.

"None," I replied.

"Not likely to be," he commented, his mouth full of bread. "Difficult for a ship to make it here this time of year. Winds are all wrong. Who goes north in winter?"

"Unless he made landfall somewhere in Greece and is traveling by horse," I said.

"That would be a foolhardy thing to do," he pronounced. "The roads are dangerous, and the weather is bad inland as well. Even worse, once he reaches the mountains."

"I have faith in him," I said piously. "He'll be here."

He tore off another piece of bread and scooped up a helping of stew. My stomach was feeling worse than my head, and the sight of him eating so ravenously did not help.

"Where will you go?" I asked abruptly. He looked up at me, puzzled.

"What do you mean?" he asked.

"If you lose your stewardship under the regency. Where will you go?"

He shrugged. "I haven't given it much thought. I'll just disappear with my letter of reference. I'll find something. Are you offering me a position?"

"Until my brother comes in, I'm in no position to make any offers. But I will keep you in mind, if you so desire."

He finished and stood to leave. "Once again, Signore, we are commencing negotiations without our armies in place. Until that time." He bowed, and I stood to return it.

I staggered through the gate into the square, blinking in the unforgiving sunlight. The market was a veritable hubbub of trade and amateur theatrics. I saw my colleague instructing assorted devils in basic pratfalls. I restrained myself from dashing over to demonstrate, but I was pleased to note that it was one area of foolery where my abilities exceeded his. He was not supple enough around the waist to execute the full twists and turns of *le tour français* or *le tour romain* and, for all his jibes at my age, I still was. Petty, this competition between us, but that's how it is when fools collide.

Of more interest was a series of tests run by Sir Andrew and his young assistant Lucius. He listened intently while Sebastian declaimed a speech from the play. At the end of it, Fabian, who was supervising, shouted, "Poof!" Sir Andrew nodded and measured out three strips of linen that he then quickly braided and dipped in a jar. He laid the prepared rope on a metal trough and indicated that Sebastian should recite again.

As the speech progressed, Sir Andrew took a lit candle from Lucius and touched it to the end of the braid. The flame reached the other end a few seconds after the speech ended.

"It's late, Sir Andrew," Fabian admonished him. "I want it to flare up right on the final syllable. We want to scare the sin out of the town."

"Do that, and there'll be nothing left to do," muttered Sebastian.

"One moment," said Sir Andrew. He measured some slightly shorter pieces of cloth and repeated the braiding and dunking. "The last word in the speech is what?"

"Doomsday," intoned Sebastian in a sepulchral voice.

"Say your piece again," commanded Sir Andrew. Sebastian went through it, Sir Andrew listening with his eyes closed, counting the beats in the lines. He touched the candle once more to the braid and watched the flame travel along its narrow path. The fire and the speech ended together, and Sir Andrew looked up happily at Fabian and whispered, "Poof!"

"Amazing, Sir Andrew, you actually got it to work," needled Fabian. "A veritable Christmas miracle. Good. Now, the second one comes after the gates fall. Sebastian will . . ."

"That's Count to you, you puffed-up turd," snapped Sebastian. Fabian looked for a moment as if he would strike his master, then breathed in deeply and let it out.

"My apologies, Count," he said. "The Count will then enter the mouth of Hell, and that's when I want the second one to go up, something a little bigger so he can make his way through the scenery and get ready for the debate. A bigger poof, if you will."

"It will light the very heavens," promised Sir Andrew, and Lucius giggled in anticipation.

I bought some bread and cheese and walked up the steps of the new cathedral to gain a good vantage point for observing the square. The scaffolding was covered with canvas sheeting, which flapped gently in the wind. I peeked behind the façade to see if anyone was there and found the Bishop staring back at me. I bowed.

"Good day, pilgrim," he said in surprise. "Were you looking for me?"

"Not in the least, sir, but I am delighted to find you. I came with the dual purpose of seeing this magnificent structure and gaining some shelter from the winds while I eat. Would you care for some bread and cheese?"

He brightened. "I would love some. I am also here for two reasons. First, to make sure the coverings are secure, and second, to dream about what it will be like when it's completed. God grant that I live to see the day. Come, take a look at what will be."

We walked through a door to see unfinished burial chambers and buttresses, vaults below and vaults above. The unfinished arches framed the sky like hands reaching and imploring in vain. "Gothic," I observed.

He nodded. "It's the style these days, isn't it? It won't be on the scale of your German cathedrals. We just don't have the population here. But it should be an improvement over the old one."

"I like the old one. It brings you in and makes you part of it. These modern structures fall towards the sky and scream at you, 'Look at the Heavens and cower.' They make you want to give up any hope of attaining Paradise."

He looked at me a bit sadly. "My son," he said gently. "We attain Paradise by giving glory to God. What could be more glorious than this?"

I decided not to get into any arguments on that score. We chatted briefly, then I thanked him for the tour and walked back to the front steps. I watched the team working on the scenery for the play. They were daubing red paint on the Devil's head, making it more Hellish by the minute. Some children were painting their idea of Paradise on a sheet nearby, a nice way of involving them. I sat down and ate, glancing about to see if anyone was watching Bobo. Or me.

And there was Captain Perun, seated as usual on his horse. I had yet to see the man's feet touch the ground. He was watching the forced antics of the demons with a trace of a smile on his visage. Actually amused? Could the chief guardian of Orsino be capable of levity?

What about him as Malvolio? Certainly the steward I knew could have been proficient as a soldier. He lacked neither courage nor strength, and in all the confusion of the combined forces of the last Crusade he could easily have winnowed his way into the Duke's service undetected as his former self. The position provided the perfect excuse for watching Bobo. He watched everyone, and who was to say if his focus had narrowed?

Isaac seemed to be a better choice. The beard, hair, and garments made for a more efficacious disguise, and his position placed him in the Duke's inner circle. At the same time, take away the beard, hair, and garments and an ordinary clean-shaven man could skulk unremarked in the shadows and alleyways of the town. I wondered how he would respond if I addressed him in Hebrew. But Malvolio may have known Hebrew. And I doubted that I could get close enough to the man while he was pissing to see if he was circumcised.

And yet I preferred the Bishop. The least suspected man in town, and privy to all families, unlike Perun and Isaac. Given the run of the Church, he would have easy access to the catacombs that ran deep underneath the town. But would Malvolio risk possible exposure by another papal emissary? It may not be much of a risk—once dispatched, Rome's missionaries are rarely followed with any zeal, and by the time anyone may have checked up on the man, their memories of his appearance would have changed.

As had mine, I realized. It had been fifteen years since I set eyes on the scoundrel, and I couldn't summon up a picture sufficiently precise to allow me to recognize the man. And who knew how Time had affected him? The strongest impression I had of him was of his voice, but a voice could change or be disguised.

Maybe it was none of these but Bobo's mystery lodger who no

longer lodged nearby. I was tired of waiting for the man to make his move. I was ready to make one of my own.

I found a paper-seller and purchased a sheet of a darkly decorated hue. To trim a gift, I informed him, but the setting of the sun spurred me back to my lodgings. I pulled my jester's bag down from its hiding place. No indication of tampering, a good sign. I pulled a small lantern and several small candles from it. I cut pieces of paper to fit three sides of the lantern and had myself a ready-made thief's lamp. I dashed downstairs, dined briefly, and had but one glass of wine to the astonishment and financial disappointment of my host.

I then nipped back to my room, lit a candle, placed it into the lamp, and concealed it under my cloak. The back stairway led me by the stables. Zeus whinnied at me, and I shushed him. He whinnied at me again, perverse beast. I passed through the gate and veered behind the unfinished cathedral, pulling my hood up. No one was following.

I measured the time by reciting an old story that I knew from experience took an hour to tell, then slipped behind the old church, waited for one of Perun's patrols to pass, and scampered across to the alleyway behind the steward's offices.

I didn't see Bobo. There were no torches to light the way and little moon. I was about to risk using the lamp when a dark heap by a pile of refuse shifted and rose. I nearly dropped dead on the spot.

"What took you?" whispered Bobo, raising the hood that concealed his whiteface. I leaned against the wall, catching my breath, while he took a small broom he had brought with him and brushed my tracks clear. "Don't want the patrols getting curious," he said. "That's the door."

I opened it slowly and stepped inside. Bobo followed and closed it gently behind him. I removed the lantern from under my cloak.

[123]

We were in a small room containing a table with a washbasin and several small plates and bowls on it.

We held still for a while, listening. The wind howled outside, the building's timbers shifted and creaked, but we heard no sound from a human inside. I pulled out the lantern and peered through the doorway. We were underneath the stairway.

"Go check the shutters," I whispered. "I don't want anyone in the square seeing the light." He nodded and crept into the room.

"Wedged tight," he pronounced. "If the building tipped sideways into the sea, it would float."

I followed him in, shielding the lamp with my cloak. Isaac's ledger sat on his desk, an enormous sheaf of paper bound in black leather. I sat quickly behind the desk, placed the lamp so it illuminated the book, unbuckled the hasp, and opened it. The first page was blank. So was the second.

"Odd," I muttered while Bobo came to peer over my shoulder. I kept turning pages until I arrived at one that was filled. Bobo laughed softly. The ledger was written in Hebrew.

"You started from the wrong end," he pointed out.

"I am quite aware of that," I said, and flipped the ledger over and began from the right side. "A good way to frustrate prying eyes. Let's hope that he at least had the courtesy to use our calendar. I can never figure out the Jewish one."

And he had, as it turned out. His hand was meticulous and neat, fortunately, and the two sets of entries were matched in a very model of clarity.

"Damn," I said. "He's also using some sort of code. I can't make any sense of these words."

Bobo cleared his throat. "Excuse me, but do not the Hebrews use their letters as numbers? That might account for it, especially as I see none of our numbers there."

I stared at him for a moment. "You have this very annoying habit of being right all the time," I said.

"I apologize," he said, shrugging. That mystery solved, I skimmed over accounts of olives shipped out, Egyptian cotton shipped in, so much contributed by various consortia, so much paid to sundry ships, until I arrived at April.

"The Venetian traffic picked up in the spring," I pointed out. "Quite a bit of activity. Looks like the locals did quite well this year. Wait a second."

"What is it?"

"I think I found the minuscule error." He glanced at where I was pointing and whistled softly.

"If that's minuscule, I'd like to know what they consider real money."

The Duke, the Countess, and the rest of the major families of the town were in a consortium for investing in trade. Most of Isaac's ledger was dominated by this group's activities, which ranged inland, up and down the coast, across to Venice and Florence, and to Beyond-the-Sea. A sum of money that would have fed the town for a year had been withdrawn in April and paid . . .

". . . to 'Aleph,'" I said, pointing to the single Hebrew character.

"And who is Aleph when he's at home?" wondered Bobo.

I read on. There was no further mention of Aleph until I reached the day when I was last in the office. An identical sum was repaid to the consortium.

"Well, then it all balances out," said Bobo. "Nothing lost, nothing gained."

"Maybe Isaac and Claudius were speculating with someone else's money," I conjectured.

"And maybe you're speculating now," snapped Bobo. I looked up in surprise. "Forgive me," he continued in unrepentant tones, "but exactly what does this have to do with Malvolio?"

"If Isaac is Malvolio . . ."

"Then he is conniving with Claudius to steal from him, then return the money after he kills him? With all due respect, Herr Octavius . . ." Never had the phrase sounded more disrespectful. "That's ludicrous."

"Maybe the speculation was profitable, and only the original stake was returned to the consortium. As for the connection . . . Well, I fail to see it, unless it was part of the whole general revenge."

"Revenge is never about money," he argued. "And who knows if that money was even returned? This is just a book with words and numbers in it. Just because it said money was returned doesn't mean it was. Accountancy is the new father of lies in this world. What we have here is embezzlement, pure and simple, and furthermore it suggests to me that these two would have ample motive to kill Orsino without any need for Malvolio at all."

"But the message to me at the Guildhall . . ."

"Meaningless. Someone merely wanted to tell you about the Duke's death as a courtesy, but the message was garbled in transit or the messenger was less than reliable. Nevertheless, you immediately leap to the worst possible conclusion and gallop off into a murder investigation. And because of that, I miss my first opportunity to attend the Feast at the Guildhall in years and have to play second fiddle to a fool who's a few hairs short of a bow and a few sheets to the wind, besides."

"Excuse me?"

"In time I may, but right now I'm wondering what we're doing here."

"Investigating suspects," I replied. "Let's continue upstairs."

I closed the ledger and buckled the hasp, then ascended the steps to Claudius's private sanctum.

It would have been charitable to call it a simple room. It would have been accurate to call it a bare one, an undecorated space encumbered only by a single chair and table. The last supported a slim wooden box about a foot high and eight inches wide. It opened from the front, a divided lid with hinges on either side. I sat down and opened it to reveal the only treasure in the room.

It was an icon, one such as travelers would carry. The center was a beautifully wrought mosaic of Our Savior, blessing the fortunate onlooker who has released him from this dark prison. The two side panels were painted with miniature scenes from two lives. On the left, a maiden was converted by Saint Paul, saved miraculously from death at the stake, saved again from death at the fearsome jaws of lions and bears. On the right, a scantily clad girl dances before soldiers, then is apparently converted and spends her life in a cave.

"Saint Thecla, I recognize," said Bobo. "Who's the holy dancing girl?"

"Saint Pelagia, I think. Strange choices. This must have come from Constantinople. Look how long the noses are, that's Byzantine."

"I agree. So what? We know he's religious. He takes time from making money to come up here and pray. It's private, and it's not a Roman church. He's a Greek, or a Syrian, or even a converted Turk. It doesn't have anything to do with anything."

I was looking at the icon while he rattled on. It was thick, thicker than one would expect for holding a tiled image of Jesus. I ran my fingers carefully over the frame. There was a faint click, and Jesus divided himself neatly down the middle as the two halves of the mosaic swung outwards. I held the lantern close and peered inside the revealed cavity. I saw myself looking back. The hidden compartment contained a mirror. No more, no less.

"What do you see?" whispered Bobo eagerly, and I stood to let him have a turn. He peered in, started, then laughed softly. "I see a fool," he said, looking at me. "What did you see?"

"An old man," I answered. "Let's get out of here."

I dreamt that night, an odd dream that disturbed my waking thoughts the next day. I was running through a forest on a moonless night as a low, evil laugh echoed around me. Branches caught at my clothes and tore my skin. I stumbled over exposed roots, cut my feet on jagged stones. Finally, I came upon a clearing, a round, flat circle in the very center of the forest. The laughter came from one direction, then another, but I could never make out the man who was its origin.

Suddenly, something came flying out of the woods in my direction. I caught it and looked at it. It was a juggling club. I hurled it back, but another came flying from a different point on the circle. This too I returned, but more clubs came from all directions. I spun like a whirligig, catching and tossing, faster and faster. I knew that sooner or later I would drop one.

TEN

"I have cap and bells," he pondered,
"I will send them to her and die. . . ."
W. B. YEATS, "THE CAP AND BELLS"

I awoke near midday once again, shivering with cold. Or with fear, or with too much drink, or not enough. The damn beard was driving my chin to complete distraction. I was weary despite the late morning, having slept only fitfully since I had that nightmare. I wish I had dreamt longer. Perhaps the forest would have revealed someone.

It was the last day of the year, and I decided I would enter the new year a clean man. The one major building added to the town besides the cathedral in progress was a public bath, located upriver from the wharves. I saddled up Zeus and took him for a much brisker ride than I truly wanted, but he had been cooped up too long and wanted the workout.

While the cathedral drew its gothic grandeur from the north, the bath clearly was modeled on some eastern design. Some Seljuk builders must have been recruited by Orsino while he was out playing Christian soldier. A low square building led to an octagonal one, surmounted by a simple dome. Wisps of steam escaped from vents in the walls, a welcoming sign. I left Zeus at the bath's stables, entered the disrobing room, and stripped off my clothing. I left my linens to be laundered, purchased a clean towel from a stall in the corner, and padded across the marble floor to the passageway to the tepidarium.

A few other men were already stretched out on slabs, getting massages from muscular young men while allowing their bodies to adjust to the heat. Steam poured in from the other end of the room, and there were roaring fires on both sides. I climbed onto a free slab and allowed myself to be pummeled and whacked unmercifully with rushes until every inch of my body was begging for relief. I tipped the lad and staggered into the last room.

There was a circular pool about thirty feet in diameter, filled with naked men recovering from their sins, their woes, or their massages. It was heated from below. I could commiserate with the teams of servants maintaining the fire in the hypocaust, especially in weather this cold, but the water was glorious. I sank beneath the surface and stayed until I could hold my breath no longer, then floated on my back and gazed at the dome, which was cleverly decorated with a map of the heavens, the gilt of the stars reflecting the torchlight. Pretty, but I had lain on my back on many a summer night looking at the real thing, and there is not enough gilt in the world to capture it.

I grabbed some soap and a brush and entered one of the seven alcoves containing smaller tubs. I plunked myself down in one as an attendant poured a couple of buckets of hot water over me and set to work in earnest. I had almost completely lathered my hair and beard when a booming voice shouted, "Beware, lads. He may be rabid."

"Greetings, Sir Toby," I said without looking up.

"Bless me if it isn't the merchant fellow," he said. He was naked, of course, and a larger mound of pink flesh I have never seen on one frame. He crashed into an oversized tub that must have been specially built to accommodate him and sighed in contentment.

"Heavenly, isn't it?" he said. I nodded. "Best thing to come out of the Crusades, if you ask me. Only good thing, in fact. Very clean, those infidels. Cleaner than the Jews, if you can imagine such a thing."

"Really?" I said.

"Of course, they don't wash together. Unclean, unclean. But the baths are splendid."

"The only thing missing is a jug of wine to go with them," I said idly.

"A jug is an insufficient quantity," he pronounced, lifting an enormous wineskin from the side of his tub. He upended it, then passed it to me. It was still the old year. I drank.

"What was it like being on Crusade?" I asked.

"Completely ludicrous," he grumbled. "We went off, puffed up with the glory of our puissant selves, arrived seasick, and lay around camp for months dying from the sun and the boredom. Broken by periods of intense slaughter on one side or the other. We saw very little of that, fortunately. Our little band mostly went plundering and pillaging on behalf of Rome, with the priests waiting to bless the hauls when we returned. Most exciting thing that happened was when Andrew got himself captured."

"And the Duke rescued him."

He laughed, sides shaking while waves of soapy water washed over the sides of the tub. "If by rescue you mean he walked up to the Muslim city and bribed them for his release, then he rescued him. But it was more haggling than it was jail breaking. Of course, they put up a fierce front. Held him for a month trying to hike up the ransom, but they let him go. It was cheap enough for them to keep him——he barely eats. They worked him over pretty well looking for information, I remember, but the man never knew a thing worth knowing in his life, so they finally gave up and let us have him back."

"Did you see combat, Sir Toby?"

"I did," he said, and took a long pull on the wineskin. "I

acquitted myself on the field of battle with honor, and I never want to do it again. Rome can fight its wars without me. I'm quits with all of them, priests, bishops, generals, the lot. We came back trumpeting our conquests, knowing ourselves to be dupes, frauds, and hypocrites. Since then I have devoted myself to nothing more profound and holy than good drink, hot baths, and a loving wife, and I've been a happy man for it." He leaned back and gazed at the artificial heavens. "Look at this place," he said quietly. "The Duke started two buildings when he returned. One for pleasure, one for sanctity. Look which one was finished first." An attendant was hovering nervously nearby, and Sir Toby fixed him with a glare. "It won't happen!" he bellowed. "Go on about your business and leave me to my ablutions." He turned to me and winked. "They're terrified of me, you know. Not that I'll harm them, but that I'll fall asleep and drown in the tub, and it will take a squadron of them to lift me out of it. Not a bad way to go, now that I think of it. Some lithe wench to straddle me as I fade away, and I'll have no need of Heaven."

"I am surprised that with such an attitude you would seek the responsibilities of the regency."

He shot a quick glance at me. "Oh, so you heard about that, did you? Well, contrary to appearances, my motives are pure. I don't care about the power or the wealth. I just want to protect the lad from the rest of them. Just until he's old enough to take care of himself. If he gets caught between the aunt and the mother now, he'll be lucky to have any kind of childhood left. Now with me he'll learn to drink, to swear, to chase women, all one needs to know of becoming a man."

"Perhaps you could hire on as a tutor," I suggested.

He laughed. "By God, you have it," he said. "I shall start my own school. Sir Toby's Academy for Advanced Wastrels, complete with wine tasting. I shall be the headmaster and chief lecturer. It will all be done through demonstration."

"Allow me to enroll immediately," I said, getting up and toweling off. He saluted me and lay back to contemplate the ceiling some more.

I wanted to talk to Viola. I had a disturbing feeling that Malvolio would be making a move soon. I still hadn't made up my mind as to whether I should reveal myself to her, but of all of them she was the one I could trust if it came to that.

Well, the mountain and Muhammad were being kept apart by a too-praiseworthy manservant. Surveillance of the house bore no fruit, so I decided to keep watch over one place I might catch her unguarded. I filled my pack with enough food and drink to last me a full day and walked up the hill to the north gate.

The cemetery lay on a rise overlooking the town, a rock-strewn plateau on which little grew. Grave-digging in that ground was such backbreaking work that most families who could afford it built mausoleums. This led to the usual ostentatious competition. The final dwelling place of the Dukes of Orsino would have been a modest enough affair if it had been placed next to, oh, say the Parthenon. Over the centuries it had gotten a bit crowded, and it was rumored that some of the oldest skeletons had been quietly removed to less desirable real estate. So far, there had been no complaints.

I staked out a sheltered patch of woods nearby, piled up some dead leaves, and burrowed into it with a blanket I had borrowed from the Elephant. Only my eyes were exposed from under the hood of my cloak. I soon discovered how cold one's eyes could become. After the weeks of luxurious living, it was pleasant to return to my impoverished and uncomfortable jester ways.

A few pilgrims wandered up the hill to pray or wish their ancestors a Happy New Year, but no one approached the ducal sepulcher. As the sun set, I could hear sounds of revelry from the town. Good job, Theo. You've added the feast of Sylvester and New Year's Eve to the fun you're missing on this mission.

And then, in the gloom, when the cemetery was deserted by all but the dead, I saw a slight figure creeping up the hill. I left my hiding hole and slipped behind a lesser mausoleum to gain a good vantage. It had to be her.

But, to my surprise, it was Claudius. He glanced around briefly, then entered the building. I sneaked up to the door and placed my ear against it. I heard a low, anguished sobbing.

Of course. So obvious, anyone would miss it. I sat on a low wall opposite and waited. He emerged after twenty minutes or so, his face tearstained, his eyes cast down. He plodded towards me without seeing me.

"Good evening," I said politely.

My God, he was fast! Before I could blink, his sword was out and under my chin.

"You know, this is the third time I've had a blade at my throat in the past week," I complained mildly. "It must be the beard. Ever since I grew it, people seem compelled to try and remove it."

"I would be happy to oblige," snarled Claudius. "I may take your head off with it."

"Let me make it easier for you," I said, unbuckling my sword and letting it fall. "And there's this." I pulled my dagger from my sleeve and dropped it. "Oh, and I almost forgot. With your permission." I slowly reached into my boot, removed my knife, and added it to the pile. "Now, let us proceed."

"What the hell are you doing here? Why are you following me?"

"I didn't follow you," I said. "I've been waiting here for the better part of the day. Then you showed up."

"This is hardly the time or place to discuss business, Herr Merchant," he said. His sword did not waver for an instant.

"Oh, but I think it is. Depending on the business, that is. I think that we might help each other, Signor Claudius, but I find myself in a bit of a quandary. I have stumbled upon a secret of yours, but in order to confirm it, I would have to reveal one of my own."

"You speak in riddles, merchant."

"Sorry. Force of habit. I must say I admire your attachment to your late master. Far beyond the usual clerical loyalty."

"You insult me. He was an excellent man." Tears welled up, but whether of anger or grief I could not say.

"A most excellent man," I agreed. "And a devoted husband. Wouldn't you say so, Duchess?"

He glanced behind him quickly, then back at me. "There is no one here besides the two of us. Who were you addressing as Duchess?"

"You," I said, then gasped as the blade touched my neck. "Really, Viola. The last time I saw you wield a sword, it was most unimpressive."

"Who are you?" he whispered—she whispered.

"It's Feste, Viola. Shave my countenance in your mind, subtract the years from your memories, paint me in whiteface, and see me as I was."

She shook her head vehemently. "No. Feste wouldn't come back here. Not unannounced. Not in disguise. Who are you and what do you want?"

"Put me to some test, something only Viola and Feste would know."

She frowned under the beard, thinking. "The first time I saw Feste," she said falteringly, "he sang to Orsino, to my husband. Sing that song, and I'll know your voice."

A good test, and all too appropriate under the circumstances. I cleared my throat. "Come away, come away, death," I began. "And in sad cypress let me be laid." The tears fell, the sword dropped. "Fly away, fly away, breath; I am slain by a fair cruel maid."

"Feste," she breathed and fell into me, clinging hard.

What a strange sight we would have made for any onlooker, two middle-aged, bearded men embracing on a moonlit night on a wintry burial ground. I cared not. These were but masks. Underneath them, Feste held Viola—Theo held Viola—I was holding her and I didn't want to let go. But I could do nothing more than continue singing.

> My shroud of white, stuck all with yew,
>   O, prepare it.
> My part of death, no one so true
>   Did share it.
> Not a flower, not a flower sweet,
>   On my black coffin let there be strown;
> Not a friend, not a friend greet
>   My poor corpse, where my bones shall be thrown.
> A thousand thousand sighs to save,
>   Lay me, O, where
> Sad true lover never find my grave,
>   To weep there.

She released me when it ended, smiling ruefully. "I suppose some explanations are in order. For both of us. What miracle brings you here in this masquerade?"

"Did you not send for me?"

"Did I? No."

"I thought not. Tell me, Duchess, how did your husband die?"

It was cruel, but I had to be for the sake of the truth. "He fell off a cliff," she said.

"Do you believe it was an accident?"

She looked up at me, not wanting to speak. "No," she said finally.

"Do you think he took his own life?"

"I don't know," she said, choking on the words.

"May I see him?" I asked gently. She was surprised but nodded and led me inside.

He had been laid inside a simple sarcophagus for the time being. A more elaborate one had been commissioned and would be completed by the summer, she told me. It suited me fine. I pushed the lid back and looked at the corpse of my onetime friend and lord.

The long, frigid winter preserved him well enough for my purposes. His face was smashed beyond recognition, though the blood had been carefully cleaned away. Age had taken its toll as well, but it wasn't his face I was concerned with.

"I was summoned here by news of his death," I said, watching her closely. She was looking away from him, but I could tell she was startled.

"Who summoned you?" she said. "Why?"

"To lure me here, I believe, to investigate the murder of your husband."

She turned to look directly at me, pale in the flickering torchlight. "Murder? Why murder? And why you?"

"For revenge, Milady. May I?" I indicated the body. She nodded. I reached gently under his head. "There. Forgive me, but I need to prove this to you. Feel here." I took her hand and placed it on a portion of the back of his skull that gave to the touch. "It's broken. Crushed."

"He fell off a cliff!" she screamed, yanking her hand away.

"And landed on his face."

"What?" she said incredulously.

"A beach dweller named Hector saw him fall. Fall without

screaming, without moving like a man who fell by accident or who had flung himself over the edge. And he saw him land on his face. That wouldn't cause this injury."

"Hector is a drunken old man."

"So am I, Duchess. But he has a sharp eye for all that, and if you remove all the veils from his stories, you are left with the truth, exposed for one patient enough to look for it. Your husband was dead before he fell, struck from behind."

"But Hector saw him alone. That's what he told us at the time."

"The angle of the cliff could have concealed the assailant. Or it was done by some missile. But Orsino was murdered, Viola."

She fell to the floor. I thought she had swooned, but she was sobbing. "He didn't kill himself," she said in a quick burst. "They all hinted he did, that it was only his position that allowed him to be placed in consecrated ground. I hoped it wasn't true, but I thought I would never know."

"I'm sorry."

"No," she said, allowing me to pull her to her feet. "I was afraid it was because of me, somehow. But it wasn't. It was . . ." She staggered again. "Revenge? You said revenge. You mean . . . Not Malvolio?"

"I think it may be," I replied, and touched on what I knew of his journeys as well as I could without revealing any secrets of the Guild.

"And you came to our rescue in disguise," she said, marveling. "But this other fool, is he a companion of yours?"

"Indeed he is. And I would appreciate it if you would order your very effective servant to allow us entry to your villa from now on. It would improve communications."

"Done. Now, how did you find me out? That's the second time, you know."

I closed the sarcophagus and removed the torch. We went outside and I collected my weapons.

"It was a combination of small signs," I said as we walked back to town. "Brought to the fore by your appearance here. You smelled of pine when I first met you."

Her hand reflexively stroked her beard.

"I am an old hand at false beards, although that one is quite good, and I finally realized why I recognized that scent. The resin you use to glue it on, am I right?" She nodded. "Then there is that very interesting icon in your upper office."

She glared at me and I shrugged.

"Forgive me, I have been poking my nose into many places it doesn't belong. But I could not figure out why anyone would want to conceal a mirror, of all things. It's clear to me now. You use it for assuming your disguise. You slip in and out of there in the guise of an old woman servant, and Claudius remains inside a cabinet."

"The sad thing is that it takes very little to make me look like an old woman these days."

"Nonsense, Duchess. Then there was the choice of subjects for the icon. Saints Thecla and Pelagia. Both women. Strong and devout women. And women who escaped persecution by disguising themselves as men."

She looked away from me. "It was a gift from my husband," she said without elaborating. We walked on for a time in silence.

"The gates will be locked by now," I commented.

"Since you know so many secrets, I will reveal one more," she said, and veered off the road into the woods. She led me to a giant oak by a stream. Its gnarled roots overhung the bank. She jumped down lightly and ducked under them. There was an opening there. She took the torch and entered. I followed.

"Every ruler needs an escape route," she said as I looked at an ancient stone-lined tunnel. "This once carried water to the Roman garrison. It's been kept up for other purposes by the House of Orsino. As you might guess, I have found it singularly useful." She lit a candle that sat on a shelf on the wall, extinguished the torch, and led the way.

"Brilliant," I said. "The whole scheme is brilliant. The best part is that having passed yourself off as a man once, no one would believe that you'd ever have the audacity do it again."

"Thank you."

"Why? What led you to this?"

A strange recounting, hearing her voice come from Claudius's lips as though she were a ventriloquist hidden behind some screen. "When the men went away and Sebastian sulked inside a cask of wine, I assumed the management of the Duke's affairs. As it turned out, I had quite a talent for it."

"I'm not surprised."

"When they came back, he was impressed but felt that it would be improper for the Duchess of Orsino to run things when the Duke was present. I had no means of asserting my desires other than those of any wife, and those weren't enough. It was maddening.

"Then, as a lark for the anniversary of our marriage, I re-created my guise as Cesario. It was quite a success, and I even succeeded in deceiving many of the visiting lords and ladies. My husband was quite . . ." She paused, and even in the candlelight I could see she was blushing. "He was quite taken with the costume. He found it . . . exciting. Since his return from the Crusade he had been prone to fits of melancholy such as he suffered when I first met him. This guise aroused him, rekindled much of the fire that was missing from our marriage. I was pleased, so it continued. Eventually, I developed Claudius."

"Staying with the Roman emperors for your name."

"Yes. Strangely, in this guise, he began talking to me as man to man, speaking of affairs of state and commerce in ways that he never did to Viola. And he found my counsel to be worthwhile. The same words coming from Viola would be completely ignored. So much freedom in a beard, so much power from a little thatch of hair. I thought the arrangement quite intriguing, and when I proposed that Claudius become steward, he agreed."

"But how did you find the time?"

"Oh, it was complicated, but when one is Duchess, one is not expected to do much other than preside over social functions. The raising of my children had been snatched away from me by nurses and tutors, and I was never one for needlepoint. With peace at hand, even the commercial affairs were not that difficult. I recruited Isaac to keep the books, and the estates virtually ran themselves. We have prospered mightily with Claudius as steward."

"How many knew of your double life? Isaac, obviously."

"Yes. Three servants, one who has been doubling for me under a veil on occasions that demand the presence of both of us. Olivia knows. I felt with her position and her investment in the consortium, she was entitled."

"And Sebastian?"

"No. At least, I've never told him, and I've asked Olivia to keep quiet. I'm afraid he still resents me for taking over from him. I can't trust my brother with any secrets."

"The good Captain Perun?"

"Who knows what he knows?" she said. "I've never liked the man, but Orsino insisted. He has many sources of information. He may know, others may have guessed over the years, but I couldn't tell you for sure. I trust my servants, I trust Isaac, I don't trust Olivia anymore and I'm not sure who my husband may have told. We're under the villa."

The tunnel widened into a chamber with a rough-hewn table and a small cabinet. She opened the cabinet and removed a simple dress and cloak. She began unfastening her tunic, then glanced at me.

"I'm so used to being alone here, I almost changed in front of you. I realize you theatrical people have loose morals, but do me the courtesy of turning your back."

I bowed and faced the wall. The moment I did, her blade was at my neck again. "For your information, I am now very good with a sword," she said. "My husband tutored me in many of the manly arts. I have risked much tonight in trusting you."

"And I risked much in turning my back just now, agreed?"

"Agreed," she said, and sheathed the blade. I heard some rustling noises. "You may turn around."

Some people age better than others. I should know, I was one of the others. She could no longer pass for a boy, but there was absolutely no reason why anyone should want her to. Her hair was cut short but still a glorious auburn, untouched by gray. She was thicker around the middle than she was when I first met her, but that was an improvement. The face, as ever, was what held one. Not at first glance but upon careful study, upon seeing those eyes capture your own soul in their thoughtful consideration, that mouth with its slightly crooked smile. A few wrinkles here and there, trophies of an interesting life.

"You may stop staring and say something complimentary," she instructed me.

"You look better without the beard," I said, and she began to laugh, then sat on the bench and put her face in her hands.

"Oh, God, Feste," she said. "What I have been through in just one evening with you. Fear, relief, mourning, laughter. I cannot thank you enough for relieving me of the burden of my husband's possible suicide, yet you thrust a new one upon me with his murder. What can we do? Do you know where Malvolio is?"

"No," I said. "I don't even know who he is anymore. But he's close. He may go after one of us. Be guarded in your conduct. Trust no one. Not even Isaac. Can you tell me about the night your husband was killed?"

"We had several people to dine."

"I know the guest list. Did anything unusual happen?"

"Apart from Mark falling ill, no. There were no strangers there."

"What happened after Mark fell ill?"

"A bit of pandemonium. We took him up to his room, then I went to fetch the doctor while my husband attended to the guests. It took me some time to find the mountebank—he spends each night ministering to a different slattern. I tracked him down to a stable maid's loft and dragged him back here."

"And where was everyone else?"

"They had left by that time. My husband likes—used to like—walking up to the cliff every day before sunset. He was hovering about feeling useless, so I told him to go take his walk, that I had everything under control." She stopped. "That's the last thing I said to him, go take your walk, everything's under control. Only it wasn't. At least not by me. And now there's just this semblance of control. Olivia will become regent, Claudius will be no more. Viola will be ruled first by her drunken brother's wife, then by her son when he is old enough. Not exactly the life I would have chosen for myself. But then, how much choice does any woman have?"

"You've had more than most."

"Have I?" she said, rubbing a cloth over her face, removing the final traces of her disguise. "I sometimes wonder. It seems to be more the randomness of the Fates than any choices presented to me."

"Look back over the last few months. Have you seen any strangers, anyone whose actions seem odd in retrospect?"

"No," she said, considering. "Besides yours, of course. What is your plan?"

"Bobo draws Malvolio's attention, I set the snares, and the rest of you keep an eye out."

"We'll need more proof, Feste," she said. "There are forces that would prefer that my husband be a suicide with an estranged wife, the better to control Mark."

I thought for a moment. "I haven't explored the scene yet," I said. "It's been many weeks, but there may be some trace of his assailant. Do you wish to meet me there?"

"All right. Tomorrow afternoon. Both Viola and Claudius have obligations to meet before then. Feste?"

"Yes, Duchess?"

"You stopped writing."

"Alas, the delivery of mail in my particular life is a haphazard thing. But I have thought of you often. Of all of you. My condolences, Duchess. He was a good man and deserved a longer life."

She led me to a ladder and up through a trapdoor into a root cellar. She listened at a door, then quietly brought me into the villa. Malachi was standing there. He started to bow, then saw me and stepped back, a hand going to a knife at his waist. She stopped him with a gesture.

"It's all right, Malachi. I will explain everything to you, but first, show the gentleman to the gate." He motioned me forward, and she added, "With all due courtesy." He looked at her, then bowed to me. "Thank you, Herr Octavius."

"Your Grace," I said with a bow that equaled Malachi's. He escorted me to the gate and unbolted it.

"Am I to understand that we will be getting to know you better, sir?"

"Perhaps, my good man."

"Then permit me to wish you a Happy New Year, sir."

"Thank you, Malachi. The best to you and your family."

The gate shut behind me, and I looked up at the stars, twinkling brightly on the first hour of the year.

ELEVEN

Haec reticere monet stultum, ne forte loquendo secretum prodat quod reticendo tenet. (This tale warns the Fool to keep silent, lest by talking he betray the secret which he might have kept by silence.)

AESOP

"He's what?" cried Bobo, leaping to his feet.

"She's what, you mean," I said smugly, and recounted my adventure of the previous night.

He stormed around the room, then collapsed onto the bed, laughing uproariously. "It's superb, amazing," he pronounced. "By King David, if she wasn't so far gone in age, I'd say we recruit her for the Guild when this is over. What a waste of talent!"

"She's not that old," I protested. "Early thirties, or somewhere in that area. Anyhow, I told her about the two of us and Malvolio."

"Do you think that was wise?" he asked, serious again. "How can we be sure she can be trusted?"

"Because I know her," I said simply.

He threw up his hands in despair. "I am doomed," he said. "I put my life in your hands, and you throw it away on a pretty face. Was it a pretty face, by the way?"

"Very."

"Well, then it's probably all right. I firmly believe in surface appearances. What now? You've slept through half the day again. I'm beginning to think you're metamorphosing into an owl."

"Reverting to a fool's schedule, that's all. I am meeting her, or him, at cliffside this afternoon. Looking for evidence."

"Sounds good. We'll need all we can get. My God, you took a chance on finding his skull crushed like that. How did you know?"

"I didn't know, but it made sense given how he fell. If he was murdered, then that seemed the most likely method."

"And if he had a good, solid block of a head like most noblemen?"

"Then I would have apologized and slunk back to the Guildhall to be publicly spanked."

He shook his head. "You take risks that I wouldn't, Herr Octavius. Do you want me to help you search?"

"No. It might cause suspicion if the two of us were to meet openly like that. If I meet with Claudius, no one will be the wiser. See me back here in the morning."

"As you wish. Happy New Year, by the way."

"And to you, Brother Fool," I replied, clasping his hand.

He slipped out the back way, and I went down to the public room.

"Happy New Year, Signor Octavius," bellowed Alexander when he saw me. "And how may we refresh your arid palate this fine day?"

"Happy New Year, my gracious host. A flagon of cold water and some bread and cheese, if you would."

A look of astonishment mingled with disappointment shot across his face, but I held firm to my resolve. At least for one meal.

I felt giddy after the previous evening. Solid proof for the first time. No more living on hunches. The game was on in earnest. I wondered when the next move would be. And who would make it.

The sun sped westward, and Zeus and I were soon making our way to the northwest gate.

"Have you seen Signor Claudius pass this way?" I asked a guard.

"No, sir."

"Well, if he does, bid him join me for a ride. I need to turn this beast loose every now and again."

"I will, sir."

We passed through the gate. The road had been but lightly traveled since the snows came. Not unusual—the northwest road was a traders' route, and it was a time for staying ensconced near the hearth, not for wandering abroad. The farmers who came in for church used the northern road.

I kicked Zeus lightly to nudge him along, and he promptly broke into full gallop, charging up the rise as if there were a mare in heat waiting at the top. There wasn't, and I managed to rein him back to a trot before we overshot our mark and ended up in Capodistria.

The road veered away from the cliff's edge and vanished in the trees ahead. This close to the sea they were mostly laurel and holm oak, the last green even now. I directed Zeus to the left, where the rocks jutted out past Hector's shack. I glanced down, but he was nowhere to be seen, although a thin wisp of smoke rose reluctantly from his driftwood mànor.

Orsino's vantage was at the apex of a triangle formed by the rock. Behind it, about fifty feet back, loomed the forest, mostly scrub and Aleppo pine at this point with a healthy stand of brush in front. Ample cover for any halfway decent assassin. I tied Zeus to the sturdiest tree I could find and walked carefully to the edge.

A well-chosen spot. From here, Orsino could see over the barrier islands to the open sea. From here, he and his ancestors saw marauding Normans, subtle Saracens, and, most insidious of all, the merchantmen of Venice who sought to conquer with tariffs and monopolies.

I looked behind me and saw the ridge rising in the distance, broken only where the river passed through it. There was a small watch-tower where ever-present guards looked both inland and out to sea. Toby once boasted that from there he could see all the way to the Marches, but I doubted that.

The sun was starting to set, turning orange and massive at the edge of the world. All my time in Orsino, and I had never once seen the sun set from the cliffs. It was dinnertime, when jesters make their living or die hungry. So many years looking at audiences through thickened lashes, hiding behind the double artifice of masks and words. Rare to have this moment of isolation, God's glory on full display, the waves crashing below and the wind whispering through the woods behind.

"Fool," I thought it whispered.

I laughed. Theo, your self-pity is speaking to you again. I reached for my flask, unstoppered it, and placed it to my lips, then spluttered as the unexpected taste of water hit my tongue. I laughed at myself again and thought the wind laughed along with me.

But it wasn't the wind. A man laughed somewhere in the woods behind me, and I remembered that I had come because another man had been killed by someone hiding in those woods. I was standing where he stood, completely exposed.

"Claudius?" I called cautiously. The laughter grew, so like the laughter from my dream that I shivered and glanced about for cover. There was a large boulder, about twenty feet to my left. I took a step, and something went whistling by my ear and out to sea.

"Stand still, Fool," said a voice from my past. "I want to see what Time has done to you."

The fastest I've ever seen a man reload a crossbow was to a quick count of four. I made that boulder in about three and a half, diving into a somersault and rolling behind it in a tight ball. Something clattered off it an instant later.

"But this is too vexing," complained the voice. "I miss you once because of the wind and a second time because you won't hold still."

"Who are you?" I shouted. "Why are you trying to kill me?"

"Don't you know?"

"I know that you are flirting with eternal Hellfire using that weapon."

"Really? And why, pray tell?"

"Crossbows are banned by the Church. Put yours down before it's too late."

There was laughter, genuine amusement, echoing from the trees. The boulder, while providing quick cover, left me too far from the woods to risk another such dash. I slipped my dagger into my right hand and my knife into my left, hoping he'd come into the open, wondering if I could do any damage before he killed me.

"Such wit in the face of Death. I admire it. But an exception was made for the killing of infidels, and I think you fall into that category as far as Rome is concerned."

"I am as good a Christian as you," I shouted.

"Then you should be the one worrying about your immortal soul."

I peeked around the side and a bolt struck just above my head, sending a spray of rock chips into my face.

"Who are you?" I called again.

"Don't be tedious, Feste. I know you all too well, and you know me. An older man than I was but a wiser one, too."

"How dieth the wise man? As the fool," I shouted.

"Brave words. Even the fool can cite Scripture for his purpose. Here's one for you: Like a thorn that goes up into the hand of a drunkard is a proverb in the mouth of fools. We will all die, Fool, but many will die before me, I promise you that. And they all live behind those formidable walls, waiting for Death. But Death was waiting for you to return. And as a dog returneth to his vomit, so a fool returneth to his folly. Let that Proverb be your motto now."

Man knows his Proverbs, I thought, trying to guess where he would emerge. I heard slow, measured footsteps moving through the brush, and I clutched my weapons tightly, wanting one clear shot.

Then Bobo screamed, "Run, Feste!" Never one to miss a cue, I fled to the woods at my left, diving through a gap in the brush and rolling behind the thickest tree I could find. I heard a struggle some distance off, then a cry and the sound of someone crashing through the forest away from me. Then silence.

I waited. The sun hid its face behind the outlying islands, and I waited, listening for anything, hearing nothing. Finally I moved in the direction of the struggle I had heard, weapons at the ready. I stepped carefully, soundlessly, pursuing the man who had summoned me here. I left my sword in its scabbard—the forest was too thick for swordplay, and it wasn't my best weapon. On open ground, the crossbow gave him the advantage. But in the woods with a knife, I would prevail over the Devil himself. No one was going to stop me.

And no one did. It took me fifteen minutes to cross sixty feet, but I made it unchallenged. Malvolio was long gone, but Bobo was still there, lying on his back, staring at the treetops, bleeding from his scalp, the blood vividly staining the white lead. I took him for dead, but the eyes rolled in my direction and he smiled weakly.

"All right, you convinced me," he whispered. "He's here."

"Can you walk?" I asked.

"Not sure. That fortune-teller may have been an optimist." I helped him up, and he fell to his knees, clutching his head.

"Come on, my horse awaits you."

"Damn it, I botched everything," he groaned. "I had him. Another step, and he would have been mine. And then I wasted my breath saving your life."

"Appreciate it, thanks. Why were you following me?"

We staggered out of the woods and I nearly dragged him the rest of the way to Zeus.

"Father Gerald's orders," he gasped. " 'Make sure the old reprobate stays alive,' he told me. 'If he wanders off by himself, follow him. I don't want him running headlong into any nooses. He's more valuable to me than the whole lot of them.' So, I've been playing protector. Rotten job I've done of it."

"I'll be happy to debate that point when you're feeling better."

Zeus looked at us with his usual benevolence, but my glare must have been something fierce for he suffered the two of us to mount without a fuss. I pulled Bobo's hands around my waist. He clasped them weakly, and I added one of mine in a grip that made him flinch. I flicked the reins lightly and Zeus stampeded back to town.

Claudius was riding up the road as we approached and pulled up on seeing us.

"What happened?" she said.

"Malvolio tried to kill me," I said. "My colleague stopped him but got his head knocked for his pains."

"Bring him to the villa," she said immediately. "I'll fetch the doctor. Tell Malachi to put him up in the east wing." We passed back through the gates and split up.

Malachi took one look at Bobo and, to his credit, carried him straightaway to a room and a clean bed. I handed off Zeus to an apprehensive groom and followed. When I arrived, Bobo was slipping in and out of consciousness, his breathing shallow. A maid came in with a bowl of water and a cloth and started wiping away the blood. The blow had fallen on the very top of his head.

"Must have been a tall man who struck him," commented Malachi.

"Perhaps," I said. "I didn't see him."

Bobo shouted suddenly and grabbed the maid's wrist. She shrieked and dropped the cloth as he sat up, staring wildly about the room. Then he saw me and lay back.

"Apologies, dear lady," he said. "Pray continue, only leave my face on. I would prefer to die a fool."

"Live to see the doctor," I urged him.

"I've heard about this doctor," he muttered. "He may finish the job that bastard started."

"Will he jest until he's buried?" whispered Malachi.

"Why should that stop him?" I answered.

The doctor appeared in the doorway, looking around the room uncertainly until we all pointed at the patient. He nodded briskly and sat beside the bed, peering at the wound.

"Fellow looks much too pale," he observed, and Bobo laughed, though it obviously hurt. The doctor dressed the wound and bandaged his head.

"He's lost some blood," he said when he was done. "These blows to the head are tricky. He could live, he could go like that. If the wound swells, I may have to let it a bit. Too bad this didn't happen in the spring. My leeches have all died, and I can't replace them until after the thaw."

"A doctor who cannot even keep a leech alive?" cried Bobo. "I am certain for the grave. Doctor, when a leech is ill, what do you use to treat it?"

"In the meantime?" I interrupted, mostly to prevent apoplexy on the part of the doctor.

"Watch over him. If his breathing becomes shallow and irregular, send for me. Give him as much wine as he desires."

"This, I like," whispered Bobo. "They keep an excellent cellar here by all report. A marvelous physician. I take back everything I've said about him."

"Hush," I implored him. "If you don't behave, I'll let him oper-ate on you."

"No need, no need," said the doctor hastily. "Let Nature take its course."

"It always does," I said, and he left. I sat by the bed. "Now, how do you feel? Really."

"I've survived the doctor. Always a good sign. I'm just afraid that if I fall asleep, I'll die."

"Nonsense," I said, a bit too heartily. He took my hand and held it.

"Stay with me," he begged. "Tell me your stories. Sing a ballad that I don't know."

And that's when I became truly afraid. A jester cares nothing for the last rites of either half of the Church, but when he wants songs to ease his way, that's serious. I sang into the night, softly for an au-dience of one. He occasionally mouthed the words of the ballads he knew, or smiled at the punch lines he didn't know or encountered again as old friends. Finally, he drifted into sleep, and I sat by the bed, listening to his breathing. It was slow, but regular.

"You should get some rest, too," said Viola, standing in the doorway.

"How long have you been here?" I whispered, rubbing my neck.

"I've lost track. I've been listening to you sing, a long-absent pleasure. And I wanted your advice on this situation. Should we alert the town now that we know he's here? At least tell Captain Perun."

"No," I said.

"Why not?"

"Because I don't know who to trust outside of this room."

She was silent, mulling it over. "You think the Captain is in league with him?" she asked.

"Maybe. He may even be him."

"But surely you would have recognized him if that was the case."

"I didn't get a good look, I just heard his voice."

"Then you should move in here where you'll be safe."

"No. That would alert too many prying eyes."

"It would seem that part of your plan has failed. He knows who you are."

"True, damn it. I'll consider it. I can still move more freely about the town as Octavius than as Feste."

"So be it. But the offer stands. Get some sleep. We'll watch him."

I bowed. "Many thanks, Milady. For everything."

I left Zeus there for the night and borrowed a torch to light my way back to the Elephant. The guard at the gate recognized me and let me through without challenge. All was quiet. It must have been close to midnight, and even the most determined revelers were sleeping it off somewhere.

No signs of life in the Elephant, though a chorus of snores resonated from the back rooms. I drew my sword before ascending the stairs. The hallway was deserted. I stepped quickly past each doorway until I reached my room, then laughed quietly at my nerves. The room was empty.

Except that on the bed there lay a pair of yellow stockings, cross-gartered.

A few minutes later, I was banging at the gate of the villa, clutching my belongings. A sleepy and irritated Malachi emerged.

"Good morning," I said cheerfully. "Tell the Duchess I've changed my mind."

When sunrise came, I peeked into Bobo's room. He saw me and lifted a hand in greeting.

"How's the patient?" I asked.

"One night to the good," he said hoarsely. "My head is killing me."

"Mine, too."

"What's your problem?"

"New Year's resolution."

"Ah. I usually get the shakes the second day."

"Same here. Take a look at this." I tossed a crossbow bolt onto his blanket. He examined it curiously.

"Where did you get this?"

"At the cliffside where we were attacked."

He sat bolt upright in surprise, a move he immediately regretted as pain shot through him. He collapsed back onto the pillows.

"If you continue to risk your life like this," he said slowly, "then I won't guarantee its length."

"Never asked you to. Besides, I figured our visitor wouldn't be returning to that spot so soon. What do you think about that bolt?"

"It's a crossbow bolt. What am I supposed to think?"

"You're the one from Toledo."

"Oh, and suddenly I'm an expert on arms," he grumbled. Nonetheless, he peered at it more closely. "All right, look at this." He indicated the tip, which was diamond-shaped and came to a nasty little point. "That's called a bodkin point. Splits the links in chain mail from a hundred paces. You weren't wearing chain mail, were you?"

"Afraid not."

"Well, my boy, this would have gone right through you and landed in Genoa. As to where it came from, I haven't any idea. They're easy enough to make. This could have come from a foundry anywhere from Toledo to Damascus."

"Thanks," I said, taking it back from him.

"I just thought of something," he said. "There's another kind of bolt that has a square head. It'll knock a knight in plate right off his mount, and then it's turtle soup for everyone. Maybe that's how he did in Orsino."

"A broken skull and no one with him," I said. "And you could pick the bolt up when the coast is clear. Or tie a string to one end and pull it back. Of course, a well-thrown rock would have done the trick."

"Or one from a sling. But with a crossbow, you're less likely to miss. It could be his weapon of choice. A coward's weapon."

"He may be many things, but I doubt he's a coward."

He looked at me oddly. "One would almost think you admired the man," he said.

"Not in the least. But I am impressed with his cunning. This is a kind of madness, this revenge. How long has he been planning it? The disguise, the information, the infiltration. It's all quite brilliant."

"And then he missed you when he had a clear shot."

"No. He missed me intentionally. The first shot was just to toy with me. It would have been less amusing if he killed me without taunting me first."

"Maybe," he said, still skeptical. "Still, there was something odd about last night. I can't quite put my finger on it, but I'll sort it out when my brain starts working again."

"Use it now. What did he look like?"

He closed his eyes. "I came up behind him. He wore a monk's cowl, a brown one. He was moving into a position where he could shoot you when I yelled. He whirled and struck me with the crossbow. I saw a black beard, trimmed to a triangular point, a mustache coming down on both sides to join it. No clear look at the face—the sun was behind him and the hood concealed most of it. Then I saw stars in daylight, and then I looked up at the treetops for a long time. I'm sorry, that's not very helpful."

"Could it have been any of our candidates?"

"The beard didn't match any of them. In fact, our esteemed representative of the Holy Father is beardless. Either Malvolio is none of them, or whoever it was put on the beard for the festive occasion of spitting you."

"Maybe he did. Maybe he needs me to see him as Malvolio was for the revenge to be complete. I wonder if it's worth checking the monastery."

"Probably not. If he was there, which I doubt, then he's cleared out. He's probably gone to ground until he makes his next move. And what will yours be? Will you become Feste now?"

"Not just yet."

"Why not? There's not much point in the disguise if he knows who you are."

"Maybe not. But something tells me I should keep it a while longer. If I abandon Octavius, then the whole town will know why, and we'll never catch him."

He looked at me for a long moment. "If we scare him away, then we may save some lives. Have you considered that?"

"Yes. For the near future. But he will return eventually. He can only hibernate for so long before the madness drives him out again. Octavius remains."

He closed his eyes. "The way we play with peoples' lives without their knowledge. It frightens me sometimes."

"Get some rest. We've let it out that you were injured in a drunken fall and are recuperating here. No one will be shocked by the news. Would you like me to bring Fez here?"

"Good God, I had forgotten him! He'll never forgive me. Please, if you would be so kind. And I will try and think some more, since I'm of no use for anything else."

I collected Fez from the hostel and dragged him to the villa. As I was doing so, I was hailed by Captain Perun riding by.

"Well, merchant, a steed more suitable to your stature," he said. "I've seen many a speculator ride in on a horse and ride out on an ass."

"Very good, Captain. Perhaps we should race again for the amusement of the town."

He scowled. "Your time here is dwindling. Have you concluded your business yet?"

"No, but I am making progress. Thank you for inquiring."

"Yes, I know. You now reside in the Duke's villa by a clever ruse."

"Excuse me?"

"Recruiting that fool to gain entry for you. What does one pay a man to have his head broken?"

I looked at him, amazed. "Are you so cynical that you would suspect a mission of mercy?" I asked him.

He smiled, a hideous sight. "I don't believe in mercy," he said. "Remember that if you are still here five days from now." He turned and rode off.

TWELVE

The way of a fool is right in his own eyes.

PROVERBS 12.15

I spent much of the day searching the docks, the taverns, and the brothels for men with triangular beards but to no avail. It was a large town where a man could lose himself without difficulty or pay to have his location kept quiet.

I stopped by the Elephant around noon to explain my change of accommodations to Alexander and to settle my account. Sir Andrew and Sir Toby were there and hailed me to their table.

"Where've you been hiding yourself?" asked Toby. "You've missed all the festivities. Did you bathe for nothing, or did one of our village maids clasp you to her bosom for the New Year?"

"No such luck," I replied, laughing. "I've merely moved. I received a very kind invitation to stay at the Duke's villa."

"Well, well, your fortunes are improving," applauded Sir Toby. "And how is Mark?"

"I haven't seen him yet," I confessed. "But I am told he is somewhat better."

"I visited him this morning," volunteered Sir Andrew. "He's clearly on the mend, but I hope they keep him inside until spring. These winter winds could only precipitate a relapse."

"Nonsense," scoffed Sir Toby. "Just the thing for him. Get him out in the brisk air with his friends, put him on a horse. It's all of these smothering women that hamper the cure. He's being coddled to death. What about Viola? How fares the lady?"

"I was only allowed to pay my respects for a moment," I said.

"And how did sh, sh, she . . ." Sir Andrew broke off in a fit of stammering.

Toby laughed and clapped him on the shoulders, nearly shattering the poor knight. "Still afraid of her after all this time," he said, guffawing. "Fought a duel with her once, back when we all thought her a man. Funniest damn thing I ever saw, two terrified swordsmen thinking they were meeting their doom. And then we found out he had battled a maid! God, that clown Feste reenacted it virtually every night for a year and we never ceased laughing."

"Really, Toby, why can't you stop dwelling on the past?" muttered Sir Andrew.

"Because it's worth dwelling on," replied Sir Toby. "It was the best part of our lives, that time. It was the time I fell in love, and I choose to dwell there."

"I prefer to dwell in the present," said Sir Andrew.

"And yon merchant dwells in the future, being a speculator," concluded Sir Toby. "We are the very Fates sitting here, only I can't weave worth a damn. Back to the topic—how did Viola seem?"

"I could not see her face. She was still veiled."

Toby glanced at Andrew and shrugged. "To each his own, or her own, I should say. But that isn't healthy, either. She is too much in mourning. Give it a month, then move on to the next one, I say. She'll turn nun shortly, mark my words, and that'll be the waste of a damn fine woman. I hope when I go that my Maria will have a good, long cry, a respectable two weeks of bereaving, then go carousing through every tavern in town looking for a replacement."

"Why waste two weeks on you, you drunken reprobate?" said Maria, standing in the doorway.

"Good God, it's the wife!" roared Sir Toby. "Come to my arms, my love, and give us a kiss."

"In front of all these people? 'Twould be scandalous," she protested, approaching nevertheless.

"Would everyone kindly turn their back while I kiss my wife?" he cried, looking about the room. No one moved. He looked at her and shrugged, then pulled her into his embrace. "I asked, my dove, I asked politely."

"You did at that," she said. "I guess there's no help for it." She threw her arms around him, well, almost around him, and delivered her lips with force enough to drown most men and then resuscitate them. We applauded heartily.

"May I present the noble merchant Octavius?" said the knight after a lengthy disengagement. "My loving wife, Maria." I bowed low and she smiled, that same wicked grin that crossed her face when she was first enticed into forging the letter from Olivia to gull Malvolio. She had become plump since then, though still slender next to her husband.

"As one who has never married, I stand in awe of such a perfect match," I said, lifting my cup.

"Is he drinking mead?" she asked her husband. "It must be, for honey has coated his tongue. I dislike flattery, sir, except when it is directed at myself, so you are most welcome." I bowed again. "As for the two of you, it's past time you came in for dinner. Our turn for the mince pie, Andrew?"

"Oh, yes," he said. "I'm really going to manage it this year. A different house and a mince pie for every day of the twelve."

"And when your luck changes, what do you plan to do?" asked Toby.

Andrew looked startled. "I'll do what I always do, but this time successfully."

"And does mince pie truly have this miraculous power?" I asked.

"We'll see," he said. "And if it doesn't, then no harm done. And, truthfully, I do love a mince pie."

"No sign of it," said Maria, inspecting his frame critically. "Me, I just look at one and I get fat."

"I remember when you used to say that about me," commented Sir Toby with a wink at the crowd. She slapped him gently.

"To think I believed I was marrying a gentleman," she said ruefully. "It was a pleasure meeting you, Signor Octavius. We'll have you to dinner later this week." I bowed, and they left.

Fabian sauntered in a little while later, nodded at me. "Have you seen that fool hereabouts? He was to help me at the rehearsal, teaching the demons how to fall."

"Alas, he should have rehearsed himself first," I said. "I heard he took a drunken tumble yesterday and is mending at the Duke's villa."

"Bad luck," he grumbled. "Just when a fool would come in handy, and to have one actually available. Buy you a drink?"

There was nothing I would have rather had, but I declined politely and took my leave.

The shakes came that night, and I was thankful I had supped lightly during the day for I had a chance to revisit the meal. I slept poorly again, hearing the same evil laugh in my dream. It was Malvolio who became my juggling partner in the forest, sending his missiles at me at a pace that would have overwhelmed even Brother Timothy. They writhed in my hands as I returned them, and I saw that they were people, not clubs. We were juggling living souls in our duet, and Orsino already lay twisted and broken at my feet.

I woke with a sour stomach and disposition to match. I staggered to the window, threw open the shutters, scooped some snow from the sill, and rubbed it into my face. I didn't feel any better afterwards.

The first order of business was to visit my wounded colleague. Bobo waved weakly when he saw me.

"How's the search going?" he asked.

"Badly," I said. "How's the thinking going?"

"Also badly," he said. "Thinking made my head hurt when I was healthy. You can imagine what it's doing to me now. They've left me some food. Want some?"

My stomach lurched, but I forced down some bread.

"One thing I've been wondering," he continued. "How do you think Malvolio knew who you were?"

"Maybe he sought me out at the Guildhall before he came here. Maybe some spy of his sent my description to him. Maybe someone in the Guild betrayed me."

"That's a frightening thought. Any evidence?"

"I prefer to leap to conclusions without evidence. It saves time."

"Then here's another hurdle for you. If he knew who you were, why did he wait so long to attack?"

I tore off a particularly tough piece and chewed it for a while.

"Opportunity?" I ventured.

"He had ample opportunity. You thought you were unrecognized, so you blithely wandered all over the place. A dark alleyway, a quick thrust of the knife, and there's a dead merchant in town and none the wiser."

"But no gloating that way."

"True enough," he conceded. "But he could have figured out something. Why wait?"

"I give up. What do you think?"

He lay back, rubbing his head. "I'll let you know what I think when I get another thought. I've used up today's ration." He closed his eyes and soon was breathing deep.

Just like a fool to pose riddles and leave them unsolved. He began to snore, which left me unable to think at all. I tiptoed out the room to find a lady in black walking towards me. I bowed.

"Good day, Milady."

She glanced around, then raised her veil. "It's the real Duchess," said Viola. "How is your companion?"

"Not out of the woods yet, if I am any judge. Will Claudius be making any appearances today?"

"In this holy season, Claudius usually repairs to some private chapel for constant worship. The Duchess's social obligations outweigh the steward's commercial ones."

"It works out nicely. Shall we walk for a while?"

She nodded and lowered the veil.

"How fares your son?" I inquired as we ascended the steps leading into the main house.

"Much improved, thank you. Andrew's visiting with him now. He's been a godsend to Mark, reading to him, playing chess. It's good to have a man paying attention to him with his father gone."

"Even if the man is Sir Andrew?"

"That's unkind, Feste. He is a gentle creature for all his flights of folly, and such are to be prized in these ungentle times."

"True enough, Milady," I conceded. "Mark has so little childhood left to him and now has the title thrust upon him prematurely."

"I worry more about the former than the latter. He's like me—determined, intelligent. He'll run this town well enough when he's ready."

I tried to gauge her feelings about this, but her tones were as veiled as her expressions. We walked the halls with no particular end in mind, while servants scurried about with bedding, chamberpots, and fresh rushes to scatter on the floors to improve the smell of the rooms.

"What will you do then?" I asked. "Settle into the role of the Duke's aging mother?"

"But I am the Duke's aging mother. It's an easy role to play."

"And Claudius?"

"Claudius will continue to serve the Duke."

"And Viola? What will become of her?"

She stopped by a window that looked out to sea. "Who is Viola? A blank. Someone who plays parts in grand pageants not of her design. That is my fate, Feste. That of most women, only I'm lucky to have had this one adventure." She turned, and I could scarcely discern her features.

"Poor monster," I said. "You need not stop living now."

"Really? What are my prospects? I'm hardly in a position to remarry. My wealth now belongs to my child. Do I seek permission and a dowry from an eleven-year-old boy?" She laughed sadly and again looked out to sea. "You know, on New Year's Eve, I looked into my glass at midnight, just like a little girl, wondering if my next husband would be revealed to me."

"And what did you see, Milady?"

"Myself, alone. It's a silly superstition, anyway."

Something glistened under the veil, caught the light for a moment, then slid down her cheek.

"By your leave, Milady," I said bowing. "I must depart temporarily."

"There was a time," she said slowly, "when Feste would say something amusing to comfort me in my troubles."

"Who is Feste?" I asked. "If Viola is a blank, then Feste is something less than a blank, for Feste was nothing but a sham."

"Not the one I knew," she said, keeping her gaze seaward.

I bowed again and left her there.

. . .

The play was being rehearsed in the square again, providing more unintentional amusement for the onlookers. Fabian was screaming at the poor demons.

"Really, this is appalling," he shouted. "Not one convincing pratfall by the four of you. Look, Astarte, just imitate Sir Andrew and it will go just fine."

An inspired bit of direction. The four looked at one another in a shared epiphany and simultaneously fell backwards. The choir roared with laughter, and Fabian applauded.

"Now, where's the Count?" he asked, looking about. Sebastian was nowhere to be seen.

"Probably down at the Elephant," he muttered, then noticed me. "Good merchant, would you be so kind as to stop by the Elephant and tell His Eminence that he is needed?"

"I will inform him that Heaven and Hell await him," I replied, and sped down to the tavern.

He was there. He had been there for some time, judging by the level of inebriation he had reached.

"It's the traveling bachelor," he bellowed when I entered. "Come and drink, for tomorrow we may die. Or worse, be married." He wrapped an arm around my shoulder and roughly held a cup to my lips. "Drink, damn you. Drink the health of my wife."

"Forgive me," I sputtered. "I have sworn off drink for the New Year."

"So have I," he exclaimed in surprise. "How easily oaths are broken. Oaths to the New Year, oaths to the Church, oaths of fidelity. My wife fancies you, I think. So, you'd better drink her health if you want to stay on my good side."

"Some water, Alexander," I said, signaling desperately. Agatha raced over with a cup. Sebastian knocked it away and she shrieked, cowering behind the bar. I saw Alexander take a short club out of his apron but hesitate, fearing to strike the local nobility. Sebastian noticed it as well and fumbled for his sword.

"Enough!" he shouted, drawing it and waving it wildly as the nearest revelers threw themselves onto the floor. "This churl will drink my wife's health, and he will do it now before I let his blood and turn it into wine. I can do that, you know. I'm Jesus this year."

I didn't value my resolution that much, so I lifted the cup he handed me.

"To the health of your noble wife," I said, and drained it.

He looked at me wearily and lowered his sword.

"Damn you all," he croaked, and started weeping.

Fabian appeared in the doorway and took in the scene in an instant.

"Oh, dear God, Count," he sighed. "Pull yourself together. You've embarrassed yourself in front of enough people here. Do you want the rest of the town to see you like this?"

"Who cares?" muttered Sebastian.

"Now, now, you have a rehearsal to attend. Many are counting on you, Count. It's an honor to play Our Lord. Act like it."

Sebastian drew himself up in a feeble approximation of dignity.

"I will not be spoken to like that by a servant," he announced haughtily. "Conduct me to the rehearsal as befits your station."

Fabian stood still for a long moment, then turned on his heel and led the way. Sebastian followed, and I trailed them, ready to catch him if he fell.

But not ready enough, as it turned out. He stepped squarely on the first patch of ice we encountered, and his legs flew out from under him as if they were possessed. It was all I could do to keep his head from smacking into the flagstones. Fabian began laughing uncontrollably.

"Behold the true test of divinity," he howled. "For Jesus could walk on water, yet his portrayer cannot even stand on ice."

Sebastian started cursing and struggled to his feet, reaching for his sword. He slipped again, and Fabian looked down at him, his lips pursed in a precisely calculated expression of contempt.

"You are a mere shadow of a man, Count," he pronounced. "Come join us when you are able. I expect the Second Coming will happen first." He turned, took one step towards the gate, and promptly fell. Now, it was the Count's turn to start laughing. He roared, pushing himself up, using his sword as support.

"Come, fellow," he cried. "We've both kissed the flagstones, so now we're even. It is meet that two fallen souls should walk together to Hell. Give me your hand."

Only Fabian didn't get up, and the ice and snow around him slowly turned red.

I grabbed the Count and hauled him with a strength I did not know I had behind a low wall.

"What . . ." he began in confusion and I signaled him to keep still.

"There," I whispered, and pointed to the base of the door to the Elephant. The Count looked and turned pale when he saw the crossbow bolt sticking out of it. I peered around the edge of the wall but saw no one.

"Guard!" I shouted. "Ho, guard!"

Two came running from the gate, then more. Perun came galloping up a few minutes later, and actually dismounted, so horrible was the sight before him. He looked up at me.

"Who did this?" he demanded.

"I do not know," I answered. "We were walking out of the Elephant when it happened."

"We?" he said, then glanced behind me to see Sebastian cowering by the wall. Perun rolled his eyes.

"Take the Count home to his wife," he barked, and two of the soldiers, smirking, lifted Sebastian to his feet.

"But I have a rehearsal," protested the Count.

"Not anymore," snapped Perun. "One second, Count. Was this man with you when it happened?"

"Yes," said Sebastian, earning my immediate gratitude.

"You, merchant. Show me where he stood when he was struck."

"Where his feet are now," I said. "He fell right away."

"Hold him up," commanded Perun, and two of his men lifted the late steward so that his feet dangled over the last footprints he would ever make. Perun examined the wounds, both front and back, then went to the bolt and sighted back at the corpse.

"Shot from on high," he said, and we all turned and looked up. Looming past the wall was the scaffolding around the facade of the cathedral. "Go," he said, and four men ran. I must say that I admired his efficiency in a crisis. "And seize the merchant and take him to the jail." I changed my mind as two guards clapped me in irons and summarily hauled me away.

Tumbling is a handy skill when you're being hurled headlong into a cell. I broke my fall without difficulty and sat on a low bench as the door was bolted behind me. It was some kind of holding cell, large enough to hold six or seven unfortunates if they took turns breathing. Not a proper dungeon at all compared to some I have been in. Nevertheless, it was not the most convenient place for me to spend the afternoon, especially as it left me completely at the mercy of Perun. And I remembered that mercy was not one of his strong points.

The guards had taken my sword and knife but had missed the dagger in my sleeve. I loosened it for quick deployment, but there were too many doors between me and the outside. I decided to play this one out.

By the time Perun unbarred the door, I had examined every stone and traced the inscriptions scratched into them. He removed my chains himself, then turned his back on me and led me up a narrow flight of steps to his office, not once looking behind him. I followed meekly, making sure I would provide him with no excuse to defend himself.

He sat behind a plain pine table on which rested an oil lamp and a pile of maps. He motioned me to a small stool in front of it.

"I speak with prisoners in two rooms," he said. "In this one, they talk without assistance. In the other, they talk with assistance."

"I like this room," I said quickly. "I like it a lot. What do you wish to talk about?"

He leaned back in his chair and put his feet up on the desk. "You have by your appearance here created a fascinating quandary for a simple soldier such as myself."

"You are far from simple, Captain."

"True," he agreed, smiling. "But still a soldier. Send me into battle, and the subtleties of terrain and tactics are my joy. Put an unwilling informant in the rack, and I will tickle the knowledge out of him in ten minutes. Simple tasks, obvious goals, that's how I like it. But the larger intrigues are beyond my ken.

"It is no secret that I think you are a spy. Come, come," he admonished me as I began to protest. "Anyone who comes into town this time of year is a spy. Your story is less flimsy than most, quite imaginative to be sure, but I would suspect the Three Kings themselves if they appeared in Orsino on Christmas Eve."

We observed each other closely as we spoke, a little dance of the eyes. We both knew I was lying. I thought he was as well, but only he knew for certain. I am used to prevarication, but usually under the cover of whiteface. I found it harder with only the mask of my face to shield my thoughts. So he watched me to trap the lies of my words, and I watched him to trap the lies of his aspect. Take one steward, add time, hardship, imprisonment, wars, madness. Would the sum total equal Perun? I saw details I hadn't noticed before. Did Malvolio have that small scar over his left eye? That shape of a nose? I couldn't remember anymore. And scars can be acquired and noses broken and reshaped.

"I'm sorry to have spoiled the season for you."

"Oh, to the contrary. You've made it interesting. As I've said, I could take you into the other room and retrieve the information I want to know, but there's this problem." He paused for effect.

"Which is?" I said finally, picking up my cue. He nodded with approval.

"Which is that I don't know who you work for," he replied. "There are too many possibilities in these troubled times. Were I to inadvertently cause your demise in the course of narrowing them down, I might be doing the town more harm than good in the long run. Will Venice invade? Will we resist if they do? Will our distant Hungarian landlord take umbrage? What about the Saracens? And so forth. You wouldn't want to enlighten me, would you?"

"I fear I would only cloud the picture even more, Captain. I am a merchant, no more, no less."

"Well spoken," he said, slapping his hand on the table. "And I shall set you free in due course. Forgive the imposition, but I intend to use you to find out at least one bit of information in spite of yourself."

"Which is?"

"I am waiting to see which of the nobility values you enough to demand your release," he said. "Always good to know the higher relationships."

"Shouldn't you be looking for Fabian's assassin?"

"My men are searching the town at this very moment. And I am conducting my own investigation."

"How?"

"By talking to you."

I tried to look suitably surprised, but I was tired. "You suspect me of being a murderer as well as a spy?"

"No," he said.

"Then I am confused."

He took out a dagger and delicately cleaned his fingernails. "Three men walked out of the Elephant in a line. One was killed by a crossbow bolt from an impressively difficult angle and distance. Either the arcubalister was particularly good, or he missed his target and hit Fabian. Now, this steward was an irritating fellow, I grant you, but not the sort to make mortal enemies. He was too careful for that."

"So you think the bolt was meant for Sebastian?"

"Or you. Tell me, have you enemies in Orsino?"

"Only you, as far as I know, and not for four days."

He chuckled, and then looked past me. There were voices emanating from the hallway. He stood quickly and bowed, and I turned to see Countess Olivia posed decorously in the doorway. I stood and bowed, too.

"My husband tells me that you have arrested this man, Captain," she said, smiling.

"Not arrested, Countess," protested Perun. "Herr Octavius kindly agreed to accompany my men to my offices to present an account of what happened to your poor servant. I did not wish to trouble the Count on this matter."

"Very kind of you, Captain. But I need him free. He has promised me three casks of cinnamon."

I remembered promising one, but saw no purpose in protesting the matter.

"Very good, Milady," said the Captain. "He is yours."

I bowed to each in turn. She nodded, satisfied, and waved me outside. Perun tapped me on the shoulder, and I turned.

"Interesting," he commented. "You have the favors of two great houses and not a speck of spice to exchange for it. Well done. You need not worry about my being your assailant, by the way."

"Really?" I replied. "Why not?"

"Because I wouldn't have missed," he said, and smiled warmly under cold eyes.

It convinced me. I got out as quickly as I could.

"Thank you, Milady," I said when I had caught up to Olivia.

"The time will come when I instruct you how to thank me properly," she said. "And if your ships do not come in, perhaps you will come work for me. I need a new steward, you know."

I bowed yet again, and she wafted off.

It was dark when I reached the villa. Malachi had saved me a bit of mutton, for which I blessed him profusely. I gnawed on it and walked to Bobo's room, nodding at the servant who guarded it. He was still awake when I came in, reading by the light of a single candle.

"Fabian's dead," I informed him. "Crossbow."

"I heard," he replied. "He's the first we let die. Who will be next?"

THIRTEEN

He that trusteth in his own heart is a fool.

PROVERBS 28.26 (KING JAMES VERSION)

Another bad night, as Fabian joined Orsino in my dream. Fabian looked up at me reproachfully. "We were friends, once," he said. "We laughed and drank ourselves into stupors on many an occasion. Why wouldn't you help me now?" But I was too occupied in keeping the rest of the clubs from falling to answer him.

Maybe Bobo was right, I thought in the morning. His criticism had stung, but sometimes it takes a fool to set another fool right. My machinations were proving both dangerous and ineffective. Better to go for saving their lives in the short run. In the long run, nothing mattered much anyway.

It was clear in retrospect that I had been outmaneuvered on this one from the start. I had walked into a carefully arranged scenario, and even the knowledge that I was doing so was not enough for me to disrupt it. My partner was isolated and I myself was hampered by my unfoolish guise and the scrutiny of Perun. And I still couldn't rule him out as Malvolio. Indeed, the pleasure he took in toying with me put him even higher in my suspicions.

The funeral for Fabian took place that morning. I stood respectfully at the rear of the church, then followed the congregation up the hill to the cemetery. The Countess wore a mourning gown that was so cut to her figure that I am surprised it did not arouse the dead from their sarcophagi. She smiled and chatted with the townspeople as if it were a ball. Sebastian looked hungover. No, more than that. Guilty.

I spied Alexander and walked over to him.

"What's wrong with the Count?" I asked.

"Remorse over yesterday's behavior, I think," he replied. "He said if he had only shown up at the rehearsal on time, maybe Fabian would still be alive. And he feels terrible that he laughed at the man as he lay dying."

"That wasn't his fault," I said. "He had no idea."

"Nevertheless, he has sworn to stay sober until the end of Twelfth Night, and in penance will run the rehearsals himself."

"Short penance for brief guilt."

"Any length of sobriety for him will be ample punishment, believe me."

I could not argue with that.

Fabian was placed in a crypt reserved for loyal retainers of the Countess, and the crowd started back for town. The Duchess was escorted by Claudius, who detached himself from her and fell in step beside me.

"A sad thing," Viola commented in Claudius's voice. "One might almost venture to say a foolish one."

"I agree," I said forlornly. "You were wrong to indulge me."

"Not true," she said. "We can't all hide indoors for this season. A man brazen and skillful enough would have found a way. You can't blame yourself."

"I can."

"Well, if you want to feel sorry for yourself, then we might as well surrender now. Hear me, Herr Octavius. Remain yourself a little longer. If he's the man I remember and the one I think he's become, then his success will only encourage him to take greater risks. And therefore more likely to be caught."

"How many die in the meantime?"

"None, I hope. You forget that his targets live primarily in two houses. Ours is well guarded, and I've suggested to Olivia that, in the light of recent events, she take extra precautions as well. I hinted that the murder might have had something to do with her financial affairs. She turned quite pale at the thought of a threat to her money."

"What about Sir Andrew? And Toby and Maria?"

"I've rounded up some servants I trust to keep a lookout for them. It's the best I can do. But you have to find him soon. I have family to protect, and I am unwilling to go too long without getting the guards involved."

"Understood. I will try not to fail you."

"Please see that you don't. I'm trusting you, you see." And she rejoined her counterfeit.

And there it was. Me gallivanting off on a fool's errand, and here was Viola putting her life in my hands for another day. No reason to deserve her faith. No results to justify it. No recourse but to earn it.

I sought out Bobo in his room and found him rapt in a game of chess with a boy. The child had dark hair, olive skin, a strong jaw and intelligent eyes. I had seen those eyes before, and that jaw, for that matter. Bobo, seeing me enter, held his finger up to his lips. The Duke concentrated fiercely on the board in front of him, then moved his knight.

Bobo gasped in the best histrionic fashion, then flung one arm to his brow and sank back on his bed. Mark laughed in triumph.

"Well done, Milord," moaned Bobo. "You have played quite skillfully and defeated a fool."

"A good game, Senor Bobo," said the Duke. "You play better than most around here. May I come again?"

"It would be an honor," said Bobo. "But since honor means nothing to me, let me say more to the point that it would be a pleasure. And speaking of pleasures, allow me to introduce you to Herr Whatsis from somewhere, the spice merchant you've heard me talk about."

I bowed. "Milord, I trust your health is improving."

"It is, thank you, Herr Octavius," he replied in perfect German. "You are welcome to our villa and our city. Do you play chess? I've never played a German before."

"I do, and would happily accept the challenge. This evening, perhaps?"

"That would be delightful. After dinner, then." I bowed, and he skipped out.

"What an intelligent child," said Bobo. "Asked me many interesting questions about our profession. Plays a good game, too."

"You let him win, of course."

"I may be a fool, but I'm not an idiot. Naturally, I let him win. But he won't need that indulgence for long. He asked me about you."

"Which me?"

"Feste. He assumed that all professional fools knew each other, although he didn't know of the Guild. I told him I only knew Feste by reputation. He was disappointed, but I told him a few dirty stories he could pass among his mates and he cheered up nicely."

I sat down on the stool recently vacated by the Duke. "I need to pick what's left of your brain," I said.

[177]

"Good. I've come up with a few ideas since we last talked. Care for a game?"

"Why not?" He set the pieces up, taking black. I moved a pawn.

He advanced one of his own. "It might be productive if you go back to the beginning," he said. "State your facts and your conclusions, tell me why you think Malvolio is here and who he might be. Play the wise man, and I will be Marcolf to your Solomon."

We moved pieces rapidly while I collected my thoughts. "Malvolio is here," I said. "He is here because no one else would care enough to tell me about the Duke's death. He is here because the Duke was murdered, and he had reason to do it. He is here because Fabian was killed, and Fabian was part of the group that betrayed him to Olivia. And he is here because we saw him, and because he tried to kill me. As to who he might be, I don't have any more to go on than I had when I came here. He might be any of three people close to the two families, or he might be someone else entirely." I castled, sheltering my king behind pawns. "And that, pitiful though it is, is that."

He advanced a rook. "I've been a failure on this assignment," he said. "But since I can't move around, I've been using my reason. As to your proofs that Malvolio is here, let me make the following comments. They consist of an assumption, a fact, a leap of faith, and a deception."

"Go on," I said, intrigued.

"The assumption: That the message came from Malvolio, and that no one else cared enough to let you know. But some might have fond memories of you, who knew of your love for Orsino and thought that the slight effort of informing you would be worthwhile. Or there might be a motive to lure you here that had nothing to do with Malvolio."

"What motive?"

"I'm getting to that. But if your basic premise, that Malvolio sent the message to draw you into a trap, if that is wrong, then the rest all falls with it. Consider the fact: Orsino was murdered. In a town like this, many could have motive and means to do it. This may be nothing more than a shabby little crime of passion, or even worse, money. You've been looking only for Malvolio, when you could have been looking for a murderer."

"But . . ."

"Hear me out. I think you've become so obsessed with Malvolio that it's clouded your mind to all other possibilities. You leapt to the conclusion that this whole tawdry affair was set up to lure you here. You've conjured this eternal struggle between you and this Malvolio creature that you've created in your mind. He's become your opposite self, the dark assassin hiding in the woods. But the world is larger than your little ongoing drama. You may only be a minor player instead of the lead. Fabian was killed. Why Fabian? That's the leap of faith. He's also a minor character. Why not Sir Toby? Or Olivia?"

"They're still on his list. He has time."

"But by killing Fabian, he's puts himself out in the open. No mystery over the death like with Orsino, just a Jovian bolt from above. But it brings out the watch, and that just makes things more difficult for him."

"Unless Malvolio's Perun."

"True enough," he said, chewing on his lip, staring at the board. He moved his queen. "But there's the deception."

"Which is?"

"That scene on the cliffs. You said we saw Malvolio. But you didn't see him, you only heard him. And I saw a man who looked like the Malvolio of legend, down to the beard, but then I never knew him. Here's what I think about that. I don't think that was Malvolio."

If an actual Jovian thunderbolt had shot through the window and hit me, I wouldn't have been more stunned.

"Sounds more like your leap of faith," I said.

"It was Fabian's murder that struck me," he replied. "Consider the shot. From the scaffolding by the new cathedral, a hundred paces away, fifty feet up. Apollo would have found it difficult. Yet that same crossbow could not pierce you from less than half the distance on a level cliff. And he warned you with that villainous laugh first. He wanted you to know he was there and to make you think he was trying to kill you."

"He just missed me," I protested.

"He knew exactly what he was doing. He was there to make you think Malvolio was here in Orsino and seeking his revenge upon you. Remember what I said yesterday? That it didn't make sense that he would wait so long to attack Feste? Especially knowing about the Guild, and knowing that you would come looking for him the moment you arrived? But the timing of the attack was significant, don't you see?"

"No, I don't," I said, rising to my feet and throwing open the shutters. I needed air badly.

"I think you do, but you're refusing to admit it," he said softly. "You were attacked after revealing yourself to the Duchess Viola. You were attacked after stumbling upon one of her greatest secrets, perhaps more than one."

"But that couldn't have been Viola you saw there," I protested. "He was tall!" I sat down again, gulping the cold air. I no longer knew whose turn it was, nor cared.

"Yes, he was. And he had that distinctive black beard. But would Malvolio still have that same beard after all this time? Would it still be black? Would he risk discovery by flaunting it? And why would he bother putting it on just to kill you? You would know him with or without. I suspect that was someone in Viola's employ, with a little disguise to help. And we know how good she is with a false beard."

"Stop," I said hoarsely. "This is nonsense."

"Is it?" he replied, moving a piece. "Then let me ask you this. She was supposed to meet you at the cliffs. Did she?"

"She was late. Claudius had some business to take care of."

"And what business is taking place during this season? This town is dead in the winter. Without the Twelve Days, everyone would be sitting at home with the shutters closed, keeping near the fire and telling stories. It's just too convenient that she would be late."

"But Malvolio's voice . . ."

"Easily imitated. 'Like a dog returneth to its vomit,' " he finished in a passable re-creation of the voice. "I can do it, so can you. I'll wager many can do it. He's a legendary butt of stories here, half the town can imitate him."

I wanted wine, I wanted to drown myself in a barrel of it.

"Let me pose it this way. Viola kills her husband. Why, I'm not sure. From what I've seen of marriage, I'm surprised more wives don't do it. She had opportunity. He's shirking his parental duties and taking his little walk, and she's supposedly out looking for that doctor. It took her an hour, they say. Enough time to get to the cliffs, knock him over the side, find the doctor, and get back. No one's the wiser. Then, out of the blue, Feste returns. And to her absolute shock, not only tumbles to the murder but to her secret identity. But you reveal your chief suspect to her, and that gives her a way of diverting your attention. So she sets up the scene with the fake Malvolio to hammer it into your head even further. And you needed no convincing. You've been sent galloping down the wrong road."

"How does Fabian fit into this?"

"Don't forget he was Olivia's steward. This whole affair may be mercenary at the heart. Viola may have been doing some shady dealing with Orsino's money, possibly through the missing Aleph. Did you ask her about Aleph yet?"

"No," I said in chagrin.

"It may be that Fabian was involved, a conspiracy of clerks. Only with you investigating, it was too dangerous to let him live. So, he was killed. And now you're on the verge of proclaiming the second coming of Malvolio to the world. Everyone will be jumping at shadows for the next ten years, which would suit Milady just fine. Where was she at the time of Fabian's death? Can she account for herself?"

It fit. All of it.

"All right, it's plausible," I said grudgingly. "But you have no proof."

"I learned that at the hands of the master," he said, bowing in my direction. "All I am saying is that it makes a better explanation than the return of a vengeful steward. If Malvolio truly carried that hatred, he would have reappeared years ago. Why now?"

"You mentioned a motive for summoning me. What is it?"

"One more leap of faith, if you will. It may have come from Olivia."

I thought about that. "You think she suspected Viola but couldn't pursue her directly?"

"Precisely. So, she sent you an anonymous message, knowing you would arrive eventually and go after the murderer."

"That assumes she knows the true nature of the Guild."

He shrugged. "I don't think we're that secret a society anymore. She's a smart woman, sitting at the center of her web, reeling in whatever rumors get trapped in it. It's a possibility."

I looked out the window, over the wall to the river. Devoid of traffic. No ships other than the fishing boats. He was right, there was no commerce this time of year.

"I've missed everything," I said. "How could I have been so blind?"

"You mean you don't know?" he said, chuckling sympathetically.

I looked at him in dismay, tears blurring my vision.

"I'm sorry, but it's clear that you're in love with her. Probably have been from the moment she walked into town disguised as a boy. She was more like one of us than one of them, wasn't she? But you had to carry out the plan, like a good fool, so you did. And now, you've come back to save her. She probably saw this when you revealed yourself and has been playing on it ever since. It's your move, by the way."

"I'm sorry, I haven't been paying attention," I said, wiping my eyes and sitting down at the board. "Where did you move last?"

"The bishop."

"What?"

He indicated the piece with his finger. I stared at the board in confusion and followed the diagonals.

"The bishop, to be sure," I said. "And I see you've pinned my queen. Apt, very apt." I knocked over my king angrily. "Look at me, I'm losing to a man with a broken head."

He laughed gently. "That's more like it," he said. "Now, what do we do? If it isn't Malvolio, then it really doesn't involve the Guild. We could just abandon the assignment and sneak out of here with dignity."

"No," I said. "There's still a murderer to catch. A murderess, I should say."

He nodded, unsurprised. "Then maybe you should find out more about Aleph."

I stood and held out my hand. He grasped it. "I'm sorry for involving you in all this," I said. "I have managed to get us both lodgings in what may be the most dangerous place in Orsino for us. Will you be all right?"

"I think so," he said. "She thinks we're looking for Malvolio. She won't try anything right under her own roof. Be careful out there."

I nodded and left for the stables.

Zeus looked up at me expectantly as I walked up with his saddle. "Come on, old Greek," I said. "We have work to do."

FOURTEEN

Even when the fool walks on the road, he lacks sense.

ECCLESIASTES 10.3

I managed to hold Zeus to a slow trot as I worked my way up the riverside, past the baths, past the wharves, up to where the fresh water first meets the salt. Normally, one could take a ferry across to the south road, but this winter had been long and cold enough to ice over all but a narrow channel in the middle. Which Zeus promptly jumped the moment I gave him a little slack.

I let him fly on the open road, past snow-covered fields and occasional flocks of sheep or goats huddling together, scraping the ice away, searching for frozen clumps of weeds. The ridge was further from the sea on this side of the river, and the farms provided no cover as far as I could tell. I wasn't being followed, nor did I worry about it. Any threats lay ahead.

The south road clung to the shore, and the wind whipped up the salt spray so that I was chilled beyond the already frigid air. I was deeply grateful when the farms petered out and the forests reclaimed dominance, providing some respite from the wind, though these trees were planted, dormant groves of olive awaiting spring. I slowed Zeus down to a trot and started scanning the woods on either side of me.

No signs of recent travel, but I was looking for something older. Though I was not a woodsman by training, I have slept under enough trees to know them by name and inclination. I didn't know what precisely I would find, but I would know it when I saw it. I traveled some five or six miles in this fashion, studying the slightest break of a branch, the most casual disturbance of fallen leaves, but found nothing. Judging my travels sufficient, I turned Zeus around and trotted back to town.

Which gave me time to think about the accusation of love that had been tossed in my direction by Señor Bobo. A strange idea to a jester, long used to concealing his feelings not only from others but from himself, yet apparent to my observant colleague. Such are the perils of strolling around sans makeup. I cursed my traitorous face.

I have sung about love, joked about love, composed lengthy poems of courtship for stricken swains with coin to spare, reenacted the wooings of the mighty and the meek. But love for myself—well, there's not much I can do when it happens. A cat may look at a king and a fool may love a duchess, but only the cat will be satisfied. I had a job to do when she first strode into Orsino in boyish attire, and I had one to do now.

"What say you to this affliction, Old Greek?" I asked my steed. "If the legends have but a kernel of truth to them, then you've had much vaster experience with it than I. Is it worth the trouble?" Zeus snorted, which was his answer to everything I said. Nevertheless, a good answer.

"Well, let it be," I said to him and the wind, and we rode on in silence broken only by the muffled thuds of his hooves in the snow.

A solitary horseman was waiting as we neared the river. It was Perun, his hand resting gently on his sword, perhaps caressing it, although that may have been my imagination. I made certain my own hands stayed in sight, not wanting to give him the slightest excuse for offense.

"I thought of sending a man to follow you," he said. "But then

I realized which horse you were riding and gave up. Did you find what you were looking for?"

"My brother, you mean?" I replied.

He shrugged. "Very well, your brother."

"Alas, no. But since I am alone, you've already guessed that. Will you ride with me back to town? I assure you that you will find nothing down that road, and it's too bitter a day to venture forth. And night approaches."

He sighed. "I will send a man out in the morning," he said.

"Please, spare him. There is truly nothing to find. There is less to me than meets the eye, believe me."

"What meets the eye is always deceptive, Herr Octavius. I would employ only blind men in my service, but they are such poor marksmen."

I laughed for the first time that I could recall in his presence. The horses carried us back to Orsino in an almost companionable silence, and he saluted me as we went our separate ways.

I returned Zeus to the villa's stables and gave him a good currying to his surprise and pleasure. A willful, cantankerous beast. Clearly, we were made for each other. When I entered my room, I saw a note in a supremely neat hand requesting my company at the Duke's chess table.

I found him in the Great Hall, well remembered from formal occasions. The Duke's chair, elaborately carved from a massive piece of ebony, sat on a raised platform. Mark was sitting by the base of it, staring out the long, slender window into the courtyard.

He stood and returned my bow and motioned me to the table, an ornate affair of alabaster and black marble, with pieces carved from ivory and ebony. The castles were elephants with siege towers.

"Will you play black or white?" he asked.

"Rather than impose on your hospitality, let us leave the choice to fate," I said, and took a pawn from each side and hid them behind my back. I held my fists in front of him. He tapped the left and played white.

"Your German is quite good, Milord," I commented as we played. "You must have your mother's gift for tongues."

"Do you know my mother?" he asked.

"We've only been introduced," I said. "But her talent for languages is of great repute. Ah, I see what you're doing."

"But can you stop it?" he crowed.

I scanned the board, then held out my hand.

"Skillfully done, Milord."

He took it and pulled me closer.

"You're very good," he whispered. "You let me win with much more subtlety than that fool did this afternoon. Now, let's play a real game. And don't worry. If you beat me, I promise not to have you beheaded."

I grinned. "Then it's my turn to play white."

We reset the board and began anew. He was an excellent player for his age and managed in a short time to erase whatever vantage the white pieces gave me. We ultimately drew.

"Much more fun," he pronounced. "I wish people wouldn't treat me with so much deference."

"Unavoidable, I'm afraid. Until you are of age and assert yourself, people will approach you with care."

"Maybe I should assert myself now," he mused, sitting back on his chair. I shrugged. He looked sadly at the board.

"My father gave me this," he said. "It was a present when he returned from the Crusade."

"He was gone a while, wasn't he?"

"Yes. And now he's gone for good. It's too short a time to have a father. I did not want to be Duke yet."

"My sympathies, Milord. There's nothing I can say to comfort you, except that such a man has certainly gone to Heaven. Be grateful for the times you had together. Think of the best of them when you miss him the most."

"He took me to Venice, once," he said, brightening. "And then to Rome. I had never been overseas before. We saw everything. I even met His Holiness!"

"And think of all the sons who never traveled with their fathers. My father traveled the world seeking spice and would be gone for years at a stretch. You've probably spent more time with your father in your short life than I did in my long one."

"That is true," he said. He yawned, looking again like the boy he was. "I must get my rest. I'm trying to get my strength back enough to be in the Play."

I stood and bowed. "May I thank you for your splendid hospitality, Milord."

"You probably should thank Mother for that," he said. "I've guessed that she's the one responsible. But it's fine with me. A fool and a chess player as gifts for Christmas. Good night, Herr Octavius."

"Milord," I said, and with one last bow left the room.

"You're very good with him," whispered Viola. I had spotted her passing a doorway during the game and guessed that she had observed the whole interlude.

"He's a fine boy," I said.

"And you're a good chess player. You let him draw the second game, didn't you?"

"I confess it."

"And yet that time he didn't catch on. You have more facets than a diamond, Feste. Do you have children of your own?"

Something in my face must have closed shut, for she immediately backed off.

"I'm sorry," she said. "I don't mean to pry. I've just realized that there's so little I know about you."

"As it should be, Duchess," I said lightly.

She shook her head. "No, it shouldn't be. You came to help us when you were called. You didn't have to come, but you did."

"I did have to come. There was no other choice."

"That says quite a lot. When this is over, we will sit down and have a good, long talk. Perhaps a game of chess. And please, Feste, don't hold back when we play."

"Milady," I said, bowing. She brushed my cheek lightly with her hand, then turned and left.

And what was this? May a Duchess look at a fool? Or love a cat?

In the morning, I sought the only creature who truly understood me. I fed him, saddled him, and rode through the northwest gate. Looking back, I saw Perun standing on the wall, watching me. He waved. I waved back. It occurred to me that I only had two more days of protection from his challenge.

Zeus took his usual pace up the hill but uncharacteristically slowed as we approached the point where the path to the cliffs veered off. I urged him along the road instead. He seemed nervous about entering the woods. I could hardly blame him. I was nervous, too.

I slowed Zeus to a walk and commenced my search. The road was wide enough to accommodate a good-sized wain, though none had been by recently if I was any judge of tracks. I was surprised that Perun's patrols didn't extend this far, but perhaps he limited his bailiwick to the town's walls during the winter. Only a fool would be out traveling this time of year, and such would be left to the Lord's protection, for he scarcely deserved Perun's. The sun was over the eastern ridge, and the light was filtering through the trees at a high angle. There was little wind, and the brush and evergreens closer to the cliffside had prevented much in the way of drifting.

The road was as well preserved as an amateur woodsman and tracker could possibly desire.

I spent the better part of the journey examining the sides of the road, looking for suitable locations to wait in ambush. I recalled halfway through that it was not so very long ago that I had been attacked from these very woods. The sound my sword made as I drew it from its scabbard seemed absurdly loud in the emptiness. I can't say that it gave me any comfort.

About five miles in, a branch hung at an unnatural angle. I reined in Zeus and dismounted cautiously, sword at the ready, hoping I wouldn't have to use it. It was a recent break, and the surrounding brush also showed evidence of some disturbance. I squatted down to examine the ground. The snow lay smoothly. Too smoothly, in fact. I took a few steps past the brush into the wood proper and saw a crude path made recently in the snow, a profusion of footprints with two shallow grooves running through it such as would have been made by a pair of heels dragging. The smooth snow separated this track from the road, and there were slight ridges at the sides of it, where the brushing had been slightly less meticulous.

"Have you come about the dead man?" screeched a voice from my left. I whirled, pointing my sword in its direction.

He looked at me, more amused than threatened. "I am unarmed," he said more gently. "And a peaceable man. I didn't mean to startle you. It's been a while since I've spoken to another person."

"I didn't hear you approach," I said apologetically, sheathing my sword. He was clad mostly in blankets, draped over his shoulders and belted haphazardly around the middle. On his feet were sandals, stuffed with rags. An ineffective way of keeping out the cold, I thought, but he seemed to pay it no mind. The hair and beard were long and matted enough to afford a little extra warmth. His eyes, which were the only feature I could make out clearly, were blue and gentle. As for his age—all I could do was estimate the length of the beard and add sixteen. Maybe thirty, maybe fifty. Only a shave and a bath would reveal it.

"Yes, I would very much like to see this dead man of yours."

"Oh, he isn't my dead man," he replied. "But there is one about, and you're the first person come by since he came on the scene. I thought he might be yours."

"Not necessarily," I said.

"But you were looking for something. Will a dead man do?"

"Quite possibly. Let me take a look at him, and I'll be able to answer you better."

"This way, then," he said, and turned. I reached out and stopped him. He looked at me quizzically.

"If you don't mind, walk uphill from these tracks," I requested. He nodded and continued on. I followed, leading Zeus by the reins. This was an old section of forest, with trees reaching high into the heavens and little undergrowth. Enough sun fell through the branches to let us pick our steps with confidence, although he looked as if he knew the woods well enough to do it blindfolded.

"How did you find him?" I asked.

"The screaming," he said shortly. I waited for him to elaborate. "I was praying in my cave, off a ways yonder. Then I heard it."

"I take it you're a hermit?"

"Neither by choice nor by inclination, but recent circumstance has made me one."

"Would I be correct in guessing that you are one of the Perfect?"

He laughed quietly. "No, my friend, I am one of the Flawed. My name is Joseph, by the way."

"I am Octavius of Augsburg. Forgive me, I did not mean to be facetious. But you are a Cathar?"

"A name given to us by others. They call us Cathars, Patarines, Bogomils, damned Manicheans, any appellation they can attach before they light the pyre. They burn us because they think it spills no blood. I've seen burnings. It isn't true."

"What do you call yourselves?"

"The Good Men. Which is about as arrogant as anything else, when you come to think of it. But it provides us with a worthy goal, if nothing else. By the way, would you happen to have anything to eat that you could spare?"

I rummaged through my saddlebags. "A bit of bread and cheese, if you like."

He shook his head. "No cheese. Nothing that comes from coition. But a scrap of bread would be most welcome." I gave him the whole thing and he nodded his thanks as he tore into it. "The ignorant believe we live off the elements. The truth is, we depend on the charity of others in the winter."

"Where are your companions?"

He shrugged. "Fled, I suppose. We lived at the sufferance of the Duke, and when he died, the food stopped coming. I think he kept his support a secret, given the way things are nowadays. That bishop bears us no love, and Perun would happily launch another Crusade in our direction. So, between the lack of food and the fear for our safety, the group just fell apart. Part of our history, it seems. We were a schism of a schism, anyways. Kept finding out that the elders who administered the consolamentum had committed fornication or some other mortal sin, so there'd be arguments over who was pure and who wasn't. And we'd start over with a new round, and then the same thing would happen again. A small band of us settled here and dwindled down. Now, it's just me and the wolves."

"And the dead man. Tell me about the screaming. When did you hear it?"

He counted back on his fingers. "Nine days ago, in the early morn."

I calculated quickly. "Morning of the Feast of Saint John?"

"I'm afraid that we do not recognize your saints, so I couldn't tell you. When every local village can purchase a sainthood from the Church for their local legend, it makes the whole idea pointless."

"Yes, it's who you know, isn't it? But I would like to know when you found him."

"It was the morning of the day after the snowfall."

"Tell me as much as you can."

"As I said, it was far away. But it went on for a while. Then it stopped. When I got here, he was already dead."

"Did you see who did it?"

"I must confess that I didn't try. As I said, I am unarmed and not particularly adept at defending myself. I couldn't do anything to help the poor fellow, so I decided to do nothing to join him."

"Sensible. What could you hear? Any words?"

"It was not in a language that I recognized. But it went on for some time. Here's where I found him."

The snow was greatly disturbed and heavily stained with blood. It was clear that the forest denizens had come afterwards to partake of the feast, but enough of an impression remained to show me where the body had lain. The footprints were too closely overlapping for me to get any kind of read from them. There were several deep holes dug in a snowbank nearby. I tiptoed around the edges of the scene, squatting to examine it.

"Are you a huntsman?" he asked, watching me curiously.

"Neither by choice nor by inclination, but recent circumstance has made me one. Where is the body?"

"This way," he said, and we walked a short distance through the woods. "He was already dead when I found him. He was stripped of his garments and appeared to have been tortured. I administered the consolamentum. It normally takes more than one of us laying on hands, but in an emergency . . ." He trailed off.

"What is that, exactly?"

"The imposition of hands, the ritual of blessing and acceptance, the forgiveness of the rebellion against Heaven that is within us all, allowing the forgiven to return there. If he wasn't sufficiently pure, then metempsychosis will take place."

"If at first you don't succeed, try, try again."

"That's one way of looking at it. In any case, that was all I could do. He could be brought into town to have the Last Rites administered if you would prefer."

"I'm sure your ministrations were fine." He led me to a rough cairn, stones piled haphazardly over the body.

"What happens to the body is irrelevant," he commented as I stood before it. "But I thought it might have mattered to others. The ground is too hard to dig a grave in the winter. Normally, I wouldn't build anything like this. It's too much like that feast of stones that they call a church. But I thought it might keep the scavengers away."

I removed some stones from the head of the cairn. The man inside was maybe twenty-five, no more. A short life, ending in horror and pain, judging by his face. He had been beaten savagely, one ear hacked off. I removed more stones to find more signs of torture, slashes to the body, fingers missing.

"Odd how little blood there is," I commented, trying to sound dispassionate, failing miserably.

"He's very clean," agreed Joseph. "He was like that when I found him. It was all I could do to drag him over here."

"Why didn't you report this to the town?"

"As I said, I don't trust Perun. He'd hang me for the death of a squirrel if he could tie me to it."

"But you trust me. Why?"

He shrugged. "You came looking for him. I assumed that you cared about him. Did you know him?"

"I never saw him before in my life, and that's the Lord's truth."

He looked at me, perused me for any signs of dissembling. "I believe that. And now I am puzzled. Was I wrong to trust you?"

"No. I am trying to prevent a great evil from continuing. Will you assist me further?"

"If I can."

"Then tell no one else of this matter. I will return tomorrow to bring back the body. Will you be here?"

"I'll be here," he said. "And so, I expect, will he. Will you explain your actions to me?"

"Not now. You're safer not knowing."

"That I believe more than anything else that you've told me. Until the morrow, then."

I hastily reassembled the stones and rejoined Zeus.

The last thing that I wanted to do when I returned to the villa was play another game of chess, but it is rash to ignore the summons of a Duke, no matter how young. I duly presented myself for another skillful drubbing at his hands, but he motioned me to be silent and dashed around the room, drawing the curtains and shutting the doors.

"May I request a favor of you?" he whispered.

"Certainly, Milord," I replied, a bit apprehensive.

"Would you listen to me recite?" he asked.

Dear God, more amateur theatrics. I assented immediately and composed myself upon a cushion, prepared for obsequious praise. He stood solemnly before me and placed his right hand upon his breast.

"Hard ways have I gone," he declaimed. "Many sorrows have I suffered. Thirty winters and thrice half year have I passed in living here . . ." He passed from rote to role as the spirit began carrying him away. Altogether too young to be playing Our Savior, but hearing His words in a child's voice was chillingly effective.

He ran through each of the speeches in turn, then looked at me expectantly when he was done. "Was it all right? I took great pains to con it, but I've got all the words in the right order."

"You do, and you must let them speak for themselves. Listen to the words, Milord. The poetry will carry you if you allow it the privilege. And let me show you one useful technique." I stood behind him and placed my hands on either side of his waist. "Say ah, and hold it," I instructed him.

"Ahhh—HUH!" he cried as I squeezed.

"You see, Milord, the air is propelled from your lungs when you breathe from down here. You'll be heard at every corner of the square if you do that."

"Will I? Thank you," he exclaimed. "How did you know about that?"

"A very harsh singing instructor during my youth," I said. Which was true, as it happened. "I take it you are planning to assume the role of Our Lord?"

"I'm going to try. Mother doesn't want me to go out, but I am feeling well enough."

"A boy should listen to his mother, Milord."

"But I am the Duke," he said, drawing himself up. "And it is important that the town see that I am there."

I looked at him. There was strength there, an iron will that would prove formidable with that intellect. I bowed. "As you wish, Milord."

He sagged suddenly. "I don't know if I can do it," he whispered.

"The role?"

"The role. And the role. Being Duke. I can't even bring myself to sit in the chair. It was his, not mine."

I glanced at the chair seated on the platform. "Allow me, Milord," I said. He stared in shock as I calmly walked up to the chair and sprawled languidly across it. "Fetch me some food, Mark," I commanded him.

He was seized by rage. "Get off of there immediately!" he shouted.

I leapt down and knelt before him. "Of course, Milord."

His anger melted as suddenly as it had emerged. "Why did you do that?" he asked.

"When I sat in that chair and commanded you to get me food, did you do it?"

"Of course not."

"Yet when you commanded me to get down, did I not immediately comply?"

"You did," he said slowly, realization creeping across his face.

I patted him on the shoulder. "The power isn't in the chair, Milord. It's in the Duke. The chair is merely a prop."

He looked at me, then the chair, then walked up to it and sat down.

"How do I look?" he asked.

"Like a duke," I replied. "Like your father before you."

He smiled, and I took my leave.

I sought out Bobo's room. He sat up when I entered and was about to speak when I heard footsteps approaching. I glanced into the hallway and saw Viola bearing down on us.

"A word with you, Feste," she snapped.

"I will speak with you on the morrow," I said to Bobo. He shrugged, and I accompanied the Duchess to her anteroom, where she turned and folded her arms.

"I have been informed by my son that he is going to perform in the play," she said icily. "And he told me that it was at your behest."

"Not exactly," I said. "I counseled him on asserting himself as befits his position."

"When I need your counsel on raising my child, I will ask for it," she said. "It's too dangerous for him to be out there unprotected."

"He won't be unprotected," I said. "I'll be there. Nothing will happen to him."

As a prophet, I turned out to be an excellent fool.

ƒIFTEEN

We enjoin you, my brother, to exterminate from your churches
the custom or rather the abuse and disorder of these
spectacles and these disgraceful games so that their impurity
does not sully the honor of the Church.

POPE INNOCENT III, *CUM DECORUM*

"Be glad! Oh, be glad, for the Lord is risen!" cried the Bishop, and the congregation shouted, "Alleluia!" He raised his hands and beckoned to the rear of the church. The doors were flung open, and a boy clad in a white tunic and hose was led in, riding on the back of an ass bedecked in red robes.

"*Orientis partibus, Adventavit asinus, Pulcher et fortissiunus, Sarcinis aptissimus, Hez, Sir Asne, hez!*" the choir sang raucously. The congregants reached in to stroke the flanks of the beast and passed the touch on to their neighbors for luck.

The ass was led to the altar, as all asses inevitably are, and the boy got off and stood and faced the assemblage. He took an enormous breath and sang out, "*Kyrie eleison,*" in the purest of sopranos, holding each syllable for an eternity and embellishing it with such elaborate melismata that Jubal, Father of Music himself, would have wept in awe upon hearing it. The deacons responded with a trope of further praise, and the Bishop stood behind the boy and held his arms out from his sides as if in supplication. "*Christe eleison,*" sang the boy, and the choir sang it back to him as two subdeacons appeared on either side of the Bishop and carefully removed his vestments. "*Kyrie eleison,*" the boy sang again as they transferred the vestments to him, a midget bishop in oversized clothes. The Bishop himself removed his miter from his head and held it over the boy. *"Christe elei-son,"* the two sang in unison, and on the last note, the Bishop placed his miter on the boy's head, covering it entirely.

As he did, cymbals clashed, horns blared, and the choir launched into a supremely discordant hymn. The Feast of Fools had begun.

A rabble of satyrs burst through the doors, blowing on ram's horns, beating on goatskin drums, squeezing bagpipes, playing every possible instrument that could be made from a goat or sheep. Men in donkey's heads, bull's heads, all manner of horns. I spotted Alexander wearing an elephant's mask, appropriately enough. They hurled ordure into the congregation, which screamed with laughter and dismay. Women groaned as they were spattered, but their gowns were obviously not the good ones worn at Christmas Mass. A grotesque parody of a priest staggered in, wearing an enormous carbunkled nose and drinking from a jug. He whirled the censor like a sling, and whatever was burning in it gave off a foul stench. An old boot, I guessed. I saw the Bishop himself, rudely transformed with charcoal rubbed into his face, playing dice near the altar. Men danced in women's clothes, women danced ring dances, leapt on the pews, and undulated suggestively. A football was introduced from somewhere and was booted from one end of the church to the other.

I was having a wonderful time until I remembered that I had to stay in character. I then scowled disapprovingly at everything. But it was marvelous, I must say, and from a critical standpoint, it was only missing one thing.

Me. Feste, Lord of Misrule.

Black puddings made especially for the day were produced from a hundred pouches and handed around. I broke down and accepted one. The Mass was celebrated by the boy Bishop, his speech muffled by the miter. The deacons were portrayed in uproarious manner by the subdeacons, the subdeacons by the boys in the choir, and quite a few bawdy references were made to local townspeople. Some of the jokes were old enough to have been started by me and probably were. The crowd laughed at them anyway. All part of the tradition.

Throughout, I kept my eyes peeled for the Duke, but Mark was nowhere to be seen. Neither was Viola nor her substitute. I decided to go outside and look for them.

The scenery for the play had been finished just in time. Paradise hung on the steps of the new cathedral, the sheet flapping noisily in the wind. The mouth of Hell was truly impressive, the features fearsome, the gaping maw hung with damask. All of the townspeople as well as those from the surrounding farmlands had assembled in the square, the ones in back standing on wagons. Younger children perched on shoulders, the older and more daring clambered onto the roofs of the shops and offices. Those who could not cram into the church gathered as close to the scenes as they could, awaiting the beginning of the play.

The saturnalian band spilled back out onto the streets, scattering the crowd before them. The choir quickly assembled on the cathedral steps near Paradise, and the revelers gradually quieted as a single ram's horn was blown repeatedly in the center of the square.

I sought out Viola and found her at the side of the old church, fussing over Mark, who was clad in a beautifully tailored gold dalmatic. "Are you sure you aren't too cold?" she asked.

"Mother, please," he protested futilely, as all boys have done to their mothers from time immemorial. She tucked a scarf around his neck, which he deftly discarded the moment her back was turned.

I maneuvered my way back to the square to find a good vantage point and ended up on one of the lower steps to the cathedral. A voice at my shoulder whispered, "What do you think, pilgrim?" I turned and nearly jumped out of my skin. A man was smiling at me, the smile framed by a black mustache and triangular beard.

The Bishop laughed. "My apologies for startling you, but you've been looking so serious. This is a joyous day. Partake of the joy, and you will share in the holiness."

"I'm sorry, Holy Father. Your traditions are different than ours, and with that beard you look quite Satanic. Where did you get it?"

"An anonymous gift, left outside my doorway. The note wished me well and asked that I wear it for the Feast. Rather becoming, don't you think?"

I bowed and excused myself. I was quite flustered by the experience. My invisible enemy was playing tricks again. I wondered how close he was.

I noticed Sir Andrew standing on a step nearby, watching the proceedings intently. I walked over to him.

"I'm looking forward to your triumph, Sir Andrew," I said.

He started upon being addressed, then relaxed. "You are too kind, Herr Octavius," he replied. "I decided that Lucius was fully capable of handling the job. I really wanted to see it for myself, rather than hide behind Hell and hear about it afterwards."

"And who will tell Lucius?"

"He is young. When he has apprenticed long enough, he may stand here and feast his eyes. I love this day. Don't you?"

"We do not have such spectacles where I come from."

"Then you really should. The one this year is so important, coming after Orsino's death. I must say Sebastian has surprised me. He's kept his vow, stayed sober, and speaks his part beautifully. And he helped organize everything after Fabian . . . Well, I'm sorry Fabian couldn't see this. But it will be quite a day for Sebastian, mark my words."

"And for the Duke, I hear."

"Really? How so?"

"He will be assuming his place in the role of Our Savior after all. So Sebastian will miss the performance. But I agree he certainly is due credit for everything else."

"Mark's playing Jesus?" exclaimed Sir Andrew. "I had no idea. I've been so wrapped up in my preparations, I haven't been outside my laboratorium for days. How utterly splendid. But I hope he's not outside prematurely. I fear for his health in this cold."

"He seemed hale enough when I saw him."

"Well, I wish someone had told me," he said, frowning slightly. "We cut the fuses specifically to time the flash with the last word of Sebastian's speech. If Mark doesn't follow the same cadences, it won't work as well."

"I'm sure Mark knows that. He's a bright lad."

"Of course. Look, it's starting."

An Angel of the Lord ascended slowly into the air, two burly farmers carefully turning the windlass. The whining boy of a few days past had been transfigured into a thing of glory. The winds that were whipping up the square caught his wings and sent him spinning around, to the amusement of the crowd. The farmers caught his feet and twisted him until he was facing forwards. He gulped, took a breath, and screamed, "All harken to me now!" The ensuing silence astonished him. Emboldened by the realization that he commanded the square, he continued in full, jubilant voice. "An estrif will I tell you of Jesus and Satan. Of when Jesus was to Hell to bring thence His own and lead them to Paradise. The Devil having such puissance . . ."

People gasped and parted as the Cross was wheeled in with Mark splayed pitifully upon it. In brief dumbshow he was taken down and placed in the sepulchre. He lay still until his mourners left, then stood and rolled aside the rock. The choir sang of Resurrection. When they finished, he strode confidently to the mouth of Hell. He turned to face his audience, his hands out to bless them as the Prologue ended.

"Hard ways have I gone," he declaimed forcefully and clearly. "Many sorrows have I suffered." And the sight of this noble boy who had so recently lost his father brought tears to the cheeks of many. Mothers wept who had lost husbands and sons, sons wept who had lost their fathers, Sir Andrew wept beside me.

"Listen to him," he whispered proudly. "Was there ever such a boy?"

As Mark finished his speech, Satan leapt on top of the Gates, his red cloak swirling around him.

"Who is this that I see here?" he cackled. "I bid Him speak no more! For all that He may do He shall come to us, too! How we play here He shall learn, and find how fierce our fire burns!"

"Who is that?" I asked.

"Stephen, first son of a wealthy merchant," replied Sir Andrew. "A natural choice to play the Devil, some say."

"He certainly is enjoying the role."

The demons trooped out. What was an inept band of amateurs a few days ago was now an expert comedy team. They had maintained the ice patch in front of the Devil's mouth and used it to full advantage. One in particular, a skinny, trembling fellow, drew the most laughs, and several people pointed knowingly in Sir Andrew's direction. He seemed oblivious to them, concentrating on the dialogue.

The Keeper of the Gates appeared, a demon with an oversized key. The choir sang, and Sir Andrew nudged me.

"The powder is in those two bags on top of the Gates," he explained. "There will be two flashes. The first is when Jesus enters the Gates. That's the one on the right."

"The three bags, you mean," I said.

"What?"

"There are three bags up there."

He looked where I was pointing.

"That's odd," he muttered. "There should only be two. I put them there myself. Why . . ." His eyes widened, then abruptly he leapt down the steps, shoving people out of his path with surprising force. "Let me through!" he shouted. The onlookers laughed at the ridiculous knight. Many, seeing an opportunity for mischief, crowded into the poor man who bounced from one to another with increasing panic. With sudden foreboding, I ran after him. I incurred my own pummeling but managed to keep my balance and spin through until I reached Sir Andrew. Together we formed a two-man wedge and pushed through almost to the front of the crowd, some thirty feet from the performance.

"Mark!" he shouted, jumping and waving his arms to attract his attention, but the choir drowned him out and the Duke was concentrating on his role. As they finished, Mark stepped before the curtains at the entrance to Hell and held up his hand.

"Hell's Gates will I fall, and take out Mine all," he intoned. "Satan, I bind thee! Here thou shalt lay, until finally cometh Doomsday!" He parted the curtains and stepped inside. In that instant, a huge flash of red flame and smoke shot from the top of the gates. The spectators cheered and applauded. In a last burst of strength, Andrew broke through the front of the screaming crowd, slid on the ice patch into the mouth of Hell, and tackled Mark. There was another flash, and the screams turned to terror as the flames roared swiftly through the entire construction. Mark looked up in terror as the roof of the set began to collapse on him. Andrew dragged the boy through the damask curtains just as they ignited, and I caught the two of them and pulled them to safety.

Spectators next to the Gates fled, shrieking as their garments caught fire. The more quick-thinking villagers grabbed them and threw them to the ground, rolling them in snow to douse the flames. The crowd, which had overflowed the square, was now trying to flee it, and many were trampled as they fell beneath the feet of their faster companions.

Viola ran up, screaming for Mark. I waved her over, and she

dived at him, locking him in a tight embrace, crying. I pulled them up. "Get him out of here," I shouted. "Get yourselves home and guard the gates." She looked at me dumbly, then nodded and hauled him away. He was dazed but all right.

The flames raced along the set in an unearthly fashion, as if they had a malignant will of their own. Perun galloped up. For once, I was glad to see him.

"Get back!" he commanded the crowd. "Guards, ho! Pull that thing down." Two guards came running with long metal poles with hooks at the ends and began tugging at the top of the set. The intense heat forced one of them back. The other bag of flash powder went off, causing more panic from the crowd. The winds powered the flames and carried pieces of burning debris about the square. Paradise caught fire, and the two thrones quickly followed.

"Get buckets!" shouted Perun. "Get the water barrels."

"No," I yelled at him, and he looked down at me in astonished fury. "Get sand from the shore. Don't you recognize it? It's Greek fire. Water won't stop it."

As realization dawned, he spurred his horse to the edge of the crowd and commandeered a horse and wagon from a farmer. "Come on," he ordered me, and I jumped on the back with two guards and a townsman. Perun snapped the reins, and the startled animal galloped through the crowd at breakneck speed, people leaping out of our path on all sides. One of the guards jumped off as we passed through the southwest gate. He collected some shovels from the guard tower and ran after us to the beach.

We dug through the snow to a patch of sand and frantically filled the wagon. More wagons joined us.

"Back!" shouted Perun. "Don't waste time filling them up. Get what you can and get back to the square."

The horse labored heavily as Perun whipped it back through the gate, and we leapt off the wagon and pushed it to speed things up.

We got back to the square to find the Devil's head burning furiously. The whole thing must have been drenched with Greek fire. We grabbed shovels and started heaving the sand onto the flames.

Perun was next to me, working like a demon. "How do you know of Greek fire, merchant?" he shouted as we shoveled away.

"I saw it used in Aleppo once, to repel a pirate fleet," I replied. "They sprayed it on the ships from towers by the harbor. They burned like kindling even though they were in the middle of a thunderstorm. All the crews perished. It is a sight one does not easily forget."

"Nor is it a sight often seen," he shouted. "You are no merchant, whatever you may say."

"I am a friend to this town," I retorted.

The Bishop ran up, his false beard still on. He clutched Perun by the shoulder. The Captain whirled and shoved him away, not realizing who was beneath the disguise. Then he recognized him and started to apologize.

"The Cathedral!" screamed the Bishop. "Save the Cathedral!"

The sheet from Paradise came loose from its moorings and soared through the air, flapping and flaming like an avenging angel. It came to rest on the scaffolding. We hadn't had any snow since Saint Stephen's Day, and the wood and canvas were bone-dry. They started to smolder, then catch.

Perun turned to me. "If you are a friend of this town, follow me," he said, almost mockingly. He drew his sword and ran to the scaffolding, then began to climb it, ignoring the spreading flames.

And I, being a fool, followed him.

"I hope you aren't afraid of heights," he yelled. "We have to get to the top and start cutting the canvas loose. With luck, we'll save the building."

I pulled myself up after him. The height didn't bother me. The flames snapping at my heels did.

Perun reached the top and began hacking away at the knots binding the canvas to the scaffolding. I ran to the other end and did the same. The top row of canvas sheeting fluttered to the ground as we met in the middle, and two of his men pulled it to the middle of the square. We had five rows to go, and the middle one was burning fiercely now.

"Hurry," he commanded, but I needed no urging. I grabbed a crossbeam and swung down to the level below. I wasted no more time with the knots but sliced through the corners where they were tied. Swordplay at last, I thought. The smoke swirled around me, and I quickly wrapped my scarf over my mouth and nose to buy some time. The second row came down. It was winter, and I was sweating like a baker.

The scaffolding below us ignited as we clambered down to the next level. We were still thirty feet above the steps. I could see over the wall to the Elephant and the harbor beyond. "How do we get down if it goes?" I yelled to Perun as we worked our way to the middle.

"Quickly, I imagine," he replied. "Go, if you want."

What possessed me, I do not know, but I attacked the canvas with a fury unlike anything I had felt in years. No subtleties with this enemy. He was licking at my boots, and either I sent him packing or I would end up a charred morsel for crows. My feet grew uncomfortably hot. I looked down to see flame burst through the platform, then it buckled underneath me. Perun's hand snaked through the smoke to grab mine in an iron grip. He hauled me to momentary safety.

"No time for the canvas," he decided. "Let's cut loose the entire scaffolding. You get this end, I'll get the other. When you finish, get down." I attacked the ropes that held the framework to the Cathedral while he worked his way through the flames to the other side, negotiating the slenderest of beams with ease. I finished the last of them and slid down a pole to the steps. I yelled to the guards with the hooks to drag the scaffolding down and started pushing it from the other side as Perun reached the steps. Slowly, the structure began to topple away from the Cathedral. Then it collapsed in a flaming heap at the base of the steps, pinning one guard underneath a pile of burning canvas. He screamed in agony while his fellows picked their way to him and carried him to safety. His face, unprotected by any armor, was horribly burned.

Dear God, I thought. We just risked our lives to save a church.

The Bishop stood a safe distance away, looking at his future seat of power, tears streaming. I turned to see how it had fared. Not too badly. The marble was scorched here and there, and some of the mortar had cracked in the heat.

"This is terrible, simply terrible," wailed the Bishop. I looked at him, then at the burned guard, who was being carried away by his fellows. I said nothing.

The crowd reappeared slowly, silently looking at the damage. Adam and Eve clung to each other and wept. Masks were removed, instruments lay silent. Then another hideous scream rent the air.

"Murderers!" howled Sir Andrew, staggering through them, holding the limp body of Lucius in his arms. The boy was badly burned, his face barely recognizable, but that was not the cause of death. His chest was stained with blood, the haft of a dagger still protruding from it.

"Cowards!" cried Sir Andrew. "Which one of you did this?" He collapsed in a jagged heap near the ashes that had been the gates of Hell. "He was just a boy," he whispered, and rocked the unfortunate lad in his arms. Perun knelt before them, removed the dagger from the boy's body, and examined it. Then he walked to where I was standing.

I was numb. I hadn't expected any of it. A woman ran up screaming and buried her face in Lucius's chest. His mother, I guessed. I looked at the boy again, and the last piece of the puzzle fell into place.

"I suppose someone killed the boy and rigged that set to burst into flame," said Perun. He looked older, to my eyes, weary from his exertions, his face covered with soot.

"It does look that way."

He looked at me coldly. "I don't much care who you work for anymore," he said. "The Twelve Days are over, and with them ends your shield. I shall meet you on the morrow."

"Give me one more day, and you shall be satisfied," I begged him. "You owe me that much for helping you."

He looked out at the scene. The smoke rising, the burned guard screaming, Lucius's mother, the Bishop, and Sir Andrew crying, all for different reasons. He laughed suddenly, an unexpected sound.

"Why not?" he said. "None of it matters. One more day of life, merchant. Enjoy it while you can."

$\mathscr{S}$IXTEEN

Mès meuz vaut apert folie ke trop coverte felonie.
(But open folly is much better than concealed villainy.)

FROM THE PROVERBS OF MARY MAGDALEN

I noticed one of the villa's burlier servants leaning against the wall near Bobo's room, casually cleaning his nails with a long knife. I nodded at him pleasantly, and he ignored me, concentrating on his cuticles. I ducked through the doorway and whispered, "Pick a language."

He glanced at the door and said, "How's your Spanish?"

"Adequate," I replied, and we continued in that language, speaking in hushed tones.

"I'm being watched," I informed him.

"And I'm being guarded," he replied. "Their caretaking has been unusually solicitous since yesterday."

"You heard what happened."

"Yes, we chatted. Quite a day you had. And Sir Andrew's a hero, I hear. Of all people."

"He saved the Duke's life. But he's quite broken up over Lucius."

"You can't save everybody," he said, looking at me sharply.

"No," I agreed. "But I'm going to try and save what's left of them and end this game today. How are you feeling?"

"Much improved, thank you."

"Able to move in a hurry if things go badly?"

He laughed. "You mean they can get worse? What is your plan?"

I leaned forward to whisper. "I've discovered an unlikely ally. Mark seems to trust me. He's agreed to summon all the principals of the town together this afternoon."

"I hope they don't expect me to entertain," said Bobo with a sigh.

"I'll take care of the entertainment," I promised. "Follow my lead. And just in case, I've moved Zeus and Fez to the Elephant's stables. From there, you can cross the river easily and head south to Spalato." There were footsteps nearby. We clasped hands and I left him gathering his gear into his bag.

Mark was waiting in my room, seated on the windowsill, looking out towards the gap in the eastern ridge. "I've done what you wanted," he said. "Will you tell me what this is all about?"

"All in good time, Milord," I said. "You will learn much that will distress you. Be forewarned, and be brave." I hated using the boy like this, but I had to.

"Why is it that I trust you so much on such short acquaintance?" he mused.

"Milord, men are ultimately unknowable," I replied. "As Duke, you will make great decisions about whom to rely upon with scant information about them. Some you may trust upon short acquaintance, others you may know a lifetime and still never be sure of their motives. Some men live their lives trusting no one, some trusting all. Neither way is right, but in between lies uncertainty. Be certain of this, Milord. I am here to help you, to protect you and your family and your town. You will know me better by the end of the day, that I can promise you."

He walked to the door, then turned. "And tomorrow, Herr Octavius?"

"We shall see," I said. "I haven't thought that far ahead."

He left, and like a good professional, I took a nap. Who knew when I would sleep again?

I was roused by Malachi, who shook me none too gently. "I have carried out your instructions," he said softly. "All is in readiness."

"Thank you."

"I warn you, if anything happens to the Duke or the Duchess, I will hold you responsible."

"I place myself at your mercy, good Malachi. Now, may I beg of you one more small service?"

He smiled grimly. "None of them has been small so far."

"This one is but a trifle. A bowl of warm water and some soap, if you would be so kind."

He looked a bit puzzled but bowed and left. A good man. I enjoyed being waited upon, I must say. It had been a long time.

Viola appeared shortly thereafter, holding a parcel. "You needed this?" she asked, pulling the icon from the wrappings.

"Thank you," I said, taking it and placing it on the table by the window for the best light. I opened the wooden panels, then the false front to reveal the glass within. I gazed at my reflection for a moment, then turned to the Duchess.

"I cannot judge my own face," I said. "It looks worn and old to me. Has life etched any character in it?"

"Chiseled more than etched, I would say," she replied, inspecting it critically. "It has been much exposed to the elements. But the foundation seems strong. Much could be built upon it."

"Then first I must clear it of tree and brush," I said as Malachi returned and placed the bowl and soap in front of me.

"What are you going to do?" she asked.

"I'm going to shave off this damn beard," I said, reaching for the soap.

I peeked through the curtain of the Great Hall, watching them mill about. The original players, the new suspects, the casual bystanders, the greedy, the needy, and the disinterested. Isaac looked around curiously as if he had never been there before. Perhaps he hadn't. Bobo rested comfortably on a chair, chatting amiably with well-wishers. Clumps of conversation formed, broke off, drifted towards the food. Olivia sat serenely amidst a group of men, gossiping about recent events. I lifted the hood of my cloak over my head and waited in the shadows.

Mark and Viola made their entrance, and everyone bowed. Many sneaked glances at the Duke, trying to gauge how he had fared in the fire, while Perun leaned against the far wall, watching everyone. I smiled to myself as Mark strode to his father's chair and sat in it, prompting a few admiring gasps.

"We have summoned you here on a matter of great import to our town," he said. "We are under attack from within. Two murdered, and a treacherous attempt on our own life." He exuded such command that one forgot it was emanating from an unbroken soprano voice. "We give thanks to our friend, Sir Andrew." The room applauded, and the knight blushed. "And we commend our Captain in the heroic performance of his duties." More applause, albeit uneasier in tone. Perun bowed.

"There is a man who seeks to shed light on these dark events," continued the Duke. "He has our ear, but we will not act unless you are convinced as well. He has requested that we use our office to provide him with a forum for your enlightenment. We know no more of what he will say than you do, but we urge that you give him your attention."

Sounded like a cue to me. I parted the curtains and entered slowly. Some woman shrieked at my cloaked visage. Sir Toby chuckled.

"You're late for the Feast, whoever you are," he cried. "The time for costumes is over."

"Better late than never, Sir Toby," I replied, pulling down my hood.

"Well, bless me," he said. "It's the merchant, and he's shaved."

"I have," I admitted. "How do you like it?"

He shrugged. "A man's a man, whether bearded or no," he pronounced. "It's all the same to me."

"And you, Countess?" I asked, turning to Olivia. "What think you of this shorn face?"

"I liked the beard better," she said. "The face underneath is rather ordinary. What is this about, Herr Octavius?"

"An ordinary face. My blessing and my curse throughout my life. An unmemorable one, wouldn't you say?"

"As faces go, yes. Yet . . ." She paused, uncertainly. "Have we met before?"

"That is the magic of beards," I said. "How they change our appearance. They make a weak chin into a strong one, men out of boys, and disguise our faces as well as any mask. Yet start with a beard, then shave it, and you'll be even more unrecognizable. I notice that it is generally not the fashion of this town to sport them. Isaac does, of course, because of his religion. The Captain has a fine one, but he's not from here. And Claudius . . . Where is Claudius, by the way?"

"On holy retreat, at the Cistercian Monastery," said Isaac smoothly.

I shrugged. "That's unfortunate. But to the point. I would like to thank all of you for the hospitality you have shown this humble traveler. In return, I would like to extend the festivities for one more day. After all, as they say, Twelfth Night is for revelry, Thirteenth Night for revelations."

"And what revelations do you have, merchant?" asked Sebastian. "That your spice scheme is a fraud?"

"That, among other things, Count. I will reveal myself and others before I am done. But first, I must teach you a little more about disguises. Beards are but one method. A much better one . . . Well, let me propose it this way. Milord, are you fond of riddles?"

"I fancy that I am rather good with them," replied Mark.

"Then puzzle this one out. Never seen, never felt, never heard, never smelt. Those who have me may enjoy Life, yet in the end I will destroy Life. What am I?"

"Time," he answered promptly.

"Very good, Milord. Your wit rivals the best. Time, lords and ladies, is the great disguiser. It changes faces, bodies, hair, voices. Most of all, it changes the memories we have of people from our past." I walked over to the table and sat with my back to my audience, placing the icon and my bag before me. "How may we defeat Time, Countess?" I asked, opening the icon to reveal the mirror.

"We may not," she said. "But we may create the illusion that we do."

"Excellently put," I applauded. "And what do you use to create that illusion?"

"Secrets, Herr Octavius. Secrets found in ointments and powders."

"The Countess is refreshingly honest about her artifice. Cosmetics to preserve one's youth and one's beauty. Not many of you men wear makeup, although yon fool makes up for the rest of you." I opened my bag. "What is it that you use for whiteface, Senor Bobo?"

"White lead," he replied.

"Just so," I said. "I prefer wheat flour mixed with a little chalk." I rubbed it into my face as I spoke. "It is not as pure a white, but it is plentiful and cheap." I glanced at the mirror. Normally, I can make up my fool's face blind, but it had been a few weeks since I had done this. "See how Time flees before the onslaught. The cracks are smoothed, the features erased, all character lost. The face becomes a blank canvas upon which many faces may appear."

"His accent's gone," commented Sebastian.

"That voice," whispered Olivia. "I know that voice."

I outlined my eyes with a sharpened stick dipped in kohl. "I avoid white lead," I said. "There was a Roman fellow, name of Galen, who decided that lead was a subtle poison that eventually drove men mad." Rouge for the cheeks and lips. "By the way, Señor Fool, how do you know when a fool goes mad?" Finally, my signature, malachite to make two small green diamonds, one below each eye.

"I do not know, Brother Fool," called Bobo. "How do you know when a fool goes mad?"

I turned to face them. "When he acts just like everyone else," I said, and bowed low.

"Good God, it's Feste!" ejaculated Sir Toby.

"Feste," breathed the Duke in wonder.

"Now, the motley has its own tradition," I said, whipping off the cloak and revealing myself in my full foolish glory. "While many prefer fools to perform naked, that has a certain impracticality, especially this time of year. The motley is made of many colors. This is of necessity, as we must assemble it from what scraps of cloth we may find. But that is a reflection of Man himself, a thing of shreds and patches, constantly adding and mending."

"Anything that's mended is but patched," quoted Olivia. "'Virtue that transgresses is but patched with sin, and sin that amends is but patched with virtue.'"

I bowed to her. "I am astonished and honored that you remembered," I said.

"You were of great comfort to me when my brother died," she said. "I have not forgotten. Now, Feste, tell us why you are here."

"Did you not send for me, Milady?"

"No."

"Did any of you?" I asked. A negative murmuring. "Yet someone did. Milords and Miladies, to give an adequate account, I must instruct you in some of the secrets of my profession. A confession of the profession, if you will. For although the adage says that King and Fool are the only states in life to which you are born, not made, that is not in fact true of the fool. I have a craft, learned in a Guild that is dedicated to maintaining the high standards of a low life. Where you learn the seven liberal arts, we study the seven foolish ones, which are what, Señor Bobo?"

"Juggling, tumbling, languages, music, magic, repartee, and rhyming extemporaneously."

"Bravo, Señor. In my most recent sojourn at the Guild, I was given a message. Orsino was dead, fallen from on high. Incidentally, Milord, let me add my condolences now that I am in my true form. I knew and loved your father many years ago."

"Thank you, Feste. I am happy to meet you at long last."

"Milord, I advised you that I would bring you sad news today. And there are no pretty words, artifice, or magic tricks that will make it any better. But part of the paradox of my profession is that when I put on makeup and motley and transform myself into a walking mask, it gives me license to do freely what no others may do: to tell the truth."

"What sad truth do you have for me, good Fool?"

"That your father was murdered."

The boy turned pale, and cries of grief and consternation came from the assemblage. "How is this possible?" he whispered. "He fell from the cliff."

"He was dead before he fell, Milord. I took the liberty of exam-

[219]

ining his body with the consent of your mother. The back of his skull was crushed by some blunt object. Yet he had landed facedown at the base of the cliff. He was murdered, Mark."

"It's true, Milord," said Viola, placing her hand on his arm. He pulled it away, fighting back tears.

"Captain, you observed the body. Would you agree with my conclusion?"

"If the back of his skull was crushed," said Perun, considering, "then, yes. I would."

"But who did this?" cried Sir Andrew. "And what did it have to do with . . ." He stopped, suddenly fearful. "Malvolio?" he whispered.

"That was my thought," I said. "His longtime vow of vengeance was finally being carried out. So, I came here. It was decided at the Guild among my fellow fools that I would travel in a mercantile guise, to be followed by a colleague in motley. In that manner, I could investigate safely while he distracted our invisible enemy. But our plan went awry. While I was examining the cliffs from which Orsino fell, an attempt was made on my life. By crossbow."

Another round of murmuring, and Perun looked at me sharply. "Why did you not report this to me, Fool?" he asked.

"Because in my mind, you were a suspect," I replied.

He thought about that calmly. "From your perspective, I would be," he conceded. "Am I still?"

"Yes. As are you," I said, turning to the Bishop. "And you." This time, to Isaac.

"Outrageous," sputtered the Bishop. Isaac chuckled.

"I am not offended. I am suspected of so many things," he said. "But did you see your assailant?"

"No, but I heard him. His voice sounded like Malvolio's. And

Bobo, who was watching me, saw a man wearing a monk's cowl who had a beard that resembled Malvolio's."

"And Malvolio struck him," finished Perun.

"That's what I was supposed to believe," I said. "But, as Bobo pointed out to me over a chess game the other night, there was something odd about that incident. It is unlikely that Malvolio, fifteen years later, would still have the same black, triangular beard. Bobo suggested that we were meant to see him and survive to tell the tale, so that everyone would be duly convinced that it was in fact he."

"Are you now saying it wasn't?" protested Viola. "You heard his voice."

"Milady, I can do an accurate re-creation of every voice in this room. Malvolio's was a particularly easy one to imitate."

She looked at me long and hard. "You told me that Malvolio killed my husband," she said.

"When was this?" asked Sebastian. "How long have you known about this fool?"

"Whoever killed Orsino knew that he would be alone at the cliffs that night," I said. "Knowing he'd be at the cliffs was not enough. He went there every evening. His killer had to know that all three of the people who normally accompany him would have been prevented from doing so."

"That was the night I became ill," said Mark.

"And I was with him," said Viola.

"That leaves Claudius," said Perun. "Where was he? Shall I send my men for him?"

I looked at Viola. Slowly, she bowed her head. "Claudius won't be at the monastery," I said. "Claudius is here."

"Where?" said Mark.

"By your side," I said. "Viola is Claudius."

There was a moment of stunned silence, then Toby roared, "Good God, she's done it again!"

Sebastian was livid. He hurled himself at her and had to be restrained. "Why?" he screamed. "It wasn't enough to humiliate me once, but you had to continue doing it? You couldn't even trust me that much?"

"Please, husband," said Olivia. "Calm yourself. It didn't concern you."

He turned to her in shock. "You knew?" he said.

"Of course."

"I see," he said coldly. "A conspiracy of women. And the Jew, I suppose."

I had been watching the others to see who was the most surprised. The Bishop, Maria, and, I was pleased to see, the Captain all had expressions of shock and chagrin. Poor Mark looked as though he didn't know where to turn.

"So, it couldn't have been Claudius," concluded the Captain after the hubbub subsided. "Would you be so kind as to continue, Fool? This is fascinating."

"Thank you, Captain. I must give credit for this next bit of analysis to my colleague, Señor Bobo. It was he who realized that there had been no attack on me until after I had stumbled onto the secret of the Duchess's identity."

"Mother?" said Mark uncertainly. She was backing slowly towards the rear of the room.

"It was during the course of that same chess game that Bobo pointed out that an hour lapsed from the time she left for the doctor to the time she returned, ample time to either kill her husband or arrange for it to be done. And then he said the thing that finally convinced me as to the identity of Orsino's killer." I turned to face her. "Viola," I said, a bit hesitantly. "It grieves me to say what I must say." Then I stopped.

Oh, if you could have seen her, standing before us in all her regal beauty. A cold fury burned within her and a presence so commanding that none could take their eyes off her for a moment. She raised her right hand and snapped her fingers. In a trice, Malachi and three other burly manservants materialized around her. She pointed at me.

"Seize the fool and bind him fast," she ordered. I froze as they ran towards me.

Then past me.

He put up a fierce struggle, I must say. A knife produced from somewhere left its mark on one of the men, but they were four to his one, and they prevailed. He sat, glaring, bound to his chair. I squatted down and looked him in the eyes.

"You were very good, Señor," I said. "Very good, indeed. You've studied our ways well enough to fool even a fool. The white lead was a mistake but a small one. Now, answer me a few questions. What is this?" I held up a chess piece.

"What?"

"Answer him," said Malachi, a knife at his throat.

Bobo gulped. "A king."

"And this?" I said, holding another one.

"A queen. Feste, what are you doing?"

"And this?"

"A bishop."

"And this?"

"A knight, of course. And that one's a rook. Let me go, Feste."

I stood. "Allow me to continue my discourse on foolery. As you can see, we have our traditions. Although some would trace our lineage to King David, who played the fool to escape his pursuers, we of the Guild look to the First Fool, Our Savior, Our Lord Jesus Christ."

"This is sacrilege!" thundered the Bishop.

"Bear with me. He spoke the truth as well, through parable and paradox. And at the supreme moment, when he could have saved himself by doing a few simple magic tricks for the King, he chose silence. Then, he was led in a mock royal procession through the streets of Jerusalem to his doom and saved us all." I pulled my cap out of the bag. "Consider the jester's cap, Milord and Miladies. Some say because of this tradition that the fool parodies the King, and that this donkey-eared thing is our crown. But that is not the tradition of the Guild." I placed it on my head and shook it so that it jingled. "Mark, I must catechize you for my proof. How many kings on one side of a chessboard?"

"One, of course."

"How many queens?"

"Also one."

"How many bishops?"

"Two."

I turned to the Bishop. "How many bishops in a bishopric?"

"One," he replied.

"Mark, is that not strange? Two on a chessboard and one in life."

"I suppose it is. I've never thought of it before."

"How many sections to my cap?"

"Three," he said. "And they all flop down."

"And who else in this room wears a hat that has three sections?"

"Well," he said, looking around. Then he looked at me. "The Bishop."

"Very good, Milord. As much as anything, the Guild's tradition is to mock the Church. For that reason, we wear the three-sectioned cap. The French, who understand folly better than anyone, know this and call the piece that stands at the side of the king and queen—that avoids the gallant leaping of the knight and the straightforward approach of the rook and chooses instead to stagger drunkenly through enemy lines on the diagonal—the fool. And no jester who comes through the training of the Fools' Guild would ever call it anything else, especially a bishop. It was during the course of the chess game that I realized that the wolf in fool's clothing on the other side of the board was Malvolio."

There was a long silence, broken by Bobo screaming, "That's it? That's your proof?"

"Basically," I said.

"Milords, listen to me," he begged. "I am indeed Bobo the Fool. This is madness, literally madness. I was sent by the Guild to keep an eye on Feste. We were concerned that he had lost his wits after hearing of Orsino's death. Malvolio is dead. He's been dead for years, and we have known about it since it happened, yet this poor simpleton has continued to rave about him. When he set off on this mythical Crusade, this quest, I came to prevent him from doing any harm. He is an honored fool, we owed him that much. But don't condemn me on the basis of this rambling diatribe."

"Oh, there was also this," I added, beckoning to Malachi. He left with the other servants and shortly returned with a shrouded figure on a plank. I pulled off the shroud to reveal the dead man from the woods. Some in the crowd shrank back, others leaned forward. "Captain, your professional opinion, if you please."

Perun stepped forward and examined the body. "He was tortured," he said immediately. "His ear was cut off, as well as two fingers. There's . . ." He stopped, puzzled. "There's very little blood, all things considered."

"Yes," I agreed. "After I realized that Malvolio had come in the place of the fool I was expecting, I went looking for the original. I believe that this is the real Señor Bobo. I found him a short distance

[225]

from the north road. My guess is that Malvolio was lying in wait for me, having sent the message to the Guild after killing Orsino. Instead, Bobo showed up. The poor fellow was ambushed, taken and tortured to reveal what he knew. Learning that I was not acquainted with the fool I was expecting, Malvolio improvised a clever plan: He assumed Bobo's identity, gained my confidence, and continued his revenge under the best of covers. He took the poor fellow's earring and finger rings the hard way, then scrubbed the body until no trace of makeup remained. One Bobo leaves the Guild, and then another arrives in Orsino."

I took the washbasin and a cloth and began scrubbing the makeup off his face. "Then he staged the attack on the cliff to throw me off the scent. Brilliantly done, sir. I heard Malvolio's voice from your own mouth, and the minor injury you inflicted upon yourself added to your bona fides. It also gained you entry into the Duke's villa, the very heart of your enemies." It was done. A bald, clean-shaven man glowered at me from the chair. The crowd gathered around.

"It could be him," ventured Maria.

"It's him," said Olivia. "I think."

"I really can't say," said Sebastian.

"Well, there are ways to find out for sure," I said. "We can send to the Guild for someone who knows the real Bobo. Or perhaps we could call on the skills of the good Captain. You could use that other room you mentioned."

"Delighted to be of help," said Perun.

"Please," said Bobo. "I can prove to you I had nothing to do with any of this. Brother Fool, may I catechize you now?"

"Be my guest."

"First, at the cliffs, did you not find me lying on my back, with my head bleeding?"

"I did."

"Did you find the crossbow which I supposedly used to attack you?"

"I did not."

"Very good. How did it vanish from the scene if I used it to attack you? Second, was I not in the Duke's villa from then on?"

"You were."

"Malachi, please remove that blade from my throat and answer me this: Did I ever leave that room from the time I was brought in until just now?"

"You did not," replied Malachi, the blade remaining in place.

"Then I conclude: It was impossible for me to have killed Fabian or arrange the fire at the play, because I never moved from that spot. Or are you accusing me of sorcery as well?"

"I never said you killed Fabian," I said mildly. "Nor did I ever say that you acted alone." Glances shot around the room again, then bounced back in my direction.

"It is clear that you had to have had a confederate. There was more than one set of footprints at the site of Bobo's abduction and murder. Someone struck you on the head to enhance the deception, ran away with the crossbow, then used it to kill Fabian. The confederate had to have been someone with the knowledge that Viola and Claudius were one and the same, because he knew he could guarantee the Duke's isolation by the simple expedient of poisoning Mark."

"Poison?" gulped Mark.

"Yes, Milord. Nothing fatal, just enough to make you ill for some time. But it had to be poison, because no one else at the meal suffered any consequences from the food."

"Go on, Feste," he commanded.

"It goes back to the events of fifteen years ago," I continued.

"Another wronged man. One who has undoubtedly picked up a little knowledge of Greek fire and herb lore in his studies, who was of Orsino's inner circle, who was in fact sitting right next to Mark at that fatal dinner. . . ."

"Please," said Sir Andrew. "I don't want to hurt her."

He was standing behind Viola, a knife at her throat.

"When did he recruit you, Sir Andrew?" I asked. "When you were imprisoned in the Crusade? Later on, with some promise of hidden knowledge of the Elixir of Life?"

"Andrew! What on earth is this about?" cried Sir Toby. "I thought we were all friends."

"F-f-friends?" stammered Andrew. "You left me there for a month! They tortured me, you know. Wanted to know what I knew, but I never knew anything because none of you bothered telling me. And it was a month because Orsino was haggling over the ransom. For God's sake, I wanted to die in there. Friends! You've been sponging off me for fifteen years, and what have I gotten in return? Couldn't find poor Andrew a bride, could you? I lost Olivia, and not once did someone think to toss me the slightest bone of a girl, not once."

"Andrew," cried Mark. "Why did you try to kill me?"

"He didn't," I said. "That fire was meant for Jesus. For Sebastian. You pulled Mark out in the nick of time, after you found out he was taking over the role, didn't you?"

"Yes," he shouted. "I saved you, Mark. I would never let anything happen to you. I would have been a real father to . . ." He stopped short and screamed, "No closer! I will kill her." Perun, who had been edging along the wall, stopped. A drop of blood slowly crawled down Viola's neck. She winced and stayed as still as she could.

"You killed that boy, didn't you?" accused Olivia. "Because he would have known how you arranged the fire. You stabbed a child in the heart, Andrew?"

"I had to," he mewled. "I won't go to prison again. I'll kill her if you try and stop me from leaving here."

"Excuse me, but I haven't finished my lecture," I said.

"Really, Feste, this is hardly the time," protested Sir Toby.

"Oh, but it is," I replied. "Timing is one of my great skills. Behold!" With a flourish, I produced my marotte from my bag. "Observe, *mesdames et messieurs!* The jester's scepter. The French, bless them, have a separate word for it, *La Marotte.*" I shook it, and the tiny bells on its cap tinkled merrily. "Most useful for defending one's person from thrown vegetables. Regard the head, Sir Andrew." He gawked at it. "See the skull beneath the makeup, grinning at us all. There is one more tradition associated with fools. Death, Sir Andrew, the greatest mocker of them all, the Fool who brings all men down to the same level." I began shaking it over my head in a peculiar rhythm. "You've studied much ancient lore, Sir Andrew. There are secrets of smiths, of midwives, and of fools. Ours are rarely invoked, for it is a poor fool indeed who resorts to such drastic measures. But Folly walks hand in hand with Death and may call upon him in dire emergency. It would be a terrible thing to die unconfessed, noble knight. For the love of Mark, spare his mother or I will pronounce your doom."

His hand shook but stayed where it was. "Very well, then. Just as the setting sun marks the end of the day, so the descending skull marks the end of your days. Watch it closely, Sir Andrew. It will be the last thing you ever see."

I began waving it back and forth, slowly lowering my arm to point in his direction. He couldn't take his eyes off of that little skull with the tiny green diamonds under each eye. He peered over Viola's shoulder, his mouth hanging open.

"Kill her, you idiot!" screamed Malvolio. "Kill her now!"

The marotte came level. The knife fell from his hand, and he staggered back, clutching his throat, coughing violently. The expression? Horror? More like an accusation, but whether it was directed at me, Malvolio, or the whole assemblage was too difficult to say. He stumbled over a low stool and fell backwards. It was his final stumble.

Perun rushed forward, sword at the ready, but there was no need. He bent over the dead knight, then looked at me. "Neatly done," he said. "How did you do it?"

I shrugged. "I didn't say I would reveal every secret I knew, Captain. Oh, by the way. You challenged an Augsburgian merchant to a duel tomorrow. The merchant is no longer here. Would a postponement, a permanent one, be acceptable?"

He drummed his fingers on his sword, looking at the Death's head on my marotte.

"Perun!" shouted the Duke. The Captain turned, startled, as the boy strode up to face him. "This fool is under our protection. No harm shall come to him from you or anyone directed by you. Need I remind you where your loyalties lie?"

Perun was silent for a few seconds. Then he bowed. "Not at all, Milord. There is no need for concern. There is no honor in dueling fools."

"None whatsoever," I agreed. "Thank you, Milord. Now, if I may prevail upon the Captain to escort Malvolio to his new quarters, we can then conclude. I will visit you in the morning, Senor. I'll bring a chessboard."

He grinned wolfishly. "You'll lose again, Feste. You can't beat me."

"I think I just did," I said. They carried him away.

"What now, Feste?" said Sebastian. "Are you going to sing us something to finish?"

"I am finished, Count," I replied. "I am a bit weary, so I will, with your permission, remove myself. But you have some work to do. The world is changing too rapidly to delay appointing a regent any longer. The boy will rule like his father all too soon. I urge you to set aside your squabbles and choose now." I swept my gear into my bag, leaving the icon, and turned and bowed.

"Milord and Miladies, *mesdames et messieurs*, good night."

$\mathcal{S}$EVENTEEN

Mock on, mock on——'tis all in vain!
You throw the sand against the wind,
And the wind blows it back again.
WILLIAM BLAKE, "MOCK ON"

In my dream, I juggled once again with an unseen partner in the forest. Then the trees parted like a fog in an unexpected gale, and Death walked towards me, tossing the clubs harder and harder, the grinning skull gleaming under the cowl, pure white broken only by green diamonds under each eye.

I woke with a cry, sitting up so hard I nearly wrenched my back. A figure stood in the doorway, holding a lit candle on a dish. Still between dream and reality, I gaped at it in terror.

"Are you all right?" asked Viola, entering the room.

"What's the hour?" I asked.

She shrugged. "Late. Near dawn, I think." She sat down on the edge of the bed. "Olivia is now the regent until Mark is considered of age by vote of the leading families. Claudius is no more."

"What about Isaac?"

"He becomes the steward for both the Duke and the Countess. That was my price for going quietly. May I?" She indicated my marotte, lying on a table by the bed, its head not far from where mine had rested. I nodded, and she picked it up gingerly. "Is it safe?" she asked.

"At the moment."

She turned it in her hands, inspecting it from every angle. "I give up," she said finally. "How does it work?"

"The staff has a thin tube inside, with a spring that catches near the handle. It shoots a small metal dart. Poisoned, of course. I can hit any target I want within fifteen paces. I put it into the back of his throat."

She shuddered. "How close was I to dying just then?"

"From me, not very. From him, too close for me."

"Did you know he was going to do that?"

I sat on the edge of the bed, rubbing my temples. "I hoped he would do something. I didn't think he would do that."

"How did you know he was involved?"

"Little things. The most glaring, and I curse myself for not seeing it sooner, was when he rode into the square on the Feast of Saint John. He had been out looking for the Stone, or so everyone thought. But he wouldn't look for the Stone after the snow had fallen. He told me so himself. And that was the morning my colleague was killed, according to what Joseph told me when he led me to the body. By the way, did you resume his food supply?"

"Yes."

"Thank you. Even a holy man cannot live on prayer alone. I believe that Andrew used this quest for the Stone as an excuse to go out every day and wait with Malvolio for Feste to appear. Only I came in by boat, and they got poor Bobo instead."

"When did you realize this?"

"When I saw him holding Lucius's body. I saw the loneliness of the man, the desperation. I thought of how he, as well as Malvolio, was left out of the general happiness of our original adventure. The fire, the poisoning of Mark—these are the tricks of an alchemist. When I exposed you as Claudius, I watched his face. Many were surprised. He wasn't. I don't know when he stumbled onto your secret, but he knew. None of this would have been enough to accuse him, but I went ahead and did it anyway."

She shook her head sadly. "Poor Andrew. I cannot find it in my heart to hate him, even knowing what he's done."

"Who's Aleph?" I asked.

She looked up, startled. "How did you know . . ." she began, then stopped. "Am I to have no secrets at all?" she protested.

"I am sure there are many more," I said. "But who's Aleph? We saw it in Isaac's ledger. Why was he given so much money, and why did he pay it back months later?"

"Aleph is a *colleganza* of the powerless," she said. "Jews, slaves, and wives. We borrowed from the Duke's funds, speculated on ships, returned the principal, and kept our profit. Every now and then, a slave would purchase his freedom, or a woman would find the wherewithal to flee her marriage. As for the Jews, they store away and prepare for the winter."

"A worthy cause," I said.

"You see much that others don't," she observed. "I've been trying to decide whether or not I forgive you."

"For exposing Claudius?"

"No, you had to do that. It was inevitable. I was fooling myself to think that it could last, but there was no graceful way to end it. But I was thinking of something else. I've been seeing things that I didn't notice before, either."

"Such as?"

"A shipwreck with no wreckage. The survival not only of a pair of twins but of their belongings, washed up intact on shore. And at every turn, there was you, dashing madly about. Knowing what I know now, I no longer believe in fairy tale romances. Well? What about it? Come, Feste, I've never known you to lack for words. Tell me how you manipulated my feelings."

"Did you love him?" I asked, my voice sounding harsh to me.

"How much choice did I have?" she said. "I was thrown into this bizarre situation, not knowing whether my brother was dead or alive, wondering how I would survive. And then I fell in love with my benefactor. Who wouldn't?"

"But did you love him?"

"I was tricked into it."

"Did you love him or no?" I persisted.

"Yes," she snapped. "I loved him. But I would like to have had the choice myself."

"You did," I said. "What would have happened to you if you never came here? Have you ever considered that? Your parents were dead. You would have been dependent on Sebastian. Do you really think he would have let you have your own choice of husband? Assuming that I had something to do with this, you still ended up marrying a wealthy, powerful man whom you loved for himself, and you had a good, long life together. How many could say the same?"

"And the seed for his murder was planted at the same time, thanks to that arrangement."

I could not answer. She buried her face in her hands.

"I'm sorry, Feste. He could have died sooner a thousand different ways. But he died this way, and once again you came galloping in to change my life forever. They won't even let me raise my own children, now. I am deemed too strange—untrustworthy even though all that I have done was for the benefit of Orsino. Now, I can do nothing. I shall sit in a comfortable room with a large window overlooking the sea and be paraded out for state occasions and do needlepoint for the rest of my life. And you won't even be staying around to entertain me, will you?"

"I don't think that would be possible under the circumstances."

She began crying softly.

"There's one more thing," I said hesitantly.

She looked up.

"Venice attacks in the spring. They seek dominion over the Dalmatian coast. I cannot advise you what course you should take, whether to fight or to negotiate, but you should know that it's coming. You may be able to work through Isaac. He has Venetian contacts. He may even be their spy."

"Of course he's a spy," said Malvolio, standing in the doorway. He looked haggard, perhaps the result of some time with Perun, and was still wearing a dead fool's motley. He held up a crossbow and leveled it in Viola's direction. "Look what I found. Move away from the bed, Feste, and leave your sword there. Or I will kill her."

I moved, my back to the window.

"Your problem, if I may be so bold as to venture some criticism after that brilliant performance of yours, is that you think too small. Do you really think that I would undertake to assail this town with just a whimpering simpleton to aid me? I had others. One is Perun's lieutenant, who was kind enough to assist my escape. I have quite a talent for corruption, you know."

"Let her go," I said.

"Maybe, maybe not. The scandal made when the Duchess is found in the Fool's bed would be delicious. But I really wanted to pay my respects to you before I left. You, after all, were the original author of my humiliation."

"You deserved it."

"Why, Feste?" he protested. "For falling in love with a countess? Was that such a crime? Or did it just not fit in with your grand design? If it was a crime, then you are the greater criminal, Fool, for you desired an even greater prize."

"What is he talking about?" whispered Viola.

"Haven't you told her, Feste? My, my, all that grandiloquence about telling the truth, and you can't even tell her that you love her.

But that isn't surprising, is it? That's the way of your cowardly little guild, running your second-rate conspiracies all over the Mediterranean. Believe me, Duchess, if I had the time I could tell you all about the secret workings of this organization. They put the Templars to shame. But I digress."

"Still working for the Saracens?" I spat at him.

"Politics," he said dismissively. "Was that the problem? Really, Feste, the whole history of this world is of one nation conquering another. What does it matter who wins? You know, the irony is that I was willing to let the whole matter drop at the time. Oh, well, I said, chalk it up to experience. But then, one sunny day, I chanced upon a troubadour singing that charming little ditty you concocted. There I was, immortalized as one of the great dupes of all time. It was the last song he ever sang, believe me, and now, I've come to have the last word. A parting shot, if you will." And he shot.

I stared dumbly down at the end of the bolt protruding from my thigh. Ah, I thought. That's what it feels like. Then the pain hit in earnest.

Malvolio drew his sword. "You didn't think I'd allow you a quick death, did you?" he said. I tried to move, but the bolt had pinned my leg to the wall. Then I heard another sword being drawn from a scabbard.

Viola walked towards him, holding my sword in front of her. Malvolio looked at her in disbelief.

"Really, Milady, this is beyond ridiculous," he said wearily. "I've seen you . . ." He barely got his blade up in time.

She attacked him with a methodical fury that caught him off guard, but he fended her off. He began driving her back, his madness a match for her rage. And she was tiring. My blade was too heavy for her. It was clear he would prevail.

I tried pulling my leg away, but it was no use. Blood was leaking out of me at an alarming rate. I reached with my good foot to the boot holding my knife, but it was too far. The room was starting to blur. Then I remembered my dagger and slid it into my hand. She was between him and me, and I shook my head, trying to focus for a clear shot.

Then I thought, idiot, he's taller than her, and I whipped it at his head. He saw the motion and ducked to the side just enough so that it merely creased his temple.

But it distracted him long enough for her to get under his guard. She grasped the hilt with both hands, planted her feet, and drove my sword upwards through his neck with so much force that it embedded the blade a few inches into the opposite wall.

I would have liked very much to see him suffer, to see him die in agony with the full awareness of his sins, but the truth was that he was killed instantly. She let go of the hilt and staggered back, clutching her mouth with both hands. He hung there, supported by the sword. She looked back and forth at the two of us, and a high-pitched giggle fled her throat.

"I seem to have a collection of fools pinned to the wall," she said. "How chic! So much more interesting than butterflies, don't you think?"

"Very good, Milady," I gasped. "But this butterfly would like to forgo the honor." She flew to my side and examined the bolt.

"I think I can get it loose," she said, and carefully pried the head from the wall. I sank gratefully to the ground.

"Now, get out," I commanded her.

"What?"

"Get out. I don't wish to sully your reputation any further. Leave me here."

"Nonsense," she scoffed. "You need help. And I want full credit for Malvolio."

She ran into the hallway. "Ho! Malachi! Selena!"

Footsteps clattered in the distance.

"Hot water and bandages immediately. And send for that surgeon. I don't care who he's sleeping with, find him."

She came back and cut my leggings off.

"I think it missed the bone," she said. She lopped the fletches off the end of the bolt. "You might not die. We may even be able to save the leg." She gave me an odd look and kissed me suddenly. "Looks like you're going to have to stay with us a little longer."

"One way or another," I said. I was fading.

"Get up," she commanded, and helped me to my feet. A maid ran in with a basin and bandages and nearly fainted upon seeing the macabre scarecrow on the wall.

"I'm going to pull the bolt all the way through," she said. She handed me her handkerchief. "Hold this between your teeth. I'll count to three. This may hurt."

"It already hurts." I turned and leaned against the windowsill.

"One!"

And suddenly I was praying, praying as I never could before, praying forgiveness for my sins, praying that I would live, that she might be mine. Praying that I would at least see another sunrise.

"Two!"

And there it was, climbing the gap in the eastern ridge, our daily miracle, God's only sun, sent forth to redeem the world once again.

"Three!"

The night was over, and darkness fell upon me.

A NOTE ON THE TRANSLATION

The translation is taken from a fifteenth-century copy of the original manuscript (made on foolscap paper, of course). The copy was part of a collection preserved to the present day, as so much was, in the library of an obscure abbey in western Ireland, the precise location of which I have agreed to keep secret in exchange for further access.

The original appears to have been lost, so its authenticity is ultimately unverifiable. Believe me, I wish more than anyone that I could verify it, for I anticipate being besieged by Shakespeareans (and Baconians) who will say, "But didn't *Twelfth Night* come from several sources? Didn't Shakespeare (or Bacon) cobble it together from *Gl'Ingannati*, Forde's *Parismus*, Riche's tale of Apolonius and Silla, etc.?"

To which I can say two things, one speculative, the other even more speculative but intriguing.

First: It apparently was the practice of the Guild to conceal their exploits by retelling and distorting the events in ballads and other compositions. It is entirely possible that the original story had, over the centuries, been broken up into its various components, which in turn surfaced in the retellings and adaptations upon which Shakespeare relied.

However, at the abbey itself, a more interesting story is told.

There is no record of Shakespeare (or Bacon), or any William of Stratford, or any other such name, ever traveling to Ireland to visit this abbey. But a sixteenth-century friar in residence does mention in a letter that has been preserved that a student, one "Wil [sic] Kempe," was expelled from the abbey for allegedly pilfering manuscripts from the library. One William Kempe later shows up as an actor in London in the company of Shakespeare and Burbage. Mr. Kempe's specialties were portraying women and fools.

Could it have been the same Kempe? Could one of the pilfered manuscripts have been Theophilos the Jester's original account of the events later portrayed in *Twelfth Night?* There is no way of knowing for sure and perhaps never will be. But it is as good an explanation as any.

The language originally used was the Tuscan dialect, similar to but predating by several decades that used by Dante. It was written in prose, thank goodness, as my Italian is barely up to the task of translating the Tuscan of this period, much less achieving the equivalent of the Dantean terza rima. I would at this point extend my thanks to the young Jesuit scholar who assisted me in the translation. His identity must also remain secret, but I look forward to his new version of the *Purgatorio* in about five years or so.

The excerpts from *The Harrowing of Hell* are freely adapted from a thirteenth-century English version of the passion play. I would like to acknowledge both the New York Public Library and the Queens Public Library for their excellent collections, as well as the several authors who have written on the history of the medieval fool.

Some may take me to task for not rendering the language in pseudo-antiquated English. This was meant to be a translation, that is, a transformation into the language of our own time. The contemporary equivalent would have been a thirteenth-century Middle English that Chaucer would have found tough going. Theophilos used an earthy, colloquial style, and I have attempted to re-create it.

HISTORICAL NOTE

There is scant historical evidence for the existence of the Fools' Guild. This is that rare secret society that actually succeeded in remaining secret. In *The Age of Faith*, Will Durant writes of "a confrèrie of minstrels and jongleurs like that which we know to have been held at Fécamp in Normandy about the year 1000; there they learned one another's tricks and airs, and the new tales or songs of trouvères and troubadours" (p. 1054). Frustratingly, this is virtually the only unfootnoted line in the entire book, and I have yet to discover his source.

The distaste of the Church for the troubadours is well documented. Many perished during the persecutions of the Albigensian Crusade later in the thirteenth century for suspected sympathies with the so-called heretics. The Feast of Fools remained a thorn in the side of the Church for another two centuries before its official eradication, but its traditions lingered long after that. Fools continued both their mockery in high places and their charitable works. Many bequeathed their wealth to charity. One Rahere, fool to Henry I, founded Saint Bartholomew's Hospital in England.

This tradition continued to the present day. Noble societies formed to re-create foolish traditions for charity. The Compagnie de l'Infanterie Dijonnaise was well-known in seventeenth-century

France for their foolish revels and their fund-raising. More recently, the Shriners in the United States have, with their Mummers' Parades and general clowning, raised significant amounts for children's health. Finally, one may only look at Comic Relief, the banding together of professional comedians to benefit the homeless, to find shadows cast by the original Fools' Guild.

Read on for an excerpt from Alan Gordon's next book

JESTER LEAPS IN

Available in hardcover from St. Martin's Minotaur

What think you of this fool . . . ? Doth he not mend?
—*TWELFTH NIGHT*, ACT 1, SCENE 5

The sun rose through the gap in the eastern ridge where the river cuts through. I watched it come up, lying on my back on the riverbank. A few months ago, I had prayed that God would grant me the gift of seeing one more sunrise. He had granted that prayer, along with a few others, in a manner more generous than my situation merited, but that's the sort of thing He does. I make no pretense of understanding His ways, but ever since I survived that dreadful night, I've made a point of trying to see every sunrise that I could. And I've continued to pray. Not for myself, mind you. I've been rewarded enough so that I can pass along some prayers for the rest of the world. It seems only fair.

As the warmth of the rays began removing the night's chill from my limbs, I took my right knee, brought it to my chest, and held it there for a slow count of ten. Then I did the same with the left knee, though the leg protested vehemently. Pain coursed through it, rounding the turns at my ankles and surging back toward my hip until I released it, gasping. Then I repeated the exercise, right knee without pain, left with.

I sat up, kept my right leg straight, and brought it up by degrees until it was pointing to the sky. I let it drop, then looked at my left leg as if it belonged to some stranger, one who had yet to earn my trust. Reluctantly, I grabbed it and started pulling it up.

I couldn't get it to the vertical, and had to settle for the diagonal. I thought I could hear the scar tissue cracking, but that may have been my imagination. I let it go and stood up.

Roosters crowed on the farms surrounding the town. I stripped to my linens and dove into the river, kicking hard. The water came directly from the snow still visible on the distant mountain peaks, pausing on its way to the nearby Adriatic to chill me to the marrow. I made it across to the opposite bank, then swam back. I did five circuits before the left leg gave up; then I dragged myself back up the bank like a shipwrecked sailor. Not bad, I thought. Only four months since a bolt from a crossbow had fixed my thigh to a wall, one month since I could walk without crutches. Lucky I still had a leg to stand on.

I dried myself off, donned my motley, and rubbed the flour-chalk mixture onto my face until it took on its normal macabre aspect. Kohl for the brows and lines, rouge for the lips and cheeks, then malachite for the green diamonds under the eyes. Finally, the cap and bells on my head, and I was ready to face the world again.

"Good morning, Fool," said a woman behind me.

I spun, startled; then I relaxed and bowed.

"Good morning, milady," I said. "I trust you slept well."

"Quite well, thank you, Feste," replied Viola. "I am ready for my lesson."

She glanced around and made sure that no one was near. Then she walked up to me, placed her arms around my neck, and kissed me.

"There, you've gone and smeared my makeup," I protested, admittedly some minutes later.

Viola stepped back and surveyed the damage. "I suppose some of it got on me," she said. I nodded. She pulled out a handkerchief and wiped her face while I made repairs to mine. "The perils of kissing a fool," she remarked. "I had no idea that loving someone so simple would be so complicated. How is your leg today?"

"Improving. Still weak and stiff, but less than before. Now, my lovely apprentice, let's see how you've progressed."

She took three balls out of a bag and started juggling.

"Good. Switch hands."

She shifted the pattern from a left-handed start to a right-handed one.

"Good. Two and one. Other way. Over the top. Excellent. Overhand grabs, now. Have you tried going under the leg?"

"In my room," she said, concentrating on the pattern. "But I can't do it here in this gown. Oh, dear." A ball dropped out of her reach and rolled toward the bank. I retrieved it before it plunged into the river and handed it back to her. "Why did you go over there?" she asked it sternly.

"Because that's where you threw it," I replied. "Start over."

She sighed and sent them aloft. "When do I start on four balls?"

I tossed another one at her. She wasn't expecting it. She made a late grab, and three of the four balls ended up at her feet.

"When you've mastered three," I answered.

"Yes, Teacher."

She went back to work while I resumed my stretching.

"That trick won't work on me again, you know," she said, tossing one behind her back and catching it over the opposite shoulder.

"That's today's lesson," I replied. "A good fool is ready for anything at any time. We'll start on four balls tomorrow. In the meantime, switch to clubs. When you're ready, we'll work on some four-handed moves."

I stopped and listened. "Do you hear that?"

She nodded, pulling three gaily painted clubs out of her bag. "Someone singing. Coming from the town toward us."

"Not just someone."

In the Fools' Guild, we are trained how to make contact with each other. The exchange of passwords is one method, of course, but only when you know where to find a particular colleague. In the vast expanses of the world, however, we have many ways of signaling when we need to find each other. A certain type of birdcall; a peculiar clapping rhythm; a song.

Our troubadours call it a *tenso*: a debate in verse and melody, a call and response between two singers on any topic, though usually on love. The best can improvise on a theme for hours at the contests held at the Guildhall and the great tournaments in southern France where a sparrow hawk is perched on a tall pole throughout and awarded to the winner.

But this particular song was a call to any Guild member to respond in kind. The verse was sung, and then the singer paused, waiting. Then he moved on and repeated it.

Thus it was that I heard in the distance a sweet tenor soaring over the faint strummings of a lute:

> *How sweet to meet the soft-lit Dawn*
> *When the world lies still aborning.*
> *Farewell, Philomel, I must move on.*
> *I have miles to go this morning.*

I cleared my throat and sang out in the direction of my unknown friend:

> *Yet stay, I pray, my pretty Faun,*
> *Or my love you will be scorning.*

The Sun will run, and then be gone.
Let tomorrow's Dawn be our warning.

"Shouldn't the second part be sung by a woman?" asked Viola, keeping her eyes on the clubs dancing in the air over her head.

"When one's available," I replied. "Now, hush, Apprentice."

Tantalo once told me that the art of being a troubadour is to sing, play the lute, and look magnificent in a cape, all while simultaneously riding a horse. And there he was, the embodiment of his own definition, perched on a beautiful, black, Spanish stallion prancing daintily down the hill, both horse and rider bedecked in black-and-red checkered silks. His Insouciance guided his steed without reins, leaving his hands free to continue plucking away at a lute that was far nicer than mine. His horse, I swear, kept time with its hooves. They descended the slope toward us. When they stopped, Tantalo swung his leg over the saddle and leaped lightly to the ground, continuing the melodic line in the lute without break.

"You must teach me how to do that trick," I said. "You're in fine voice this morning."

"This morning, this afternoon, yesterday and tomorrow," he replied. "You, on the other hand, sound a touch hoarse."

"I've been swimming," I said, a bit defensively.

He turned, doffed his plumed hat, and nodded to Viola, then turned back to me.

"Introduce me to your charming companion, if you would be so kind."

"Viola, this is Tantalo, an old friend. Tantalo, this is my apprentice, Viola."

"Apprentice?" he said in surprise. He leaned toward me and muttered, "Looks a bit long in the tooth for an apprentice, don't you think?"

I reached forward and caught a club an inch away from his skull.

"Oops," said Viola sweetly, keeping the other two clubs going with her right hand. I tossed back the wandering third. She caught it adroitly and continued practicing.

"Rather ungallant for a troubadour, commenting on a lady's age," I admonished him.

"Oh, a lady, is she? Forgive me. I mistook her for a fool's apprentice. As a Guild member, it is my right and obligation to insult apprentices, and their responsibility to come up with some witty retort."

"You're funny-looking, and your horse smells," Viola called out.

"All right, so that part needs work," I said hastily. "But she's no ordinary apprentice. She's fluent in nine languages, sings and plays beautifully, and is a superb actress and mimic. I can vouch for that."

"Well, if you say so," he said, somewhat dubiously. "Anyhow, that is not my business here."

"What *is* your business?"

He straightened up and puffed out his chest. "Theophilos, I have traveled from the Guildhall to Venice, and by boat from Venice to Capodistria, and then ridden down the Adriatic coastline to this lovely town of Orsino, to ask you but a single question: how is your leg?"

"Is that personal or official?"

"Both."

"Personally, it hurts like hell. Officially, I can no longer do a standing back flip, and I still limp fairly badly, but I am otherwise back to my old self."

"Good," he said, nodding. "Your report of your success here was duly noted. Father Gerald was so delighted, he was observed to kick up one heel. More cannot be expected of such an ancient. But you are back in his good graces."

"Hooray for me. What does the Guild want?"

"Now, now, gossip before business. You know the rules."

I debated with myself over whether or not I would intercept the next club flung in his direction. He pulled out a large handkerchief, opened it with a flourish, and placed it on the ground. He then sat upon it and leaned forward.

"You'll never guess, my friend, who showed up at the court in Hagenau recently."

"I haven't been in Germany in years. Tell me."

"Alexios."

"Which Alexios?"

"Alexios of Constantinople. Son of the usurped and blinded Isaakios, former emperor. Nephew of the usurping and blinding Alexios the Third, current emperor. Alexios, who seeks to become Alexios the Fourth, the next emperor."

"Which would be a neat trick, considering his father and uncle both live. When did he escape?"

"Sometime in the fall, we think."

"And this was not the Guild's doing?"

"By David's lyre, no. The Guild has no interest in disrupting the Byzantine throne. The results are too unpredictable, and besides, they do a fine job of that all by themselves. The immediate agents who arranged his escape were Pisan, but we suspect his sister Irene was behind it. She's married to Philip of Swabia, you know."

"He escapes, goes north to big sister, and has a ready-made entry to the German court. What does that have to do with the Guild?"

"Well, there's this little matter of the Crusade gathering in Venice."

"Which is going to Constantinople, according to Domino."

He shrugged. "Maybe. Domino's been the chief fool in Venice forever, and usually knows which way the wind's blowing. But not

[251]

everyone in the Guild thinks Constantinople is the intended target. There's a whole lot of French and Flemish soldiers sworn to liberate the Holy Land, and nothing but the Holy Land. Then there are some who want to invade Egypt first, one infidel territory being just as good as the next. So, most of us thought Constantinople was a long shot. But Alexios's arrival complicates matters. You know who else was at Hagenau? Boniface of Montferrat. Here the Guild is, making every effort to keep the Crusaders from slaughtering Christians, at the very least, and now the commander is meeting with the chief claimant to the Byzantine throne."

"What's the Guild doing about it?"

"The usual. The troubadours are in a tricky position. Unlike you, we can't just go around making fun of our patrons. We're supposed to be out there singing their praises. And if the particular lord is taking the Cross and swearing to bring an army with him, then we're supposed to be out rousing the rabble. So, we roused them. Now that we've roused them, we're trying to douse them. Lyrics that once glorified the noble quest now speak of the girl we leave behind. Some of our gallants are becoming homesick before they even depart."

"Very good."

"We're also taking the opposite tack of inflaming their fervor to such a pitch that they must to Beyond-the-Sea immediately. Several hundred have skipped Venice altogether and dashed off to Apulia, which is doing a nice business in transporting them. They'll arrive in inadequate numbers to fight the Mohammedans, while depriving their Venetian-bound comrades of their promised numbers. We're hoping that not enough of them show up in Venice to justify the journey. In Venice itself, we're spreading rumors that the Crusade is being subverted to Venetian ends.

Some of those who came there because they took the Cross are now crying betrayal and going home."

"Well done. But it won't work. Venice has committed too much of its monies to this expedition. If they don't get repaid with profit, they won't be happy."

"Agreed. And just when we were hoping everything might fall apart nicely, along comes little Alexios with his big requests. Oh, you should see how grown men and women weep to hear of his travels and travails. Fortunately, Rome won't support him. Innocent may be one of the most conniving popes in recent memory, but even he won't absolve an attack like this. Unfortunately, events have their own momentum, which is why the Guild wants you to go to Constantinople."

I was waiting for it, I was expecting it, and he still managed to sneak it in and wallop me.

"Constantinople? Me? Now?" I almost shouted.

He looked at me and shook his head sadly. "Theo, you have to do better than one-word questions if you're to uphold your reputation as a wit. But to respond in the same manner: Yes. You. Now."

"But doesn't the Guild have half a dozen people there already?"

"We did," he replied.

Suddenly, I was afraid. "What happened to them?"

"We don't know," he said slowly. "That's what we'd like you to find out. They've disappeared. All of them."

"Dead?"

"We don't know. We received word from Fat Basil in Thessaloniki. The troubadour riding the circuit from Constantinople reported that all of the fools had vanished without explanation. He left, saying he would try to find out what happened. That's the last we heard."

"When was this?"

"Maybe six or seven months ago."

"Who did the Guild have working there?"

He counted on his fingers. "The dwarf brothers were with the Emperor. Thalia was with the Empress. Tiberius and Demetrios worked the streets, the Hippodrome, and the Great Palace. The troubadour was called Ignatius."

"You're using the past tense. About people that I know."

"Then I hope that you may know them again. Thalia was a particular friend of yours, was she not?"

Some troubadours should stick to singing. When they talk, they just get people in trouble. I glanced over at Viola, but she was absorbed in her juggling, some distance away.

"When can you leave?" Tantalo asked.

"There's a complication," I said.

"What is it?"

"I'm married," I replied, indicating Viola. "Meet the Duchess."

"Married?" he guffawed. "Well, my goodness. Congratulations, I suppose." He turned to Viola. "And to you, Apprentice." She nodded, and he turned back. "I guess..." Then his jaw slowly dropped in the first uncalculated expression I had ever seen on him. "When you said, 'Duchess,' you meant... Good God, Theo, you've rejoined the gentry!"

"Dragged me down to his level, more the like," said Viola.

He got up and swept his hat off in a superb bow.

"Forgive me, milady. Little did I know that such magnificence was consorting with such a lowly man as this."

"You're still funny-looking, and your horse still smells," she replied, curtsying.

"Ha, ha, excellently put, milady," he said, rolling his eyes at me. "Well, this is a priceless piece of news to take with me. I could dine out for a month on it at the Guildhall."

"Fine, so long as you don't noise it about locally. As you might suspect, it was done in secret."

"I'm certain of it. Last I heard, she was a recent widow and you were a bedridden cripple. Did she nurse you back to health?"

"She did."

"Then you fell in love and married in secret. What a scandal!"

"There might have been a greater scandal had we not married," I said. "And we had been in love for a long time. We just didn't realize it."

"Now she's your apprentice. How much have you told her about the Guild?"

"Who we are. What we do."

He sighed. "Is that all? After all these years, you'll give up our secrets for love?"

"Because I trust her, and because she'll become a member in due time."

"But that takes years of training, Theo."

"As I said, she has a head start. All she really needs is repertoire, juggling, and tumbling, and she'll be ready for initiation."

"I imagine she could give you a pretty good tumble if she wanted to," Tantalo whispered, leering. Then he turned and caught another club directed at his noggin.

"Oops, again," called Viola.

Tantalo flipped the club experimentally, then lofted it high over her head. She walked backward, gazing upward while keeping the other two clubs going in one hand. At the last moment, she tossed them high, cartwheeled backward, and caught all three. Tantalo and I applauded.

"All right, she does show some promise," he said begrudgingly.

"In the meantime, she has taken the Oath of Apprenticeship and will honor it," I said.

"How much does she really know about you?" he asked quietly.

"More than you do," I said. "She knows my real name. I had to give it to the hermit who married us."

"My word," he said, impressed. "But there is quite a bit more to you than that."

"True. I've promised one revelation for each wedding anniversary."

"Then, milady, I wish you a long and happy life together," he said, bowing again. "You'll need it if you want to learn all of this fellow's secrets."

"Oh, I have a few of my own," she replied.

"No doubt, no doubt. Well, Theo, you're right. This is a complication."

"Not necessarily," said Viola.

I looked at her for a long moment.

"Will you excuse us?" I asked Tantalo.

He bowed and withdrew. I turned to my beloved. "What are you up to?"

"A good fool is ready for anything at any time," she replied. "The answer is simple. I go with you."

"Impossible."

"Why?"

"Because it's dangerous. You have no idea what you're getting into."

Her face darkened. Always a warning signal, although one I usually catch too late. "I married you. I became an apprentice of the Fools' Guild. I made both commitments knowing what they involved. I knew that at some point the Guild would be sending you on another mission. So, I'm going with you."

"What about your children?"

"My opportunity to be their mother disappeared when my sister-in-law was appointed as their regent. Mark is a few years away from his independence. Once he has full power as Duke, maybe I'll be allowed to be his mother again. But for now, I choose to be your wife rather than a useless appendage to my own family."

"You may get killed in the process."

"As may you. Don't forget, I've already had the experience of sitting home while my first husband went sailing off to the Holy Land to fight Saladin. Years of wondering if he was coming back. I won't do that again. I refuse to grow old waiting to see if you've survived. If you're going to die, I want to be there." She stopped. "That didn't come out the way I meant it to."

"Viola, this is no pampered life. A traveling jester lives on his wits and a handful of bronze. You'd be sleeping in haylofts if you're lucky, and on the cold, hard ground if you're not."

She walked up to me and looked up into my eyes. "But I'll be sleeping with you," she said simply.

I thought about that for all of a second. "All right, you can come. But your training continues. When we are working, you are my apprentice, not my wife."

"Agreed," she said, and she went back to her juggling.

I walked back to where Tantalo had withdrawn, a distance far enough to appear discreet while allowing him to hear every word we said.

"Problem solved?" he asked innocently.

"We'll leave tomorrow morning. Can you stay until then?"

"Alas, no," he said, mounting his horse. "I have a few more errands to run before I rejoin the Crusade."

"You're going with them?"

"Someone has to keep an eye on them. There'll be a few of us. Raimbaut's with Boniface, of course, and some of the other high and mighty are bringing along troubadours to record their prowess in verse. Things should get going this summer. The fleet will probably work its way down the coast demanding support. Most of the towns have quietly gotten in touch with Venice to arrange peaceful passage. Including yours, milady."

"We know," she said.

"Yes, that Jewish steward of yours is very efficient. You should get by with a relatively minor tribute and a few dozen men. But I have to visit Zara next. The Doge has it in for them, and they may want to consider some serious negotiating before the fleet shows up at their doorstep."

"I hear the place is a haven for heretics, brigands, and exiles."

"My kind of people. Well, I'll see what I can do about persuading them to settle peacefully; then I'm back to Venice. I'm worried Domino may take it upon himself to dive into the Grand Canal with a spike in his teeth and scuttle the fleet single-handedly. Oh, by the way, Brother Dennis was inquiring after that horse he gave you."

"Zeus is well," I said. "His manners have not improved overmuch. Does Brother Dennis want him back?"

"No. He said, and I quote, "If he can stand that vicious, willful, cantankerous bastard, he might as well stay with him." "

"That's a fine way to speak about a horse."

"He was talking about you. Good-bye, Theophilos."

"Good luck," I said, reaching up and clasping his hand.

"And to you," he replied. "Perhaps I'll see you in Constantinople."

He started strumming his lute as his horse turned north back toward the town.

"One more thing," I called. "Let's say I'm sitting there, and war breaks out. What does the Guild want me to do?"

"Try and stop it," he called back.

"How?"

He shot us a wicked grin over his shoulder. "Do what you always do. Improvise!"

Viola watched him leave, flipping a club in her right hand, gauging the distance.

"I don't think you can hit him from here," I commented.

"I'll wager a kiss that I can," she said, still eyeing him.

I took the club from her hand and kissed her.

"I prize them too highly to cheapen them by wagering," I said. "Let's go pack."

A chilling new mystery from the
Edgar Award-winning author of
A Cold Day in Paradise

WINTER
OF THE
WOLF MOON

AN ALEX MCKNIGHT NOVEL
Steve Hamilton

On Michigan's northern peninsula, ex-cop Alex
McKnight enjoys the solitude of his log cabin. But when
a young Native American woman comes to him asking
for help, his peace is shattered. And when she suddenly
disappears, McKnight is plunged into a dangerous investigation that will reveal the dark secrets and evil motives
hidden in a town called Paradise...

"The isolated, wintry location jives well with
Hamilton's pristine prose, independent protagonist,
and ingenious plot. An inviting sequel to his
Edgar Award-winning first novel."
—*Library Journal*

NOW AVAILABLE FROM ST. MARTIN'S PRESS

WOTWM 5/00